NO LOVE SONGS

NO LOVE SONGS

S.A. FANNING

NEW YORK   LOS ANGELES

Jacket design by Rejenne Pavon
Jacket Copyright 2023 by Winding Road Stories
Interior book design by A Raven Design
ISBN#: 979-8-9871737-4-9 (pbk)
ISBN#: 979-8-9871737-5-6 (ebook)

Published by Winding Road Stories
www.windingroadstories.com

To the invisible kids. Overlooked and underestimated, this book is for you.

1

———

I START TO BACK OUT WHEN HANK'S TRUCK PULLS IN THE driveway. The door opens and he eases out, taking his time to gather his thermos and lunch box. Unlike me, he's in no hurry at all, and it's all I can do to squeeze the steering wheel and curse under my breath as he approaches the car.

Hank's lips, lurking in his silvery goatee, coil like a serpent in grass. I go to set the window down, but he only shakes his head and motions for me to get out of the car.

"Going somewhere, Myles?"

I close my eyes. Obviously, I'm not going anywhere. Not now, with his truck blocking me in. Not as I step out of the car, while Hank acts like a sheriff pulling over a speeder. I wipe my hair back. "We've got a show tonight."

"A show, huh?"

He knows this already. It's our biggest show to date. The skate competition at the warehouse starts in forty minutes, but we still have to set up and run through soundcheck. Not that Hank cares. He'll only ask why anyone would want to hear us play such garbage. Hank only likes music with lyrics about hunting, fishing, or defending freedoms—none of which I've ever seen him do.

He studies the station wagon, the drums stacked neatly in the back. "And you're taking Nan's car?"

"Yeah, I told you about—"

Hank holds up his hand. I stop talking and gaze past his left ear, close enough that it looks like I'm paying attention when really, I'm watching birds across the street. It's a method I've honed over the years, as Hank is big on eye contact, but I can't quite face those sunken black pits that flank his nose.

"Yeah, maybe you did. But I specifically remember asking you to do some things around the house." He makes a show of looking around. "Doesn't look like any of that happened."

My pocket buzzes—either Noah or Mal wondering where the hell I am. I'm stuck with all our equipment, trapped in my own driveway as Hank edges closer, placing himself within striking distance.

I choose my words carefully, checking my tone. "Hank, tomorrow is Saturday. I can do whatever you need. I'm free all—"

He cuffs the back of my head. In a blink, he follows it up with a quick slap to my ear. It doesn't hurt so much as it makes me feel like a dog. I step back against the car and brace myself for more.

"I know what day it is, Myles," he huffs, already panting. "Right now, I need you to change the oil in the station wagon. Go get the tools and the oil pan."

The words get tangled up in my throat. *No. I have to leave. The car doesn't need an oil change. Why are you doing this now?* But I close my eyes, the slap on my ear a hot, pulsing warning of more to come. I stuff it down and reach into the car, pop the hood.

Change the oil, huh? I never saw that one coming.

Hank starts back for the truck. He returns with an auto store bag containing an oil filter and several quarts of oil. My phone buzzes again as I grab the tools and slide under the wagon where I loosen the plug. The oil drains out of the engine, clean and golden, like my syrupy will to stand up to Hank, as he goes on about how I should be thankful I've learned to do these things for myself. But for the millionth time in my life, I find myself wondering what my grandmother ever saw in him.

Thirty-eight minutes later—two minutes before showtime—Hank slowly backs his truck out, his meaty forearm hanging over the door as he tells me not to be late. Chores tomorrow. Early. No drinking. Lock the car. I'm sure there's more, but I get on my way.

I'm twenty minutes late by the time I get downtown. There's already a crowd gathered along the cobblestone road, cars cramming the curb and skaters hanging out near the steps. My heart races as I turn down the narrow alley between warehouses and spot Noah and Mal sitting on the loading dock.

Mal hops to her feet. Even annoyed, she's stunning with her blue eye shadow—not that she needs much help in the make-up department. Her hair is pulled up in a messy top knot, wavy dark curls falling to her shoulders. The white Party Trash t-shirt contrasts with her tawny arms.

Staring at her, I lose track of Noah until there's some banging on the back window. His spiky red hair pulls me away from Mal. "Okay, okay." I hit the locks, pull up on the curb, and leap out of the car.

"Sorry. I had to do some stuff."

Mal's eyes flash. She knows how things go down at my house. Some of it, anyway. More than anyone else. Noah mutters under his breath about soundcheck, frantically collecting his set. Mal blinks as she steps closer to me. "Everything okay?"

"Yeah," I say, looking down to find a splotch of oil on my shirt, grit in my fingernails. "Hank wanted me to change the oil in the car first, so..."

Mal's jaw tightens at the mention of Hank. Her eyes search mine. "He knew we had a show."

Nothing to say there. Of course he knew.

"I figured it was something, like that," she says, then lets it go. "So, you're good?"

She shields her eyes, squinting against a shaft of evening sun wedging its way into the alley. I juggle my car keys. I've known Mal for almost two years. She's my friend and bandmate. But sometimes, when she looks at me like that, it gets confusing. I shake it off. "Yeah. I'm good."

I smile. Because I am. I'm good now.

We rush to get set up, fly through sound check, and agree on a setlist. As we start and stop through a few songs, more kids are filing in, providing background noise. Skateboards hit the floor. I forget about Hank as we fall into riffs. I'm enjoying myself up until Noah informs me we're live streaming for the skate competition. Another surprise. My back stiffens. I glance at Mal. The fact that anyone in the world can see us makes me acutely aware of my father's scuffed guitar in my hands, how I sound, or what my face is doing. That splotch of oil on my shirt.

Too late now. Time to do this.

We plow ahead, loud and fast. It works. I do my best to forget about Hank and soon we're clicking. But the stream, the stares, the way Mal is putting a little something extra into her already killer smile—it feels like I'm one step behind.

Near the end of our set, a buzz hums over the room, our thrumming guitars colliding with the clicks and clacks of skateboards on the smooth concrete floor. Most of the attention is on the ramps, but somewhere along our set, thirty or forty kids found their way toward us, a mass of sweaty rebellion inching closer, lured by our lead singer's gravitational pull.

Mal once said there's no bigger stage than the one you're standing on. We were working on a song together, and her hazel eyes shined with sincerity even as her smile couldn't hold the joke. Kidding or not, it stuck with me. And now, as she stands front and center over the crowd, chest heaving, bass guitar dangling at her waist, I'm thinking she had it all wrong. It's her. She's too big for the stage.

It's mostly guys in the crowd and she plays it up, wiping back her sweaty hair, eyes spanning left to right as she holds them captive with the hint of a smile. When she catches my eyes again, I already know what's coming.

She wants to do her new song for an encore. It's why she's smirking at me, eyes glistening, daring me to stop her or at least look away.

When I don't, Mal shoots me a wink, having won our silent battle. Back to the microphone, she licks her lips, makes them wait. I turn away and tend to my guitar.

Sometimes it would be nice to just play music—to not worry about Hank, to not look to the left and fall to pieces over our lead singer, to not find my best friend rolling his eyes. To stop thinking about my long-dead father and wonder why the music itself wasn't enough for him.

I'm adjusting a string when Mal nods my way, breaking me from my thoughts. I shake my head. *No, we're not doing it. It's stupid.*

She lifts one eyebrow. *Oh, but we* are *doing it. And it's not stupid.*

The crowd chants. Guys with skateboards. Girls with skateboards. Everyone alive and flushed from bashing into each other. They wait eagerly for Mal to entertain them, to lead them, to tease out the next song as a single industrial light plays with her eyes, casting a honey glow onto her skin, glinting off the gold Egyptian coin she wears around her neck.

She bites her lip and fiddles with the mic stand, still playing to the crowd, taunting them. Taunting me.

"The next song is a new one."

A few dozen people lose their minds. It's all Mal needs to continue. She knows I don't want to do the song, but she also knows I have no choice. It's not like I'll walk off during our biggest show to date. I glance back at Noah, his spiked red hair glistening with sweat. He edges up on his stool and shrugs.

Before I can do anything else, Mal lays into *Oh That's Nice!*

Noah hits the kickdrum a few times as I rev up the feedback. Mal comes in with the bassline. The song is easy, loopy and basic because Mal's… um… lyrics, are the focus. And now that it's two against one, my fingers find the chords. I'm left with no choice but to join in.

Oh, you're dating Bryce?
Oh, that's nice
You cheated on him twice?
Oh, that's nice

Mal sways left, then right, wielding the bass guitar like a magician as the crowd roars to life. She sings as though it's personal, her voice strong and confident with a perfect dash of sarcasm. It's like she's determined to prove me wrong about her song—basically a diss track aimed at all the popular girls at school. I'd told her at practice it still needed some work, a lot of work. Apparently, she disagrees.

And she's right. It works. I smile at Mal, then Noah. Not for the first time, I wonder where in the hell I'd be without them.

After the show, I'm rolling up cords and hauling out amps as the warehouse clears out. Mal, still bouncing around from all the excitement, attracts a crowd. Stragglers find Noah, smacking hands and asking about the next show. I watch them as I work, smiling to myself, a slight ringing in my ears. I love these nights.

Noah's all over the promotion, working the fanbase and giving out social media handles, when a couple dudes roll up and give Mal an all-too-sketchy onceover.

The taller of the two nods at her. "That was hot."

I stop rolling the cord. Mal narrows her eyes. I instinctively slide over to her, but Noah is all over it.

He rushes in, throwing his hands out. "Thanks, guys. But I'm not looking for a relationship at the moment." He sets a hand through his sopping red hair. Sweaty and flushed from bashing away on the drums, he's got the smell to prove it. The guys shake their heads and back off.

Mal glares at me. I raise my hands in mock surrender. We've been over this before; she can handle herself. Besides, most of the people at our shows are cool, but there's always a few of these types around. When they mess with Mal, it's hard to let it go.

We get outside. Mal checks her phone. "Well, Mom's running late with her banquet thing, which means Charley's all alone. I'm under orders to get home."

I look around, still on alert. "I can walk you to your car."

Mal rolls her eyes. "Myles. I got it, okay?"

Some skaters in the alley, kids lingering along the curb as no one wants to go home. The warehouses on the lower basin sit like tombstones against the moonlit clouds. Cigarettes, mohawks, box vans, and pallets. It's cool playing the old shoe factory because of the acoustics, but the river smells like spoiled fish sticks. I do another quick scan for those two dudes who harassed Mal.

"You sure?"

"Yeah. But hey, I need to talk to you about something."

My heart reminds me who's driving. "Okay."

She doesn't have time to spill it, though, because Garrett, the promoter dude, comes rushing over. "Damn, guys. Sorry about that. Got caught up."

Noah and Mal huddle with him to talk money. I stay out of it and continue loading up, half listening to Garrett tell Mal how one day, he's going to tell people she played his gigs.

She laughs it off. But I don't. She put on a show tonight.

I open the back tailgate to Nan's station wagon. Barbara, as Mal calls her. A 1994 Buick Roadmaster Estate Wagon with wood panel sides. It's one-part hearse, one-part muscle car. All parts beastly. It really is the perfect roadie car for a band.

Garrett rushes off and Noah trots over to start loading his kit but stops. He gestures to my shirt. "Hey man, I thought we talked about the clothes."

I don't feel like explaining, not after what it took to get here, so I change the subject. "What was that about? With Garrett?"

Noah grimaces. "Well, good news, bad news."

"Bad news first," I say. Always take the bad first. My life motto.

"Okay, well..." Noah digs in his pockets and pulls out some bills "We only got $100, not the $150 I thought we'd agreed on."

"What?" I search for Garrett. "Why?"

"Probably because of the way you're dressed, I don't know. Not enough skaters? You know how Garrett is."

"Damn, there were a ton of kids in there."

On cue, one of the skaters wipes out. An explosion of laughter erupts as he rolls over on his side. Noah nods, counting out two twenties. "This is it, man. Sorry."

It's more about the music than the money for us, especially for Noah and Mal. But every dollar counts for me. I'm saving up so I can move out of Nan's house the second I turn eighteen. Still, I don't need sympathy pay. I wave off the twenties.

"Just wait until you have change."

Noah shrugs, still holding out the money. "You sure?"

I nod. He pockets the cash, takes a breath. "Sorry, man. It is what it is."

I pick up an amp, sneak another glance over to Mal, and catch her eyes. She shoots me a smile, and it cushions the blow with Garrett.

"Now for the good news," Noah continues. "Garrett said we can come back for the next skate jam."

"Yeah?" I say, still watching Mal. She's like a celebrity over there.

When Noah mentioned the live streaming, all I could think about was how people could see me, view me, judge how I played. But Mal simply flipped a switch, brightened, and stepped up her game. It was more than music. It was a performance. And it was great. Still, I can't shake the uncomfortable tingle in the back of my head, the small voice telling me it was too good.

Noah sets his cymbal in with practiced delicacy. Even worked up, he treats his set like fine china, at least when he isn't beating the shit out of it.

"Yep. I told you man, we gotta keep grinding," he says, ducking out of the car. He grins. "Oh, so check it. Heather and Traci," he nods over his shoulder towards the warehouse, where a couple of girls are busy scrolling on their phones. "We're going to hit up a party over in Boonsboro. Remember Blake Alsten, dude who crapped his pants in the eighth grade? He's having people over."

Noah has a way of remembering things. I shrug. "Yeah, I know Blake." I glance over to the two girls. Mal's song comes to mind, and it makes me chuckle. "But I'm not feeling it tonight."

"Come on, Myles. What else are you going to do?"

Mal rejoins us, throwing up a peace sign. "Okay losers, I'm out. Practice tomorrow, right?"

A guy wearing comically large sunglasses walks up to Noah. "Dude, you're a beast on those drums."

"Ah, thanks." I hear Noah and Sunglasses slap hands. They go on about the show and how awesome we were. How much we rock. We're bound for greatness. Blah. Blah. Blah. I straighten one of the cymbals.

"Dude." Noah shoves me out of the way. Sunglasses laughs, takes a swig from his beer. He slaps my shoulder. "You too. Great show, my man."

"Oh, thanks."

He smiles and offers me the other can of beer.

"Yeah, I'm good."

Sunglasses shrugs, sets the beer in the back of the car, where Noah is still fixing his drum set just right. "There you go, dude." He steps back and nods to the car. "Nice truckster."

Mal steps forward. "Um, excuse me?"

Again, Mal loves Barbara. She even composed an ode to her full leather seats, her five built-in ashtrays, the tape player. And who can forget the towing package?

The guy turns to Mal, his glasses like mirrors distorting the glow of the streetlights. His smile doubles. "Well, hey there."

She glares at him. "Do *not* make fun of Barbara."

"*Barbara?*" Sunglasses repeats, backing off as Mal stonewalls him. He wanders off, calling out to another cluster of skaters. When he's gone, Mal nods to me, as though to prove she doesn't need protection. Then she glances over to the giggling girls near the wall. "So, you boys headed out?"

I wipe my hands on my jeans. "Nah, I'm sort of tired."

Noah ducks out of the wagon and scoffs, mocking me. *"Nah, I'm sort of tired."*

"I don't talk like that."

"You do."

"Boys," Mal chides. I turn and find the Mal I've known for almost two years, eyeing me. Something about the careful way she watches me tonight makes me wonder about the smiles, the vibes she was giving on the stage. Was that for real or for show?

It doesn't look like she's going to tell me tonight. And the last thing I want to do is go home and think about it, so I turn to Noah. "Okay, whatever, I'll go to Blake's."

Noah gives me a shove. "That's what I'm talking about." He claps his hands and heads over to the two girls he pointed out earlier, Heather and someone. "Hey ladies."

I roll my eyes with a smirk. Mal steps forward. "So I think we should—"

I snap to life, hopeful. Too hopeful. Mal looks around, rocking back on her heels. "I mean, we should probably work some more on my song tomorrow. Will you help?"

"Yeah, sure." Then, so I don't come off too desperate. "I mean, it could use some tinkering."

She slaps my arm and shoots me a smile. "Whatever, you know it's good."

"It's got potential."

"Bye, Myles."

"Bye, Mal."

She starts off for her car but gets stopped by a fan yet again. All packed up, I lean against the car and watch her nod and take compliments before Noah hustles over and says it's all set. I open the door to get in the car when Mal breaks off from a group of kids and runs back to us. Noah watches me over the roof of the car until Mal slides up beside him.

"Forget something?" Noah asks.

"Well, Mom just got home, so… let's go to that party."

Noah nods his head. "Oh hell yeah. The Wide Awakes, baby."

Mal winks at me before she hip checks Noah out of the way. "Shotgun."

Noah throws his head back. "Oh, come on, Mal."

I duck into the car to hide my cheesing. Maybe Mal and I will have that talk tonight, after all.

2

—————

WE STOP AT NOAH'S HOUSE TO UNLOAD HIS DRUMS, AND so he can change clothes. Sure, we're all sweaty after playing, but Noah is extra ripe from all the drumming. He starts inside when Mal calls out to him in a gentle voice. "Oh, and Noah? Maybe try, some, you know..."

She gestures to her armpit. Noah sniffs his underarm. "Oh, right."

I raise my eyebrows. She smiles. "What? I'm only trying to help. He can't go meeting up with those girls smelling like butt sweat."

We get back in the wagon, Mal sets her head to the seat with a smile. "Speaking of girls."

I turn to her. "Butt sweat?"

She shrugs, then her face lights up with a smirk. "So what did Jada think of Barbara?"

Jada. I roll my eyes. A girl I hung out with as a tagalong for Noah. I spent the evening trying to figure out something to say while she sat glued to her phone. Bored out of my mind, I tried jokes, self-deprecating humor. I even tried making faces at her. The scowl remained. She did say our lead singer had a killer voice. She did not mention the guitar playing.

A quick glance at Noah's house. "She didn't say."

Mal runs her finger along the door. "She didn't compliment the faux wood grain finish?

"Well…"

She smacks her leg. "The functioning tape player, with Dolby Surround Sound auto reverse and seek option?"

"Mal."

She shimmies her shoulders against the seat. "What about the luscious leather interior?"

"We only hung out once. It was dumb." The plea in my voice only makes it worse. Mal's smile widens. She's having too much fun as she leans in, hair falling over her face.

"I mean, that's two rides in Barbara, there and back. I'm astonished that after two rides she didn't mention it. Honestly, I'd say she's not worth your time."

It's typical Mal, but I'm not in the mood for it tonight. I thought she wanted to talk about something important, not this. I grip the steering wheel when she waves her hand to get my attention. "Hello? You okay over there?"

I turn to her, and she raises her eyebrows. I get back to the steering wheel. "It's just, she didn't say anything about the car, okay?"

She holds up her hands. "Okay, okay. Sheesh."

Things get silent. Mal fiddles with the radio.

Mal and I met in art class sophomore year when she transferred in from a private school. It was the first day of second semester, and she walked in and took the spot beside me. She had my attention from the start, but it was her voice, so rich and full of confidence, that stuck with me. Once we realized we both liked old punk no one else listened to, we were like a team. Everything else was easy.

Occasionally in class, when she was working on a sketch, her arm would brush against mine. She never seemed to notice, but it sent shockwaves through my body that stayed with me the rest of the day. From the start, I was thinking about her too much.

It was a few weeks before I told her about the band, or whatever it was Noah and I had going then. As soon as I said it, her eyes lit up in a way I've since gotten used to but can still make my stomach drop like a sudden dip in the road.

She said she had to hear us. I told her we didn't have a singer. She smiled and told me I'd just found one.

I'm about to say something about the show when Mal stops on the oldies station Mr. Irvin likes. She starts bobbing to the corny song.

"Your kiss," she turns to me, singing along. I start to tease her for being a goof, glad to have the old Mal back, until she takes my hands and sings directly to me. I'm lost all over again when the back door opens and things get pungent.

Mal drops my hands, blinks several times. She sits back in her seat and coughs, wiping at her eyes. "Um, wow."

Noah, lathered in Axe body spray, scoots to the middle of the backseat. "What?"

Mal's hair shakes with her head. "Nothing, just don't get near any open flames tonight."

Noah doesn't respond. A first. Mal sets her window down, and I'm cracking up when I catch a glimpse of Noah staring blankly at his house. I cock my head. "Everything cool?"

"Yeah, just... parents fighting again."

Mal turns in her seat, but Noah is already shaking it off. "Just go man. I'm ready to party."

We drive out to Blake's and park near the road because the mile-long driveway is lined with cars. Hiking up, Noah jokes about how Mal went off on Sunglasses. I laugh, though it's clear he's still in a mood after whatever was going on at his house. Mal keeps singing oldies until he starts venting.

"I mean, I get why Myles likes old punk. It's all the stuff his dad played. And I do too, but come on, Mal. As a band we need to grow."

We've had this conversation too many times to count. But tonight, as the summer day's humidity clings to the evening, Noah's griping only eggs Mal on. She leans into him, tugging on his shoulder and singing into his ear. It works. In the dark, our steps crunching in the gravel, I can practically hear Noah's face come back to life. My face does the same thing, and I realize it's probably what I love most about Mal, how she can always put us back together when we're down.

"Okay, okay." Noah ducks away from Mal with a smile. He mentions the money from the show, and Mal says we can settle up later. But it reminds me of Garrett, and how I need every dollar I can get my hands on.

"I'd like to know what happened with that, anyway."

Before I can finish grumbling, Mal grabs my shoulders and leaps onto my back. I stagger a step back before shifting her up on my hips. My chest tightens as I take her legs at the bend of her knees. Mal's not heavy, but with her hair tickling my cheek, and her quick breaths in my ear as she's still humming the cheesy old song, it's all I can do to put one foot in front of the other.

Noah starts up once again about how we're like a couple of grandparents. Mal only sings louder.

I carry her all the way up the drive, until she leaps off as we get to the porch. Noah takes off and does Noah things, smacking hands and greeting everyone he sees.

We watch him go, our social butterfly, before Mal turns to me. "You think he's okay?"

I stuff a hand in my pocket. Find a drill bit from work today. "Hope so. I'll talk to him about it later."

Noah waves for us to follow him inside, where there's a poker game going on at the huge dining room table. The radio blares some pop hit, and some people in the kitchen are all talking at once. Noah continues his meet-and-greet while we hang back. Mal leans her head on my shoulder, and I can tell what she's thinking: *Soon I'll be gone.* Because it's the same thing I'm thinking: *Soon she'll be gone.*

We stroll through the house and end up out back, where I study the placement of the pavers and the design of the fire pit. They're the sorts of things I've been building with Mr. Irvin this summer. Whenever we go to a party like this, I find it hard to believe people actually live in these houses. The back lawn, even in the dark, is lush and green with mowing strips leading up to the perfectly placed trees. Not that anyone here cares, the fresh mulch is littered with Solo cups, cans, at least one sock, and some cigar wrappers.

I follow Mal off to the side, where we sit on the wall and do more people watching. A group of dudes huddled together laugh hysterically at a video playing on the phone. Another guy tries and fails to tie his friend's shoe. Two girls pace, texting furiously in a gust of urgency. "Are. You. Serious?"

Mal looks up at me. "Well, I'm sure glad I didn't go home."

"Yeah, me too."

I try to match her sarcasm, but it's true, I never want to go home. Besides, sitting with Mal at this mess of a party, the air still thick and buggy and the humidity driving her hair to Bride-of-Frankenstein madness, I'm not sure there's anywhere else I'd rather be.

As Mal watches the girls hash out their crisis, the radiance of the bulb lights strung over the patio plays tricks with her eyes and warms her arms. She turns to me, and the light glints off her coin necklace.

"Myles," she says, her gaze drawn back to the girls and their drama the way one might watch lions take down a zebra on *National Geographic*.

"Yeah?"

"Do I..."

Before she can ask, the door swings open. Noah comes stomping up to us with an acoustic guitar. "Here," he says, thrusting it at me. Mal sits up straight, eyes alive with intrigue. Noah shrugs. "Second set. Blake said I can drink for free if you guys play music."

I take the guitar and give it a once over. A decent Fender. Mal scrunches her brow. "Are you our pimp now?"

"As acting manager of the band, I made a decision." He raises a red cup, foam sloshing. "Give 'em five bucks worth."

Blake and the poker players spill outside. Someone yells, "Ayye," and suddenly we have an audience. I fiddle with the knobs. "It's out of tune."

Noah slugs down a gulp of beer, stifles a burp, then looks around. "You really think it matters?"

Mal smiles, tongue between her teeth like she's happy to have something to do. I work quickly to tune the strings as people come out and a crowd closes in, kids shouting out song requests. Not serious requests, but drunk people songs, each one cheesier than the last. We've just played the warehouse with the punks and hardcore skaters, and now we're getting badgered by Blake and the Boonsboro kids.

I strum out a few chords, and Mal straightens her posture, like *fine, we can do this.* She clears her throat, and the little gathering goes quiet. Even the guys watching the phone turn to check us out.

Messing around, Mal teases bits and pieces of whatever as I change up the chords and we figure it out. Even playing around, Mal has a voice that tucks you in like a bedtime story. It isn't blow-you-away powerful or especially high, but it's real. It massages your soul. And after her all out performance at our show, it's slightly hoarse and fragile and one note away a from coming apart.

I shake my head, laughing at the dumb requests, until Mal nudges me. With a smirk, I launch into the song from the radio trying to make her laugh. *Kiss on my List.*

I'm nodding and being goofy, but then it changes. Mal doesn't miss a beat. It's like she's still on, and she goes for it. While I'm not all surprised she knows the words—we did just hear the song— she's singing them like she wrote them.

I'm partially aware that Noah, still with the beer in hand, has his phone out and aimed at us. But like the crowd, it's blurry background stuff. I can't help it. Like the vibes at the show earlier, Mal's pulling me into it, nudging into me every time she gets to the chorus.

It's getting harder to play along with the goof, because I start wondering, *hoping,* that Mal is singing this oldies song to me. I forget we're at Blake Alsten's house, that some girl is dancing on a picnic table, even that Noah is recording us. I only see Mal, how her frayed t-shirt lays against the crook of her neck, as I play.

She throws her hair back at the end of the song. I finish up and set my arms on the guitar as we take in the applause and laughter from our little crowd. Noah holds his cup with his teeth and claps the loudest before chugging down his beer and shaking his head with a smile.

"That was perfect, you two cheese balls, just perfect."

I roll my eyes. "Thanks, Noah."

He looks back as the drama girls start for the kitchen. "Well, I gotta go do my thing," he says wiggling his eyebrows. He walks backward, holding up the phone at us. "I'm posting this, though."

Mal laughs. "Yeah, okay."

We do a few more songs, a Drop the Girl cover, The Maine, until Mal gets bored with it and we take a break to go searching for water. We find Noah in the kitchen with the girls, all three of them hunched over the phone. He's refilled his drink and takes down a gulp. "Yeah, trust me, he *wishes* they were."

I start to say something when Noah turns and sees us. He waves us over. "Holy shit. Check it out. Five hundred views in fifteen minutes."

"You really *posted* that?" Mal says, leaning over for a better view. Noah runs the band's YouTube and Facebook pages, Instagram, TikTok and other stuff Mal and I don't really understand. The genuine surprise on his face tells me something is unusual, though.

"Is that good?" I ask him, still wondering about that *he wishes* comment.

Noah nods furiously. "Yeah. It's already done better than anything I've posted."

The girls smile. The taller one shakes her head. "Sorry, but it's adorable."

Mal tenses, a block of granite beside me. Adorable? Wishes they were? Were what? What exactly is happening?

The party gets sloppier. Noah makes the most of his free beer deal, and soon things are getting crowded with people wandering around doing their own thing. Lots of smacks on the back and telling Mal and me how great we are.

It's going on one in the morning, and Mal and I are ready to go. Hank told me to be home early. Mal's dad is out of town, but her mom trusts her if she's with the band. Noah? Well, who knows at the moment. He says he's going to hang so it's just the two of us back in the car.

"That was fun," Mal says in a way that means it wasn't.

"Yeah," I say, in a way that can mean anything. I'm still hung up on what Noah was saying in the kitchen, but I'm more anxious about how I'm going to sneak back home and hopefully avoid Hank when Mal turns to me.

"Hey, can we just drive for a bit?"

I nod, turn the key. I'm still smiling as I put the car in gear. "Yeah, sure."

3

─────────

My eyes adjust to the early sunlight as my sleepy gaze roams the room. Streaks of red clay trail down the windowsill to the line of clothes leading to my bed. My boots stand a stride apart on the floor. I'm reliving the best parts of last night when Hank's plodding steps stop at my door.

"Get out here, Myles."

I know it's about the car. Or last night. Staying out so late. Anything. Another pound.

Hank's baritone drawl finds my feet from the floor. My heart picks up a gear and I can hear my own heavy breaths as I swing my legs off the bed. I manage to throw on my jeans and a t-shirt from off the floor. A quick wipe over my face, and I open the door.

He fingers his goatee. The sight of him with his big cup of soda, his basketball shorts, and the gut spilling from his XXL t-shirt sets me in panic mode. We're about the same height now, around six-two, but with his thick neck and huge head, he must outweigh me by nearly a hundred pounds.

"Mind telling me what time you came home last night?" he says, his pale blue eyes scanning over me. The ice in his cup rattles as he leans against the doorjamb, his nose twitching like a well-trained

19

canine as he tries to gather a scent of beer or weed. There's nothing to sniff out, but it doesn't help my nerves.

The worst part about dealing with Hank is waiting for him to strike. I clear my throat, try to find my voice. "I'm not sure. It wasn't late."

He snorts. "Wasn't late, huh?"

Standing before him, after being jostled out of bed to answer questions first thing in the morning, it's almost scary how much I hate this man my grandmother married. Maybe scarier is how much he enjoys this, sizing me up as he leans into the doorjamb.

He lolls his big head back toward the hall. "You hear this boy? He said it wasn't late." He turns back to me. I focus on the wallpaper behind him. "I'm asking *what time* you got home."

I shrug. "I don't know, eleven?" I look to the floor, afraid he'll see the hatred in my eyes. Or worse, the fear. "I guess I—"

"Don't guess. Know. And you left the tools out. Just ran out and saw them sitting there to rust. You know how much those tools cost me?"

Ah, the quiz game with Hank. Only there are no correct answers to his questions—questions designed to leave me soaking in shame. Another pull of his drink. Hank doesn't drink alcohol—though it might do him some good—he's too righteous for that. But Diet Dr. Pepper? By the case. We make a run to Sam's Club every weekend to re-up on that.

Down the hall, I hear Nan shuffling around, clinking and clattering in the kitchen as Hank waits me out. The urge to scream scrapes down my spine, no matter how many times we've done this.

He taps his forehead with two pudgy fingers. Fingers too short and thick to play guitar. "You don't think, Myles. You run off without a care in the world. You're too old for that."

He shifts and I step back. Hank smirks. "Go put the tools away." He points toward the kitchen. "And while you're at it, get the ladder out. You've got gutters to clean. And the trash needs to go out. Then put your laundry away." He motions past me, and I feel an inward flinch. "Your room is a mess. You're almost eighteen years old. Do you hear me?"

I nod, then turn to start for the laundry when Hank shoves me in the back. I stumble a couple of steps before I catch my balance. "I asked you a question. Do you hear me?"

A mist spreads over my eyes. I do my best to hold it together as I turn back to him, but my face is hot and my neck tingles. I tighten, flexing my forearms, more to hold it back than let it out, when Hank's glare drops to my clenched fists. Something flashes in his eyes. He moves in, his breath harsh in my face. "You got a problem with that, Myles?"

Behind him, Nan calls out "Hank."

Hank glowers at Nan for a beat, then it's back on me. Two deep, nasally breaths before he shakes his head, backing off to his den. "Laundry. Trash. Gutters. Last time I'm going to tell you."

Once he's gone, I sit on the bed and catch my breath, squeezing my eyes shut. I realize Nan is still watching me, lips parted, rag in hand, as though she actually considered standing up to him. But I know it's nothing more than a thought. And bad as it is, it almost makes me glad I'm here. What would he do to her if he didn't have me around?

I can't blame Nan. Really, I'm no better. I do the chores, starting with my laundry before moving to get the trash outside, which is overflowing with fast food bags and all the junk from Hank's truck. I keep myself together, counting down the days in my head until I hear his truck starting up. I remind myself I got off easy this time. A little shove in the back.

I head out to clean the gutters but stop first to check on Nan. She's in the kitchen, going hard—even for her—scrubbing the ancient floor so vigorously the jars on the counter clink together.

"Morning, Nan."

Two grunts in response. Even as I'm dying for a glass of water, maybe some cereal, her quick glare cuts me a warning. Do not walk on her floor.

It's okay, I'm content to wait. The house is lighter without Hank.

When he's not working or at church or doing Hank things, he hovers over the house like a storm cloud. He sets traps for me to walk into. Hank's always on the hunt, and like any good prey, my sense of danger is keen. I know when to flee.

While I don't care much what Hank thinks, it's a little different with Nan, although I have no idea what would make her happy. Maybe if I pawned my guitars, quit playing music—quit chasing the only dream I've ever had, that would do the trick. Who knows? Nan's not big on chasing dreams. But it's all I have. I'm only good at music. I hardly understand anything at all about this world, but I get music completely.

"So, big plans for the day?" I ask, leaning against the doorjamb. My voice is still a bit off from the encounter with Hank. And I'm still debating whether or not to tiptoe to the sink.

This is kind of our routine. I like to mess with Nan, part of my not-so-secret mission to make her smile. It's happened before, a few weeks ago. I'm due for another one.

I take a tiny step for the sink. "We could hit the community market?"

I almost miss playing the market. It was our band's first gig. Talk about for the love of music. We'd wake up at five in the morning on a Saturday to play for a bunch of guys in overalls chewing on straw. But it was worth watching Mal sleepwalk onto the stage.

Another step for the sink when Nan whips back her head. "Now don't go walking on my floor, Myles."

She turns and gets back to the scrubbing, the sponge disintegrating in her clutches.

"Hank's awfully upset you took the car. And about the tools."

My shoulders sink. Since Hank is gone, I'm feeling brave. "Yeah, well, since I'm changing the oil, should be no problem for me to take the car, then. Right?"

Nan grunts. And I know she's about to go into the discipline spiel. Hank was raised not to talk back. He's been working since he was thirteen. His Dad didn't take any lip. He's a God-fearing man, so now he gets to come home and make my life a living hell.

I backtrack my way out of the kitchen and start for the living room. Nan's house is old but not in the cool, fixer upper-type way. There's no crafty stair railing or crown moulding. I think it was built in the thirties with little thought for amenities. Most of the rooms have faux wood paneling and thin carpet, and the whole place smells like a furnace. But the kitchen and its green appliances stay clean thanks to Nan's weekend marathons. Thankfully I have the downstairs bedroom so I can come and go as I please.

Hank may claim the house as his own, but it was Nan's long before he arrived and established the pecking order—before he cranked up the rules, demanded respect and refused to tolerate back talk.

For all the trouble I give her, Nan is all I've got when it comes to family. I'll never count old Hank as family. My parents were a mess —my dad was a struggling musician but very successful drug addict, and my mom was a drifter who got by on her looks (according to Nan). The last thing in the world they ever needed was a baby (again, Nan), but a baby they got. Me. Anyway, all I have to remember my father by are a couple creased pictures, his guitars, some music, and fading memories that seem more and more like a movie I can hardly remember seeing.

I leave Nan to scrub, but I know that somewhere, deep down, she cares. It's no coincidence that my dad's childhood height notches on the den doorjamb haven't been scrubbed over or repainted. And even on days like this, just as I'm about to give up on her, the scrubbing stops and Nan calls out to me. "I could use some tomatoes, I suppose."

I stifle a laugh. "Okay, well come on. Let's get moving."

I'M CLEANING the gutters that afternoon when Noah texts.

Noah: Video is blowing up

It makes me laugh because I haven't thought about it all day. I've thought about the show and how I only made thirty-three bucks. I've kicked a few songs around in my head. I've run a memory loop of the late-night drive with Mal. But I've given zero thought to the video.

I get back to the gutters when my phone dings again. This time it's Mal.

Mal: You Busy?

Me: Just cleaning the gutters

Mal: Hank sucks

Me: Yep

Mal: Want to work on the song?

I'm already laughing as I type out:

Me: The song? What song?

Mal: Grrr. My house in an hour?

I play the game where I force myself to take a minute, like I'm too busy to drop everything for Mal's texts. I scoop out a handful of leaves, drop them in the bucket. Hank's been known to get up on the ladder and check behind me, so I can't skip a leaf.

Another handful of goopy leaves in the bucket before I wipe my hands on my jeans, grab my phone from the roof and ever so coolly punch a reply to Mal.

Me: K.

Well, since I have my phone out, I might as well check the video. I pull it up and nearly drop my phone in the bucket.

It's up to six thousand hits, which is crazy, but crazier still is the video itself. It's both mortifying and amazing. The way the bulb lights cast a warm glow around us, and Mal in particular, is like stage lighting. The audio is remarkably clear, only a faint murmur in the background, just enough to let you know it's live.

Then there's me. I'm all lovey eyes at Mal, to the point I almost can't bear to watch. Do I really look at her like that?

Pathetic? Yes, I'm pathetic. *So* pathetic. And Nan knows it too, because as soon as I step off the ladder and breeze into the house for a shower and change, she calls me into the den, where she's glued to *Law & Order*.

"Hey Nan, what's up?"

A quick glance at me, and her face changes. "Did you get the gutters clean?"

"Gutters?" I say, because I can't help myself. She pauses the television. On screen, the detective, his collar up against the backdrop of the inner city, is frozen in thought with a cloud of breath at his lips. I'm not sure how many episodes of *Law & Order* were made, but my nan is determined to see it through. And it doesn't do her any favors, trust me. Nan won't leave the house after five o'clock. Nothing but crime out there.

"Yes, gutters are clean."

"Good," she grumbles as she looks me over. "You going somewhere?"

"Yeah, over to Mal's. We're working on a song."

She balls her face up as though I told her we were practicing witchcraft. "You should come with me to church tomorrow."

I cough to cover my laugh. "We'll see." Nothing against God, but going to church with Hank and Nan? Give me the witchcraft.

She shakes her head and glances at the television. "Hmm. Make sure you put gas in the car."

And that's it. The detective is breathing again, cracking wise about a recent string of attacks.

Time to make my exit.

4

I get to the Kamels' subdivision around four, driving with the windows down despite the immovable summer heat. Hank looms in my thoughts, what he'll have to say about me taking the car even after I've spent roughly half my paycheck paying insurance and filling up the tank. I feel I've earned the right to drive her. Besides, any time I escape my house and drive over to Mal's house, life gets a bit better, at least for a while.

I drift down the wide streets, take in the huge front lawns with the precisely-trimmed bushes, the two and three-car garages and perfectly-shaped trees. Before I know it, I'm a world away, walking up the meticulous pavers lined with decorative grasses and mulch. I run a hand through my hair and tug at my shirt before ringing the bell.

Charley answers the door. "What's up, Myles?"

Mal's little brother is one part aspiring hip-hop producer, one part gamer. All parts dork.

"What's up, Charley?"

He nods, opening the door wider for me to come in. "Hey, you should hear this beat I'm working on. It's dope."

"Yeah?"

"Yeah, hang on. I'll get my iPad."

"Nope. No." Mal glides down the steps and sets an arm around her little brother. "I need him. We have work to do."

Charley shoots me a look, then balls up his face. "Come on, Mal. Real quick."

Mal rolls her eyes again, grabs me by the arm and drags me toward the den. "Maybe later, okay?"

Charley cocks his head. "No boys in the den."

Mal throws her free hand up. "It's just Myles."

Ouch.

We plop down on the couch. The Kamels came to America from Egypt in the late nineties and have what could be considered an eclectic taste. The sunken den is decorated in a mix of furniture from all over the globe. Mal's dad is a doctor, and her mother does something with insurance. I love nothing more than walking into their house because it's like taking a tour of the world. They've been everywhere, and the gleaming hardwood floors are adorned with Persian rugs and runners. There are statues and paintings and jungle-like plants that remind me of the Amazon Forest.

Mal bites her pen. She has her notepad, and she pulls her legs to her chest as she looks me over.

"How are things?"

It's just Myles. I turn away. "Good. Went to the market with Nan. How's your dad? Is he still coming home this week?"

"I think so. Why are you being so weird?"

I wonder if she's seen the video. And if she has, did she notice how I was looking at her? Of course she did. *Thousands* of people already have. "I'm not being weird. Am I?"

"Yes, even more than usual. Anyway. So last night, I think the song was a hit."

The song. Right. It takes me a minute to even remember the warehouse. I turn to her, shaking my head with a snort just to mess with her. "I don't think so."

She gives me a playful nudge. "You know, Myles, I'm starting to think you're jealous."

Yep, she saw the video. I shake it off and pretend not to notice her arm brushing against mine. This is Mal, my friend, my bandmate, I can't get caught up on this. I need to tell Noah to kill the video before anyone else sees it.

I shift in my seat, and she's giving me that look that says I'm still being weird, so I try to talk over it, change the subject that forever sits between us like some sort of third wheel.

"Okay, let me hear those lyrics again. All I caught last night was, 'You gave it to him twice.'"

She kicks me. Hard. "Ouch!"

"It's not *gave it to him,* you turd. It's, 'cheated on him twice.'"

"Ah, okay. That's better."

Mal is still glaring at me when Charley wanders in with the iPad. He falls into the love seat. "Okay, here it is, Myles. You think I should post this beat? It's got a Yeezy feel to it."

Mal holds up her notebook. "We're working here."

I nod. "Of course. I've heard your skills."

Mal stares at her notes, still biting her pen. "Don't encourage it."

"Really?" Charley jumps to his feet. His baggy pants turn skinny at the calf and cuff at the ankle. He's got a Post Malone vibe going on, and it's not working for him. Not sure it works for Post Malone.

"Yeah. Of course."

Mal throws a glare my way, one eyebrow cocked. I shrug. "Let me hear something. What are you working on?"

Charley smiles, gets to his feet and works the iPad. I'm not prepared for the speakers in the room to rumble as some sort of house/techno/raver beat warbles to life. Some moaning starts, I think. I can't tell what he's sampled, but he's swaying with his eyes closed. Mal grabs my arm and digs in as she covers her face with the notebook. I do my best to bob along.

Charley covers his eyes as a deep, chopped voice comes in for what I think is his chorus. "It's big bills for me, it's big bills for me, it's big—" This goes on like fifteen or sixteen times before Mal waves her arms like she's fending off a swarm of angry hornets.

"Okay, stop it. Please. Stop."

Charley uncovers his face. He turns to me, his eyes hopeful and innocent. I try to make the best out of it. "Well, I think… Yeah."

Mal buries her head into my arm, and I'm left with a pile of hair, a hint of her herbal shampoo. Charley backs out of the room, smiling. "Yeah?"

"Oh yeah."

"Sweet. Thanks Myles."

"You got it, man."

Once he's gone, Mal's head pops up. She stares at me as Charley is chanting about those big bills, no doubt to record a video on his laptop. I sit back, happy to help.

Mal's glare remains fixed on me.

"What?"

"Oh, you know *what*."

"Come on, it was good. You've gotta be more supportive."

"Oh, I'm supportive, Myles. I hear those 'Yeezy beats' every day. My dad thinks he needs therapy."

I laugh before I can catch it. Probably because it's true. I can picture Dr. Kamel, a hand to his chin, completely perplexed. I fold over thinking about it. Mal shakes her head. "Oh yeah, it's so funny. Just so funny."

I'm still cracking up when Mrs. Kamel walks in, and I'm thinking she's going to get on us about making fun of Charley, or Charles, as she calls him. Instead, she smiles at me.

"Hi Myles, how are you?"

I get myself together and rise to my feet, fixing my shirt, and trying to ignore Mal's scoffing. "I'm good, Mrs. Kamel. Thanks."

Her smile broadens. "So good to see you, dear. Your hair, it's getting longer. She reaches out and touches my hair, which would be weird, but Mrs. Kamel has a motherly way about her.

I nod, run a hand over my head. "Oh, yeah. I need to get it cut."

"And you've been working out, it seems."

Mal's eyes dart from her mom to me. But again, Mrs. Kamel has a way of saying these things where it isn't awkward. I've gained maybe ten pounds of muscle since I started hauling bricks and bags of sand around for Mr. Irvin at work. Mrs. Kamel starts in about her new workout plan, but when she flexes her arms and shows me her guns, Mal has had enough.

"Okay, Mal says, getting up. "We need to work on something, and it's not happening here." She looks at me. "Park?"

I shrug, fighting off a smile. There's no place I'd rather go.

"Sure."

5

WE HIT THE TRAILS ALONG THE BACK END OF THE PARK, hiking down to the ledge, where the rocks sit on a cliff overlooking the river and downtown. It always steals my breath how the view sneaks up on me out of nowhere. One second, I'm hiking in the woods past all the scattered trash, beer bottles, candy wrappers, cigarette butts, and shards of Styrofoam, and the next second, I turn and find a postcard view of the train trestle stretching across the small canyon, braced against the smeary blood orange horizon of the setting sun.

Before Mal, I'd been coming to River Run all my life and had no idea of all the trails and overlooks until she brought me down there to write songs. The first time I watched her leap onto the rock, worn smooth by all the hands and feet and paint over the years, I lunged after her to pull her back to safety. There's nothing but a few hundred feet of fall to the river, so it still makes my heart skip when she gets up there and stands with her arms spread apart like she's about to take a swan dive to her death. But at least I'll sit with her.

On occasion, when we hear a train rumbling in, Mal grabs my hand and squeezes tight, squealing like a little girl. It makes me hope the train will never end and keep chugging on forever. But it never does, and I've come to hate the last car of a train because it means Mal's hand is not in mine.

For now, though, all is quiet.

"You seem off today. Everything okay?" Mal asks suddenly, pulling me back in from my thoughts.

"Huh? Yeah." I shrug.

She looks me over. "Is Hank being… you know? All Hank-ish?"

Sometimes I regret telling her the bits and pieces I've told her about my life at home. Not even Noah knows how it is with Hank. I roll my neck, blow it off. "Yeah, no. It's fine."

Mal turns to the trestle, patient as she waits for me to sort through my thoughts. Ever since the day Hank moved in, he was after me to "man up." And it wasn't long before he decided part of "manning up" was to lash my back with his belt.

A gentle swoosh of traffic slips across the river. I don't want to talk about Hank, or anything really. I'm fine with the river, the trestle, the two of us. This.

Mal's got a scab near her left knee, peeking out from the hole in her favorite jeans. Her skin holds the evening sun as she cranes her neck to gaze out to the quiet. She's the only person I've ever known who can wear a sunset—its dwindling warmth finding her cheeks, casting a shine in her eyes. Below us, the water is calm, and a faint breeze tickles our faces. She meditates for a few seconds before she pulls out her notepad.

We get to work. We fix up *Oh That's Nice,* and I'm still messing with her about it when Mal gets quiet. She sets the pad down and gazes off. Something about the contemplative gesture stirs my thoughts, and I realize, as we're up there above the river and the noise, that this song isn't a joke to her. It means something. And sometimes I get so wrapped up in my own issues that I forget her life isn't so perfect, either.

She told me as much once, right here at this favorite place of ours. I was mad at Hank about something, and I blew her off. "No offense, Mal, but you don't understand. Your family is perfect."

She'd turned and glared at me, her lips parting. "Is that what you think?"

I shrugged. "It's better than what I've got," I said, as though we'd entered a competition to see who had the most messed up family.

Another glance out to the trestle. When she looked at me again, her eyes were dark and piercing. "You're wrong."

The sharpness in her tone popped my little pity bubble. With my full attention, she bit her lip, still shaking her head as she turned to me, squinting against the evening sun. "Myles, do you know how much shit my dad takes on a daily basis?"

"Huh?"

"Professionally speaking."

"Um, no."

"Well, let me help you out there. He takes it from the world. From his patients. From everyone who looks at him or hears his accent and assumes he's going to plant a bomb in a mall or on a plane."

"Mal, I wasn't, I didn't…"

Too late. I had her going now. "Seriously, he's got to be the nicest person in the world, even after what he's seen back home, you know? It's crazy. How he came here from Egypt, searching for 'freedom and prosperity,'" she said with air quotes.

"He went to medical school, *stayed* here to practice medicine. You know, to help people. And what's the thanks he gets? They call him a terrorist at a baseball game." She aims a sharp stare at me, a scathing smile, nodding. "Yep. True story. They ask if he has a flying carpet. They treat him like a criminal even after he changed his name from Jahi to *John* just to make them more comfortable."

"Damn, that's messed up."

"I know it is."

Her voice was defiant, daring me to go against her. Hurt filled the gaps between her breaths. "I know you think I live in some nice suburban house and everything is great, but it's not. My mom? No better for her. Her family hates my dad because of some religious sect or something I don't even fully comprehend. We're not even religious, probably *because* of that. My grandparents basically disowned her. For marrying a doctor, for God's sake."

She looked off, contemplating. I let her stew and throw some rocks over the cliff until I realized she wasn't finished. "Oh, then there's Charley, the boy wonder." She glared at me. "Jihadi Boy—it's what they call him at school. Did you know that, Myles? Can you believe that? Private school shits. He was making a song about it, you know, as a *joke*. I told him if he did, I would wage my own personal jihad on him."

Her eyes closed and she took a huge breath, as though she were sorting out the wreckage of thoughts and the words she'd scattered all over the place. I went to throw a rock but stopped short. "And what about you, Mal?"

She turned, stared me down. "I guess I got off easy. Sure, the girls love my *exotic* look. They rave about my olive skin and my *like, totally cool hair*." She tossed a strand of hair and fake giggled.

I turned away. "Your hair is cool."

Her voiced softened. "I could never be one of them, not that I want to be."

"Thank God."

She laughed. "But do you see? I mean, my life isn't so awesome, you know?"

It's not so easy for Mal. I know that now, as she gazes out to the trestle, hoping for a train to come and take her thoughts away. I think of how she zones out, gets quiet. How she feels guilty for her academic successes, like she hasn't earned it the way her father did. About the band, she feels like a phony because she lives in suburbia but wants play warehouses and be hardcore.

The thing is, Mal's family story *is* hardcore. Her dad is the bravest man I've ever met. And she's got to see that, see how strong she is *because* of who she is. Maybe I should tell her that more often. Remind her she's amazing.

"Mal. I like it."

She blinks, breaking from the sun's trance. I shrug. *"Oh That's Nice. It's good, okay?"*

She turns to me fully, lips curving into a smile that causes fireworks to flare in my chest. "Yeah?" I nod. She looks off, smiling. "Okay then."

We turn to something new. She's humming a melody, and I'm trying to work out some chords to go with it on the acoustic guitar. She's onto something, and I let her roam with it, swaying, taking it down, jotting. She scribbles out words, rearranges. I catch snippets of her writing: falling, trying, trusting.

I strum along until I can't help myself. I find the chords to a song I've been toying with, only I'm sort of picking at the strings on the acoustic and with the breeze. Mal looks over at me and smiles, and I realize I'm humming along now, the words in my head falling into place like puzzle pieces.

Her smile pushes me to keep going with the song, the chords making me think of my dad playing in the kitchen, which is weird because I hardly knew the dude. But it's soft and low and almost part of the breeze on the cliff. I'm still strumming it out when the snap of a stick behind us breaks my trance. I stop playing and turn to find some kids watching us.

It's obvious they're here to smoke. Mal breaks into applause, and I roll my eyes and try not to blush too hard. We hang for a bit before we get to our feet and climb down from the rock. A few of the guys watch Mal extra close. I tense up, but she brushes past them, and we hike back to the park.

I start up the wagon and put it in gear. Mal, back to picking at the scab on her knee, ever-so-casually says, "So, the video seems to be popular."

My foot comes off the gas. "You saw it?"

Her eyes widen. "Yeah, I saw it."

"I was going to tell Noah to take it down."

"What? why?"

Because I look like a fool. "I don't know, it's goofy."

"It is, but I kind of like it. And I hate to tell you this, but you can't really take it down now. It's on YouTube and other places we don't even know about. And if it keeps blowing up? I don't know, maybe Noah's right. It could help with the band. And we need help with the band right now."

True. The band needs help, but Mal doesn't. She's been getting attention from the start. I've seen her take calls from people claiming they can make her a star. Some legit, some not so much. And after last night, how she was singing, moving, *performing*, I don't know. Maybe she's looking ahead. Or maybe I'm reading too much into things.

When we get back to her house, I'm still wrapped up thinking about it. Mal whips her head around and smiles. "You okay over there, Myles?"

"Yeah, I'm cool."

She laughs, then slides out of the wagon and winks at me. "You're such a liar. I'll see you at practice."

"Yep."

She tilts her head and squints at me, something that always knocks me back in my seat. She waits for who knows what, then rolls her eyes. "You're still thinking about the video, aren't you?"

"No," I say. "Maybe."

She ducks back in the car, and I catch my breath. She smiles, as though something's just occurred to her, but then it's gone. She leans back out of the wagon.

"It's out of our hands now," she says, then pushes herself off the car and starts toward her house.

6

PRACTICE IS ALWAYS AT NOAH'S HOUSE. MAL REFUSES TO do it at her place, and it's out of the question at mine. Noah's place makes sense. His dad works constantly and his mom bakes constantly, so it all sort of works out. Plus, since Noah is the drummer, it helps that his kit stays set up in the basement when we don't have shows.

The basement is almost like a studio. Whatever problems his parents have, they take care of Noah. It's like whatever creative endeavors he can dream up, they make it happen. Guitars, drum set, there's even an old church organ. Mal loves it. She will sit there for hours if you let her, plucking out rock operas on the Harpsichord Genie.

But today, as Mrs. Connors presents a pile of jalapeno poppers to accompany all the Mountain Dew we can drink, I'm not sure how much practice will take place.

Noah is freaking out because the video is officially trending. It's shot up to 30,000 views, and it's growing before our eyes. Like, you can *see* the clicks happening. And each click means one more person saw the way I was looking at Mal.

He plays it again, and I have to turn away. Mal's face lights up with a mix of fascination and utter confusion as Noah talks about clicks and volume.

He's especially chipper tonight, rocking on his stool and going on about algorithms and hashtags. "You know what this is going to do for us?"

Mal snags a popper and takes a small bite. Noah waits for us to understand, twirling a drumstick. "Damn, you two are clueless. Well, let me help you along. This is how careers are made, if we play it right."

I'm not buying it, and I'm thankful when we move downstairs and Noah changes the subject. His dad is on some town council committee thing in Richland Hills where he is hopefully getting us on the bill for some summer festival at the park. It's Soccer Mom City, but whatever, a gig is a gig.

The stupid video keeps pulling him back. Noah checks the phone every eight seconds. He plays the video again, Mal leaning in to watch. Hearing the tinny sounds of my strumming and Mal's voice makes my cheeks flush. I grab the guitar and do some serious tuning until I hear the sloppy applause at the end.

Mal smiles. "I like it. It's cheesy but fun."

Noah howls. "Hell yes, it's cheesy. But whatever, right?"

Mal's phone buzzes. She frowns at the number but then takes the call. I glance at Noah, and he shrugs. Mal starts pacing. "Yeah, yeah. Hi!"

She waves at Noah to get his attention, then points to the door. Noah nods and Mal steps outside. Again, Mal gets calls, and so it doesn't take much for Noah to start up about opportunities and cashing in.

"You can never know what's going to pop off. The last video I posted was that show we did at the market. It got like ninety views. That one of me drumming? Forty." He shakes his phone at me. "This corny little gem has over thirty *thousand* views."

He stuffs two jalapeno poppers in his mouth once and washes them down with Mountain Dew. Almost immediately he grimaces.

"Uh, oh."

"You okay?"

Noah sets his fist to his chest. "Damn that's hot." He coughs a few times, his face turning a new shade of maroon each time. He massages his gut. "I'll be right back."

He rushes to the stairs, tripping over the second one as he hustles up the steps. I laugh, hearing his plodding footsteps over my head. Alone, I force myself to watch the video yet again, willing it to not be as bad as I think. It is. I'm about to punish myself and watch it a third time when the outside door flies open and Mal bangs in with a squeal.

"Everything all right?" I ask as she shuts the door and falls back on it, the phone by her side. Her hair flies over her face as she shakes her head. Her chest rises as she takes a deep breath then closes her eyes, her mouth an oval, a hand pressed against her cheek like she has a delightful toothache.

She nods, bites her lip, then lets out a gust of breath. Her eyes pop open again. "Oh my God."

"What?"

She jumps up and down. "That was Dave, the producer of Ripcast. They saw the video and..."

I hop up. "Wait, like, Ripcast? The thing you're always listening to?"

More crazy nodding. She's about to split open with happiness. "Myles, they want us to come on the show."

I try to process what she's saying, but she's running in place, hair bouncing to the beat of her happy dance. Another twirl, and she runs into me. She grabs my face. Her hands are hot and shaky. "They want us on the show!"

"What?" Now I'm yelling. "You're serious?" I say with a laugh. I hold my breath because my body is sort of tingling, and it has more to do with her hands on me than the podcast. It feels like I'm floating.

Mal shoves me away with another squeal. "I'm so serious."

She jumps in place again, then grabs my forearms. I can't help but join in because Ripcast is kind of big, with real bands on the show. Now they want us. Mal lets go of my arms and grabs my face again. We're still jumping when she squeals, and I kind of gush right before our smiles collide into a kiss. A pressing, wet, dizzying kiss with a hint of salt and cinnamon that lasts about *one thousand one, one thousand two*, before Mal jerks back like she's been shocked.

Her eyes go wide. She freezes, lips parted. I don't make a move until she finally blinks. A quick rush of shaky laughter that's more a sigh of disbelief. "Um… oh God, what? I'm um, wow, that…"

Mal's phone goes clattering to the floor. I see it, tell myself to pick it up, but keep staring at her because we just kissed, and I really want to do it again. But she's wringing her hands and making a point not to look at me.

I really need something to say, but it's not like words are hurling themselves through the galaxy of my brain at the moment.

"Well, I'm—"

Whatever I'm going to say is interrupted by the wrench of the upstairs door flying open. Mal and I step away from each other as Noah comes shuffling down the stairs talking about his stomach and "dropping a deuce." He hops off the last step and stops. He looks from Mal to me, then to Mal's phone on the floor. "Sooooo, what's going on?"

Mal fixes her hair. "Nothing," she says, blinking furiously, flushed and messy and glancing at me. I'm basically a useless piece of furniture at the moment.

Noah raises his eyebrows. "I heard some yelling."

Mal recovers with a laugh. "Oh, right. Yeah, *that*. Well, it's something kind of big."

"For the band," I blurt out finally, like an imbecile. But it's all I can do. Mal just kissed me. We *kissed*. Oh, and then there's the thing about Ripcast. Noah keeps looking from her to me like he's a detective on one of Nan's shows.

Mal picks up her phone and shows it to Noah. "I just got a call from Ripcast."

"What?" Noah's face trades bewilderment for surprise. I nod along, hoping I don't appear nearly as frazzled as Mal, but I'm pretty sure I'm not pulling it off. It feels like someone dropped a toaster oven into my bloodstream. Noah paces. "I told y'all! See? I knew if we got some buzz. Oh man. When?"

Mal's throat bobs. She's definitely freaked out about kissing me, and I don't know what that means. Her voice is high, and she keeps fiddling with her bracelets. "Oh, well, I mean. He was talking about next week. He's going to send me the info."

"Okay, okay so this is how it happens." Noah checks his phone and smiles. "Thirty-three thousand, baby!"

Mal sniffs. "Yeah, wow. That's awesome. He did say something about how they want to keep things simple. Like, smaller."

I glance at Mal, catching on now. Noah cocks his head, looking up from the phone. "What do you mean, smaller?"

Noah scoops up his drumsticks and twirls them. Mal walks to the organ and plays with the keys before she breaks away and falls into the tattered loveseat with the covers over the chewed-up arms.

"Like, just..." Mal sputters. I blow out a gust of breath. Noah cocks his head like a cocker spaniel.

"Huh?" Noah thinks on this, stops twirling the stick. "Oh, so they just want Mal?"

For a second I hope it's true. This would go down a lot smoother. But then I remember what she said just before we kissed. *We're going on Ripcast.*

Mal opens her mouth then shuts it. "Well, um..."

Our drummer studies the wall, taking in this new info. My guitar amp hums, the organ whirs. His eyes snap up to Mal, then me. "Oh," he says. "They want the two of you. Like in the video."

Mal bites her lip and shrugs. I try to be myself, react the way I normally would, but nothing is normal right now. I'm still flushed from kissing Mal that I can't do much more than take up space. We wait for Noah to blow up, to sling his sticks across the room, shake his head and deem us sellouts. Instead, he nods along, refusing to look at either of us. "Well, that's cool. Congrats."

At some point, we get on with practice. But it's all a bust.

There's no way we can do anything but sit in our own little thought bubbles.

Noah's elation plummets quickly, for obvious reasons. Everything is a mess.

We destroy two and a half songs before our distractions win out and everything breaks apart, and we all sort of stop playing without a word. Usually, Mal would say something about how at least we got the quitting part right, but this time she simply picks up her phone and we follow her upstairs where things only get weirder.

The delightfully buttery smells in the kitchen contrast sharply with how Mrs. Connors is laying out Mr. Connors over the phone. When she sees us, she turns and ducks down the hallway, her face flushed and teeth gritted as she continues her berating in a hushed tone. "I shouldn't have to tell you that, Will. Jesus, you know what? The sooner the better as far as I'm concerned."

Noah's mouth tightens as his eyes trail after his mom, until he realizes it and smiles to cover it up. Mal settles onto a stool at the little breakfast table in the kitchen. Noah sits across from her, and I take the middle. After another glance down the hallway, Noah leans back in his chair, drums on the table. "You know what? This is cool. Really, it is. I mean, any sort of publicity is good publicity, right? Even if…"

He lets that sit there. Mal ducks her head, eyebrows up. "What?" Noah shrugs, then chuckles. Mal takes the bait. "Even if *what*?"

"Huh? Oh, nothing."

Down the hallway, Mrs. Connors shuts the bedroom door, and we're left pretending we don't hear the muffled yelling. I shift in my seat and play moderator. "So you're happy for us?"

"No, wait," Mal says, almost turning to me before getting back to Noah. "Hang on. Even if *what*, Noah?" she demands, sounding more like herself, even managing to peek at me for one tenth of a second. Noah eats it up, his shoulders quaking with laughter.

"It's just, you know the two of you are going to have to do that song." He does a strumming motion. "*Your Kiss*, is… Damn, that's kind of lame. I'm actually glad I'm not going."

Mal throws her hair back to reveal her eyeroll. Noah keeps laughing, harder now, as though trying to cover up the hushed tones of his mom raging on the phone in the bedroom. But I think back to the vacant look on his face in the car the other night and realize I haven't seen his dad around in weeks. It seems more serious than I thought.

Mal starts to say something else when the bedroom door swings open and Mrs. Connors comes sweeping back in, blinking and sniffling and putting on a show. "Hi kids. I have pizza."

She grabs a mitt and lunges for the oven, takes out the pizza, and whirls around to the cutlery. Noah's chair comes down with a bang. "Mom, the band is going to be famous."

"Oh?" she says, absently, clanging around until she finds the pizza cutter.

Mal rubs her temples. "Noah, do you want to go? Seriously? I'll tell them."

"Go where?" Mrs. Connors attacks the pizza with the cutter. One, two, three times across before she goes for the plates. She brings them to the table before whipping around for the pizza. She places it in the middle, and Noah scoops up a slice, a string of cheese stretching and stretching as he leans back in his chair again. "Mal and Myles are going on a podcast to be goobers."

Mal scoffs. "Did you just say *goobers*?"

"Oh, Noah." Mrs. Connors laughs. She fiddles with some knobs on the stove while Noah and Mal verbally spar over the meaning of goobers. Usually when Noah and Mal debate, I find myself on the outside looking in, as both of them are super smart and strong-willed, and I'm not much on books or confrontation. But something's different tonight, or maybe I'm just too stunned from what happened downstairs to pretend anything is normal right now.

Noah goes for another slice of pizza, reading from his phone. "Synonyms include geek, dork, dweeb, goofball, weirdo. These all apply. Myles, you okay? You're kinda quiet."

"It's a *peanut*," Mal retorts, back to pretending I don't exist. "Or, like, the candy."

I clear my throat. "I'm good."

Mrs. Connors mutters something about laundry. "Okay kids, breadsticks in the oven. Take them out in five."

Mrs. Connors storms out of the room while Noah laughs, still reading from his phone. "Here it is, from Urban Dictionary. 'Goober, a lovable goofball.' So, yeah. Myles."

Mal pushes away her plate, holding up her phone with a smirk. "Southern slang for peanut."

I'm lost in thought with an empty plate in front of me. Noah sets his phone down. "Myles, spill it. You could hardly hold your guitar down there." He chews like a maniac, his face flushed. "What, you already thinking about the podcast?"

I force myself to grab a slice of pizza. "Something like that." Mal looks up from her phone and shifts in her seat. Noah laughs.

"Well, personally, I can't wait to watch you guys cheese it up. You know they're going to make this it into a couple thing."

Mal's cheeks ripen. I choke on my first bite of pizza.

7

We sit in the car outside of Noah's house, Mal an ocean away with her head against the passenger window. Suddenly everything is different, and I only want things to go back to how they were. But I also want things to be like they were for two seconds in the basement. I guess most of all, I just want to get rid of this crushing silence between us.

I put some music on and start to back out of the driveway when Mal props her head on her hand and sets her jaw with a sigh. My foot hits the brake. "Mal, look, I'm sorry."

She breaks from her daze and turns to me. "What are you sorry about?"

I set my gaze to the windshield. It's my turn to play the lookaway game. What am I sorry about? Nothing, really, besides everything. Really, I just want to know if the kiss meant something or was merely a celebration that got a little out of control. "For," I sigh. "I don't know."

"Yeah." She wipes her hair back and lets me off the hook. "It's strange, huh? Doing this without Noah? But he's been after us for months to promote, network or whatever. Now he's making fun of us." She rolls her eyes again. "It's..."

Her arms fall to her lap. She looks off at nothing as Barbara idles in the driveway. Mal sets down her window, inviting the slight breeze to catch her hair as she sets her face toward the sky. I struggle to find anything to say. Which is strange because I've never had trouble talking to Mal.

I start off for her house, pretending it's nothing when to me it's everything. I leave the windows down, if nothing else than for the rushing wind that fills the gaps and plays with Mal's hair. It's not until I pull into her driveway that she opens her eyes and turns her body to face me.

She clasps her hands between her legs. She blinks a few times, the late summer sun glittering in her eyes. "Myles."

"Yeah?"

She looks around. "We need to talk."

A quick shrug. "It's fine. I get it. Noah's just being... Noah."

I manage to turn my head to her. She closes her eyes and whispers. "Not about Noah."

For a second, as Mal's hand slides over to mine, the way she has so many times before, I think maybe she feels it, too. But she stops short, takes her hand back. "About the basement." She bites her lip, and I have to look away. I grip the steering wheel like I'm about to fall.

"Okay."

"I don't know, it just sort of happened. But we can't... I mean, it's not something we can..." She fixes her hair. "With the band and everything."

My hope lost, I puff out my cheeks. "I get it. You were happy and wanted to kiss someone. I happened to be there."

She laughs, quickly. "No." Then, more forcefully. "No! Not at all. That's *not* what happened."

She slides over, and I'm stuck, caught in in the mixed signals she's been sending since the other night at the show. Our arms touch. I kiss her head and she leans into it, closing her eyes with a smile before she jerks away. "Myles, this is... this..." Her voice holds a quiver. More nervous laughter as she glances at her house. "We just can't, okay?"

"Because of Noah?"

She sits straighter. "Not because of Noah, because of *us*. Because of everything. You're my best friend, Myles."

I groan, incapable of words. She keeps saying we can't, as though some sort of law has been written somewhere. I don't even know anymore.

"Okay," I say finally, sitting up. I put both hands on the wheel. Still about to fall. "I guess we can't. Or, you can't. So, friends."

She sighs but doesn't make a move to get out of the car. My brain screams at me to do something. To fix this. I've wanted to kiss Mal since the tenth grade but never thought she felt the same way until the other night at the show. Until the basement and maybe right now. I turn to her, and her eyes burn into me with a mix of confusion and sorrow. Maybe pity. Maybe that's all this was.

"Well, I guess I'll..." I gesture ahead, like an idiot.

She turns for the door. "Text me later, okay?

"Sure."

I nod as she slides over again and hugs me tightly. Until I'm hopeless all over again. I kiss her head again, quickly, before she pulls away and opens the door. She looks back once, and then she's gone.

8

THE ALARM GOES OFF AT 6:45. MONDAY MORNING. I SET MY feet to the floor and rub my eyes. My stomach growls as I stand and stretch. Another glance at the clock. Mr. Irvin will be over in roughly five minutes to pick me up, so I need to hustle up and get dressed, maybe scarf down breakfast. Then I remember the video. And the kiss.

A quick check of the stats sends me falling back into bed. How? How is this real? And why doesn't it feel right?

Because I hate the video. Because Mal and I kissed and she freaked out. Because Noah isn't going to the podcast with us. It's everything we've wanted, and it's all wrong.

I rush into the kitchen and find Nan at the stove. Greasy scrambled eggs sit in a pan of bacon fat. I toss some on a plate and shovel down what Hank left behind. I spill eggs on the floor, and she's ready to attack me with the broom when I spot Mr. Irvin's truck in the driveway.

"Gotta run. Thanks, Nan."

The sky is brimming with promise, burning orange with red flares, yellow at the edges. It's the kind of sky that says, "Yeah, bad things happen, but look at this."

I climb into his pick-up truck, a beige-used-to-be-white 1983 F150 with dents and rust spots that holds a completely rebuilt engine under the hood. Mr. Irvin's truck will probably outlive me.

He's got the oldies going, which reminds me of the song, the video, and the avalanche of confusion that's followed.

"How's it going, kiddo?" He says, looking me over.

I mumble my pleasantries. I have about ten minutes until I'm hauling bricks and blocks and mortar and this is usually when I sit back and catch a quick nap. Not today. Mal's words continue to haunt me.

Mr. Irvin laughs with that kind grin of his. The guy is never tired. I've worked ten hours with him in ninety-degree temps and never once heard him complain.

And maybe he's onto something. It's not so bad, being up this early. Working outside. It keeps me busy, gives my mind a break. I can let my body take over and get lost in the dust and sand as we shovel out the dirt and level the surface.

Mr. Irvin and I met at the community market last year. The band was on a set break, and I saw this old guy across the street loading cinderblocks two at a time. Wiry and strong, he looked like he could handle things all right on his own, but seeing he had an entire pallet of the things, I hustled over and gave him a hand. We got the truck loaded, and he tried to give me twenty bucks. I said no way, so he offered me a job. When I got back to the stage, Mal said it was the cutest thing she'd ever seen. Noah rolled his eyes.

The patio we're digging out today is in Boonsboro, one of those Blake Alsten-type places. Mr. Irvin thinks we can probably start paving before five if we hustle. Since I'm skipping out tomorrow to do the podcast, I get after it. While Mr. Irvin levels, I hustle like a madman, unloading bags of sand and brick after brick while the sun gets up over the tree, hot on my back as find a groove. I keep at it with the wheelbarrow until the truck is empty. I catch Mr. Irvin watching me with a smile. I'd like to think he's impressed.

Music comes first, but I do love the work, getting lost in the grunt of it all. There's a rhythm to it when my body takes over, and my brain roams. Most of the morning, I'm thinking about Mal and the rush of the kiss the other night and the awkwardness that followed. The talk in the car. How she said *we can't* like it's some unwritten rule. I wipe my forehead, load and unload. Bricks are easier to understand.

For lunch we hit Wendy's. Mr. Irvin eats his hamburger plain without cheese. He likes his fries plain, too, and he washes it all down with a small cup of water. I get two cheeseburgers with everything that will fit on them, drown my fries in ketchup, and manage two refills of sweet tea. Then I top it off with a Frosty.

"So, one more year, huh?" Mr. Irvin asks as I work on dessert. Anyone else and I'd roll my eyes, but the old man likes to keep track of things in my life. He asks questions and sits back to wait on my answers. Almost like he cares.

"One more," I say, leaving out, *and I'll still be working for you.*

"College?"

I shoot him a look. Four more years in a classroom sounds cruel and unusual. I shrug. "I really just want to play music."

He nods. A lot of adults frown when I bring up music, but Mr. Irvin, close to seventy, doesn't budge. "How's Hank?"

"A joy as usual." I scoop down a mouthful. Talking about Hank makes me pray for cavities. Drilling teeth is pleasant compared to discussing Hank.

He chuckles. "I know the feeling, about music, that is."

I set the frosty down, let my brain catch up. This is new territory for us. "Really?"

"Yep. I played piano all my life." He spreads out his fingers, as though he can barely believe it himself.

I take in his scuffed-up knuckles, the dried-out hunks of mortar in his fingertips. He wipes his chin, bristling with silver stubble, nodding along with the memory. "Not anything like you play, I'm sure. But I was accepted to the Frampton Music Academy. It's closed now, but back in my time it was somewhat prestigious. It was my dream to go there."

Some kids stroll past us, loud and laughing. Not for the first time, I wonder why Nan couldn't have met a guy like Mr. Irvin instead of Hank. I study my boss. The bricklayer, the piano player. "You didn't go?"

"No." He sips his water, crumples up his wrapper. "Went to Vietnam instead."

Damn. I'm not sure what to say, but before we can get mushy about hopes and dreams, Mr. Irvin wipes his mouth, glances at my tray, and suggests we get back to it.

I keep up my frantic pace for the rest of the afternoon, and with each brick I'm thinking about Mr. Irvin playing the piano. About him going off to war. We get some pavers going, and Mr. Irvin shows me how to cut angles until we're at a good stopping point. At a little after five, we tarp the patio, and I collect our tools and place them in the truck.

As we start for home, I ask Mr. Irvin if he still plays. He turns to me, then to the road, shaking his head. "No. Nothing worth a damn, anyway."

9

I get Mr. Irvin to drop me off at Noah's place. I'm filthy, and my shirt soaked through, nearly orange from dirt and sweat. My jeans are covered in mortar and sand, but I'm not worried about looking the part today. Something about how we left last night feels unfinished.

A few knocks on the door. No one answers, but I can hear some heavy, offkey power chords from the basement. Weird. I knock again and try the knob, but the door is locked. Another knock and the guitar stops. There's a clunk, a bang, and then a heavy thump. Like someone fell climbing up the steps.

Noah opens the door a crack, his red hair spilling out until he sees it's me and opens wider. "Hey, Myles. What's up?"

"Nothing, just wanted to stop by." I'm waiting for him to open the door to let me in, but he only hangs onto it. He's got a strange, drooping smile on his face, and his eyes are a little heavy. I pick mortar from my fingernail, wondering what's going on. "How are you doing?"

He throws his hands out. "I'm great. Just great."

I look around. "You going to let me in?"

"Well," he turns back, over his shoulder, knocking his hair from his eyes. He sways a bit, back and forth. "I'm sort of busy."

He's slurring, and his voice is higher than normal. I'm about to ask if he's drunk when again the terrible guitar playing cranks up as someone laughs. Mrs. Connors' car isn't here, and it obviously wasn't Noah plucking around. Someone else is here. Playing music.

I nod toward the kitchen. "What's going on?"

More noise shreds behind him. Then, again from the basement, someone calls up the stairs, "Yo, Noah?" A thick accent, one I'm trying to place, and put this all together. The voices, the hum of an amp. I think I hear the organ.

"Who's here?"

Another head toss. He wipes back his hair and sighs. "Nothing. Just jamming with some friends."

"Really?" I start to say about six different things—about Mal, what happened in the basement, the party, the video—but whatever is happening downstairs wins out. A flush of heat burns my face. "Is this about last night? You said you were fine with the podcast."

Before he can answer, I make a point of sniffing at him. "And dude. Are you wasted?"

He shrugs, laughs, and grabs the doorjamb to steady himself. "Nope. At least, I'm not *too* wasted. And relax, I am fine. It's just a side gig."

It knocks me back, both his breath and the idea of him playing with someone else. It almost feels like *I'm* drunk the way my head spins. "When have you ever had a side gig? Look man, we can work this out. I'll call Mal right now."

I start to pull out my phone but he's already shaking his head. "Right. No, we can't. Myles. Come on. They want the two of you. They're obviously playing the couple angle. And about that, just between us, I don't know what exactly went down between you guys in the basement, but I'd be careful."

"What does that mean?"

He closes his eyes. "With Mal. As your friend, I have to tell you that. It's all an act. You're just..." he laughs, a stinging laugh that hits me in the chest. "You need to open your eyes."

This isn't happening. My throat tightens. Hot coals in my chest. I can't keep up with everything he just said, not on top of the side band. My voice breaks. "Look. It's one stupid podcast. Then we're back. We have, what? Three more gigs before school starts?"

"Right. Sure. And I'll be there, obviously, since I'm the only one who ever does any promoting. But I'm also coming up with a backup plan."

Behind him, more thumping on the steps. "Yo, Noah."

Again, the thick accent. I crane my neck, but Noah shifts into the doorjamb. "You don't need a backup plan, Noah." I can't believe I have to say it. I try to look past him. "Who's in there?"

Noah shakes his head and smiles. "It's cool, Myles. But I gots to go, man. I'll text you later, a'ight?"

"Is it the twins?" I say, finally placing the accent, referring to the foreign exchange brothers from Romania. I'd seen Noah with them a few times in the hallway. "Seriously?"

"Later, okay?" He closes the door in my face. I'm left standing there, filthy and sweaty and shaken cold with the fear of Noah leaving the band. I start the long walk home, replaying everything he said about a backup plan. About Mal. About promoting the band. I thought he liked doing all that stuff. Now he's playing with someone else?

I need to talk to Mal, but as I get home, Hank's truck sits in the driveway. It's crazy what the sight of a truck can do to my already plodding heartbeat.

I walk in, hoping he's already turned in for the night. He does that sometimes. Comes home, eats, watches TV, then crashes.

"That you, Myles?"

No such luck. I shut my eyes. The day—with work, the thing with Noah, the confusion over Mal—I'm so done. But Hank is only getting started.

"Yeah?"

"In here, now."

I find him in the den, working his way out of his chair. That lever, the spring of the chair. It's no good. If Hank has the motivation to get off his ass, it doesn't bode well for me.

"You seen a ladder outside?"

Oh shit. I never put it away. I suck down a breath. "Yeah, I'll go get it. Sorry."

He's already shaking his head, jaw working as he chews on his peanuts. "Not what I asked. Did you see a ladder outside?"

"No, I…

A quick flash as he bops my temple with his palm. I step back, and my eyes blur as I wait for more to come.

"No, you didn't because I put it away."

My gaze falls to my feet. I blink away the blur. "Hank, sorry, it—"

"I don't want excuses from you. I want you to do what's asked."

I nod, hoping this is over. More chewing, the disgusting slurp as he sucks the salt from his fingers. He turns his attention back to the television and dismisses me. "Last warning, Myles."

With that, I turn to walk away. "And the insurance."

My steps come to a halt. "Didn't I pay it last week?" I ask, even as I know I did. I gave him eighty bucks last paycheck.

The television flashes against his face as he turns his head to me. "Well, here's the thing. You're driving the car the most, so you need to pay the insurance. This is not negotiable. I need $75 before you touch that car again. And then every month after that. Are we clear?"

I could argue the point, but the warning shot, the bop to my head, steers me the other way. "Yes, we're clear."

There's goes my cut from the other night, plus some of my paycheck. I make my escape and go take a shower.

A throbbing burns between my eyes. I remind myself it could've been so much worse.

The first time Hank used the belt, I was ten. I'd been on my bike, practicing wheelies, and at some point, I lost control and crashed into his truck. My handlebars, poking through the rubber handgrips, left a scratch on the fender. I ran in and told him, showed him the gash on my knee. I thought he might tend to my knee, wipe it clean. Instead, he walked past me to inspect his truck.

I followed him outside, where he calmly looked things over and instructed me to go back inside. He hardly seemed angry when he came in. He said to take my shirt off. I did as I was told. I remember thinking about my knee, the small patch of red blood, and my bike, still outside, when Hank unclasped his belt and began talking about discipline and scripture. Still confused, I apologized again, glancing at my bike near the peeling bark of the birchwood tree, when the first lash came down.

Like a strike of lightning, I whirled around, mouth open but useless. He took me by the shoulder and steered me back around. Another slap of leather. This time my tears blurred the view out of the window. Again, a white-hot lash came. Hank spoke of the virtues of the rod, suffering, wisdom and how he was only doing me right. He explained it all calmly, in a workmanlike way, as he instilled the discipline I so sorely needed. Like his father had done for him. He needed to teach me what my dead father wasn't around to teach.

When I found my voice, I screamed for Nan to help me. To make him stop. But she never came, not as Hank drew back again and again with the belt until the burn of the strap meshed into my spine and neck. Eventually, by the fourth or fifth strike, as Hank's exertion caused his breaths to go heavy and rapid, I could only whimper.

The memory plays until I'm out of the shower. I get dressed and text Mal.

> Me: Can you come get me?

The house, this room. The clicking and clacking of pans in the kitchen. Is this life? What happens when you grow up? Cook. Eat.

Clean. Tiptoe around the big bad man of the house? Become the big bad man of the house?

I wipe my face and look at my window. I'm all set to start walking again when my phone buzzes.

Mal: Be there in 5

10

I GET IN THE CAR AND MAL MAKES NO MOVE TO LEAVE. Her eyes never leave mine. "What happened?"

"Nothing. It's… I'm fine. Thanks for coming."

She shakes her head like I gave the wrong answer. "Myles, you never text me like that." Her eyes dart to the house. "What happened?"

Nothing, really. But my head pounds, and my vision tunnels in and out. I glance to the window to let it pass. The last thing I need is a Mal/Hank showdown. Once was enough. Last year, they had it out in the driveway. He called her an Indian Princess. She called him a fat redneck. Things got ugly.

Now, as Mal stares at me for three, four, five seconds, I feel her eyes scanning me for scrapes, swelling, or bruises before she lets me off the hook.

She guns the engine and the Honda responds with a high-pitched wail. "Well," she sniffs in my direction. "At least you smell good."

We tear away from my house, and I'm already over it. As soon as she texted me back, I was okay.

When she turns to drive, I wipe my face and ask about her day.

She laughs. "Well, I'm glad you asked. Today was officially the last day of my internship at Gillam Insurance."

I stare at her until she breaks, fighting off a giggle. "What?"

"Mal, you worked like three hours a week there."

"No. You're absolutely wrong. I pulled like twelve hours last week alone." She sits on this for a second. "You try it, okay? Go put on a skirt and pull medical files and…. *What?*"

I throw my head back, laughing at the thought of Mal in an office, pulling files and making small talk. It's too much. "Did you have your own cubicle? With like a name plate?"

She purses her lips to keep from laughing. "No. I mean, I did have one, but it was someone else's desk. Some old dude out on leave, with pictures of his family pinned up, staring at me. His keyboard was sticky. It was gross. Anyway, I'm done, so laugh it up. See if I care."

I fall back in the seat, wiping my eyes, a goofy smile on my face. Mal swats my leg, but she's laughing too. It feels good, to smile, to put distance between me and my house. To not think about Hank. And we keep on laughing until I mention the side gig thing at Noah's house earlier.

Her eyes go wide. "Noooo!"

"I honestly don't know what happened."

"Oh, please. This is typical Noah, the little weasel. Who was it? Who was he playing with?"

"I can't be sure, but I think the twins. He said he wanted to keep his options open." I can't imagine telling her what else Noah said, so I leave it out.

Mal pulls the car into an empty parking lot. She hugs the steering wheel and looks at me. "The twins? Like, Daris and Dory or whatever? Wow. That's hilarious and not too concerning in the least. So, what should we do?"

"I think it's Daris and Dorin. Anyway, I tried to get him to come, but he refused. I don't know." I sneak a peek at her. "Should we not do it?"

She closes her eyes. Her head drops and I realize how much this means to her. "Or…" I begin, with the idea that came to me as I was in the shower. "You could go, and I'll hang back with Noah." I shrug. "Maybe that will appease him."

"*Appease him?* We're appeasing our drummer, now? And here I thought *you* were the prima donna."

"Um, what?"

She sits up straighter, puts the car in gear, and backs out of the driveway, but stops the car and bores into me with her eyes. "I'm not going solo. I need you."

I ignore the flush of hope that comes with her words. "Why? You know the chords."

"Okay, one: We both know I suck on acoustic. I can get away with it if you're playing over me, but… no. Have you seen the stats?" She motions to her phone. "This thing is blowing up. I don't know how or why, but this is all his doing. It's not like we went behind his back or anything. Look, I love Noah, but he's got to get over it."

"Sounds like he *is* getting over it."

She cuts her eyes at me, and I sit back as she goes on a tangent about Noah being selfish. But I can't stop thinking about what I didn't tell her. What Noah said about her playing me. Now he's moving on, as well, and I'm trying to string him along. The dynamics are dizzying, but either way you cut it, I'm caught in the middle. I'm always in the middle.

Mal continues to lay him out, now on bullet point #4 according to the count on her fingers. "Think about it. How long as he been after us to take promotion more seriously?" she mocks in her deep-voice Noah imitation. "And now, we finally get some buzz going, and I… you know. We're a team."

She's talking with her hands, but I'm only thinking about the kiss. How her hands felt on my face as she brought me into her or we collided or whatever happened. How great things were for a few seconds. Is this her being for real or playing me? I cut a glance her way, breathing in the earthy smells of the Honda. Of incense. She's waiting for me to respond, so I throw something together. "I'm just saying, it wouldn't bother me. You going solo. I promise I won't throw a fit."

She slaps the wheel. "Haven't you heard anything I've said? You are coming. Ripcast wants *us* on the podcast, not me. Again, this helps the band. Noah will have to deal."

"Okay, okay. I'm in."

Mal's lips curve with her victory. "That's more like it," she says, slapping my leg. "So, I told you about my day at the office. How was yours?"

Her hand is still on my leg. "Oh, you know. One brick at a time."

"Huh? Oh, right, the bricks." She takes her hand back. "I have an original song I want to do. Not sure it's ready, but I want you—"

I'm already shaking my head. "Mal. I'm not doing *Oh That's Nice* on the podcast."

She slaps my leg again, harder. "Would you stop it? I'm not doing *Oh That's Nice*. That's more of a party song. An anthem, if you will. Something I wrote the other night."

"Oh." I try to sound normal, but we usually write together. Again, Noah's voice echoes in my head. I shake it off. "Okay."

"You hungry? Wanna get something to eat?" she shrugs. "Then, if you promise not to laugh, I'll show you."

I watch her carefully as we pull onto Commerce Street. She's either a first-class manipulator, or I'm that terrible a judge of character. I smile at her. "When did you get so shy?"

"Shy? No. I am not shy. It's just, this song is a little bit different."

"Oh, the possibilities. I can't wait."

She shakes her head. "Well, you have to wait. I'm hungry."

Mal asks me to grab the guitar that basically stays in her trunk. We cross the bridge and park, then hike up to the food truck near the coffee shop where I had my epically weird tagalong thing with Jada. We get some food and find a spot near the fountain at the community market where some skateboarders are gathered near the concrete steps.

Mal unwraps her veggie burger and dives in. "Well, Noah can act like a jerk if he wants, but I say we celebrate."

"To us." She holds out her soda, and we tap our plastic cups together.

I look around. "This seems like a conspiracy."

She takes a french fry and raises her eyebrows. "I know, right?"

Maybe it's the glimmer in her eyes or the rushing water of the fountain, but I have to force myself to think of Mal as a friend and bandmate and not something more. But the way her shirt hangs off one perfectly smooth shoulder is distracting.

A crush has a shelf life, right? It can't survive seasons—snowy winters, hot summers, budding springs. A crush goes dormant, dies off, or it splinters in new directions. But what I feel for Mal is crushing me.

She's doesn't seem to notice, watching the skaters and scarfing down her dinner. She wipes her mouth, her eyes flicking my way. "Okay, so my song. It's called *Where We End.*" She frowns. "It's like, sad but not. And… I was thinking of that riff you were playing by the rock. It was a few weeks ago. Right before you got stung by that bee," she says with a laugh.

"Right. I remember that vividly." I wipe my hands on my jeans and take up the guitar, surprised she remembered what I was playing.

It comes back to me. The hot, pulsing sting of my ankle. The sucker got stuck in my sock. Then before, the trestle, the rock, the chords. I start fiddling around, trying to find it, placing myself with Mal at the overlook. I can feel Mal watching me, hear the splash of water over her shoulder. And when she smiles, I find it.

It comes together, because it wasn't the place but the person that got me to the song. It was her. And with that realization comes a twinge of sadness to the notes. Because it's always going to be her.

Mal's face lights up. "Yeah, that…" Her smile widens and she whispers like a little girl on Christmas morning. "That's perfect."

I strum it out as the skaters do their things in the distance, the clatter of boards slapping the concrete, the cheers as someone wipes out. Then Mal sings, and the world drowns away.

Where we end
It's dark
I've lost you but it's okay
You've found your way
That way of yours I love so much
Now it's yours and yours alone
The way I'd always hoped you'd go

We do it once more, and it's good. Mal closes her eyes, and I manage to hold on, to do this for a friend and not be a guy who only wants to kiss her. Even if I do. All the time. Even if I want to ask who this song is about.

Where we end…

The song crashes to an end. Mal opens her eyes as though waking from a deep sleep. She grabs another french fry. "Well?"

I stop, take her in, find my water and suck it down hoping she doesn't see the chill bumps covering my arms. "It's better than *Oh That's Nice.*"

She scrunches up her face and sticks out her tongue. "You're such a turd."

"It's amazing, Mal. Seriously."

She stands and stretches, revealing a stretch of her smooth stomach, but I don't stare. She turns around, squinting into the sun. "Really?"

I catch my breath with a shrug.

"Really?"

I laugh. "I said yes."

She smiles, then walks over and hugs me. She rests her head on my chest, just below my chin. She's warm and smells like cinnamon and a little like fried food. She pulls away and stares into my eyes, the way she did before our kiss in the basement.

Two taps of her palm on my chest, and she's gone. "Okay, so we'll do the song? On the thing?"

I exhale, finding the warmth in my chest. The hot, pulsing sting now in my heart. I shake it off. "Wait, please tell me we don't have to play you-know-what. It's a deal breaker, seriously."

She narrows her eyes and takes on a boxer's stance. "Your kiss, is on my fist."

"Much better."

After the market, we wander along the lower basin near the river. We pass the old warehouse and the factories while Mal tells me how she's been listening to back episodes of Ripcast. She suggests I do the same.

"So, what do your parents think?" I ask.

"Huh?"

"About Ripcast?"

"Oh." she shakes her head and gazes off to the distance like the question might fade off on its own. "They don't come out and say it's a waste of time, but they would rather me stick to internships, you know?"

"But they're supportive?"

She leans over the railing, gazing out to the river, wide and brownish, weaving its way through our town, sweeping under us, leaving us in its rush to better things. Mal shrugs her shoulders. "It's just not something they understand. Like, they're proud or whatever, but my mom says I'm too confrontational."

"You? Nooo."

She smiles, but if fades quickly. "The sooner they understand I'm not them, that I'm not getting married at twenty and staying at home having babies, the better for everyone."

I cut my eyes to her. "You're Mom doesn't strike me as the mousy housewife type."

"No, I know, but sometimes, she'll say things like, 'You don't have to apply to colleges so far away.' It's like they want me to live in their house and wear skirts and go to the office. Then get married and come over to visit every weekend. The thought of that makes me sick to my stomach."

For some reason it hits me wrong, how the thought of living here makes her so nauseous. "Well, some of us don't have such lofty goals."

She shoots me a glare before she breaks off the railing, sweeping off on the balls of her feet like she does when she's upset. She bounces from one step to the next before she calls over her shoulder. "Believe it or not, this has nothing to do with you, Myles."

As she storms off, away from the river, the market, away from me and the song we just did, I follow a few paces behind, giving her space, realizing it's probably the closest thing to a fight we've ever had.

This new, weird silence sits with us in the car all the way home. I keep turning to her, wrestling with something to say, but nothing ever comes. Not as she's pulling down my street, into my driveway, putting the car in park and seemingly staring a hole into my house.

"Mal," I say, softly, trying to get something out of her. I can't tell if she's going to cry or erupt. I shrug. "Hey, we can work some more on your song tomorrow if you want. I'll be ready Thursday, okay?"

She nods, and I get out and shut the door. "See you."

As she drives away it feels like it did at Noah's house all over again. A snaking panic coils through me as I realize that this band, this one thing I depend on to keep my life together, feels like it's slipping away.

11

I find Nan in the den, polishing off another *Law & Order* marathon. I take a seat on the couch next to her and she frowns, which is her way of telling me to keep quiet. Nan can be fun to watch TV with. She'll snort and grumble at the detectives and talk to them directly as she cracks the case four times before the third commercial break, almost always wrong but unperturbed. But I'm not feeling it after what happened with Mal.

Nan is laying out the newest detective during commercial break when I bring up the trip to Richmond tomorrow.

"I thought you were working?" she says, halfway turning to me.

"We got a lot done today. I've cleared it with Mr. Irvin."

The show returns but Nan pauses it, aiming the remote at the TV like it's a taser. She makes the full turn this time, brow down, jaw set. "This is a music thing?"

I know where this is going. "Yes," I say with a nod.

She grumbles. Nan hates any music not sung by a choir. Music equals drugs, and drugs killed my dad. She gives me the usual gripes about work, music, and chores, until I'm tempted to take out my phone and show her the video—just to show her *something* about me. Maybe if she saw what we did, how it's been viewed by tens of thousands of people, it would make her happy or proud, or at least she would understand.

Too late. She clicks a button on the remote and her show resumes.

The detectives chase down a lead. I sit back, half watching, half thinking about whatever happened at the bridge with Mal. During the next commercial break, I start to get up from the couch when Nan clears her throat.

"You look so much like him."

I freeze. "Huh? What did you say?" I know exactly what she said and who she means, though. It brings chill bumps down my arms.

She nods. "Christopher. You've got his eyes, his cheekbones." She quickly turns away, back to the TV. "Got his sense of humor, too."

I stare at her, shocked into silence. I open my mouth to ask about him, ask about my mom, who vanished after my dad's death, my past, anything, but again I'm too late. The next thing I know, *Law & Order* returns, and that chance is gone.

Back in my room, I work more on Mal's song. We should be practicing together, working out the kinks. Instead, all I can think about is my dad. About Nan opening up to me, if only for a commercial break.

I have some pictures of him, ones I've found over the years. Still, in my mind, he's mostly a faceless tall figure with dark hair. I was six when he died, so I don't have much to go on.

I pick up my guitar. His guitar. I ready myself for tomorrow.

Suddenly, I'm transported to the old kitchen in our tiny house. It was raining outside, and my parents were together, dancing barefoot, slipping and squeaking as the ceiling leaked. My dad played the guitar, and my mom twirled and bounced and laughed as she sang along. My mom's hair took flight with her movements. It fell from behind her ears, spreading over her rosy face as she sweated it out.

They danced and laughed and sang, and we plunged away. My dirty little piece of the world was as good as I knew as I fell back and sat on the floor, beneath the smoke that hung in the room. I sat against the cabinets and thought they would fall over from the spinning and slipping and the laughter.

My dad played the guitar I'm holding now. It went through the bars and kitchens and the living rooms with him. It's been pawned a few times and has the wear and scuff to prove it. And while he isn't here to help me, the grooves and wear on the neck show me where to place my fingers, where to hold it and bend the strings to make them feel the pain I'm feeling now.

I play my father's guitar. The guitar that was with him when he died. I tell it things I don't dare tell another soul.

12

Mal beeps the horn twice. When I step outside the trunk pops. I wave to her then settle my guitar gently on the quilt she keeps in there for "spontaneous star-gazing."

In the car, she's looking sporty in one of Charley's oversized FILA hoodies even though it's already warm out. I'm not sure where we stand after yesterday, but she keeps her head down, giving me nothing to go on as she moves her backpack to the backseat. I buckle up as she backs the car out of the driveway, ducking my head to get her attention.

"Good morning?"

Mal shakes her head. Okay, so we're still being weird after our little fight, or, if we're being honest, the kiss. I set myself back into the seat, figuring I'll let her sulk. I can do this, too. We can sulk the entire trip and even through our interview and the performance. Bombs away. Fine with me.

At the first red light, she turns to me. "We have to stop for coffee."

Okay. Maybe I'm overthinking things.

We pull into Jean's Beans, but she's in no hurry. We sit in the

73

car, in a mostly empty parking lot as Mal comes to life. She yawns, does a one-armed stretch, drips coffee on the seat, and then turns to me with a bright smile.

"So, the video is still going crazy. I was sifting through the comments."

Judging by her smile, it's something about me. I turn to my window, suddenly enthralled by a tractor trailer across the lot. There's some rustling on her side, and I peek over. She whips out her phone, cocks an eyebrow. "You know you want to hear it. Ready?"

I shrug. She laughs, scrolls, then wiggles as she sits up. "Oh, here's a good one: 'The guy is effing hot. He's got that Jeff Buckley thing going on. Sexy.'"

My cheeks go aflame. "I don't have a Jeff, whatever thing. Who is that, anyway?"

She giggles. "Here's another one. 'Do these guys really exist? I mean, look at him, those sad eyes. I could make him smile.'"

I reach for the door latch. "I think I need more creamer."

She shakes her head. "Oh stop. You know you love it. There are some more, but…"

"Do I want to know?"

"Hmm," she says, sliding the phone back in her pocket. "Just stupid ones about us."

"How we're leaving our drummer behind? How we've moved on and ditched him?"

She starts the car, checks the rearview mirror. "Mm-hmm. Something like that."

We leave that alone. Mal finds the expressway, and we fall into a groove. She's awake after the coffee, and she's made a Party Trash playlist for our trip. I enjoy watching her dance and drive and occasionally sing out to the windshield.

We're more than an hour in when we pass a Riverview Mall billboard. I shoot her a smile. "You know, after this, we should get a gig at Riverview Mall."

Mal laughs, glancing at me. "We could completely sell out, get our own Nickelodeon show."

"Yes, let's go big. Disney. You could do voiceovers and theme music."

As we get closer, I take over driving duties. Mal cranks a Finnegan's mix, and we fall into the music for a while, until she points for me to turn off the interstate. From there, Mal loses the hoody, and I try not to do a double take at her fitted black tank. She brushes on some eye shadow as I take us down a two-lane road lined with abandoned factories until I spot the towers for the old radio studio.

Google Maps brings us to the mailbox, where two faded signs direct us up the gravel road. We cross over train tracks and pull to low-slung brick building that reads, WKZZ. *Today's Best Country!!*

Mal nods, "Well, we've hit the big time, I suppose."

I laugh, turn the key, and sit back. In the passenger seat, Mal has completely transformed. I smile watching her fidget with her hands, dig in her bag, pull down the sun visor mirror to fix her hair.

"You should leave it. I like it when it's all over the place."

I'm cringing at my own words as she turns to me, smiles, then slowly blinks her eyes. "Um, thanks?"

"No, I just..." I sigh, get back to my window. "It's not what I meant. I just think—forget it." I open the door and curse myself for being an idiot. The last thing I need is to make things weird right before we go on.

I grab my guitar. Mal climbs out and regards the building. Brick, boring and industrial looking. Those big radio towers in the back. We're still taking it in when a pasty, balding middle-aged guy walks out and spreads his arms wide.

"What's up, guys? I see you found our cutting-edge studio."

He introduces himself as Dave. He's wearing a faded black Dead Kennedys t-shirt that looks to be as old as he is, judging by the snug fit around his middle. He takes to Mal immediately, being how they've already spoken. I'm happy to let them do most of the talking as we head inside.

The place is a time warp, with worn carpet, wood paneling walls, gaudy lamps, and leftover office furniture.

"Okay, so…" Dave eyes me up and down. "You're a lot taller than I thought."

"Oh." I actually glance down at myself, like maybe I put on a few inches on the drive up.

Mal smirks, and Dave grins at her, gesturing back at me. "This guy always the conversationalist?"

Mal shakes her head. "No, he's just babbling."

"Ha ha. Okay, right this way." He leads us down a narrow hallway, where we're introduced to sound guys and marketing people, the names flying out of my head as soon as I hear them. We pass a few offices and smaller studios, rooms lined with soundproofing, all mics and laptops, power strips and wires everywhere, old turntables and mixing boards against the walls.

Dave keeps talking. "As I said on the phone, we usually get around six to eight thousand downloads per podcast. Some more, some less." He smiles at Mal. "We also run a low-power FM frequency, hush hush."

Mal nods at this, her gaze moving from the wall to the splotchy ceiling tiles and down to the worn, beige carpet. "This place is cool."

Dave swells with pride. "My dad owned it. It was a bigtime powerhouse station in the eighties—back in the glory days. Things went south, he wanted to sell it, but I talked him out of it. You should see the collection of vinyl in the basement. Here we are," he says, opening the door to a studio in the back. It's musty but not unpleasant, like an old book.

Dave gestures to a couple stools—two mics, headphones, and a jack for me to plug in. The two stools make me think of Noah, as Dave gushes about our video and how many times he's watched it. They all have. It's gold, he says.

"Okay, kids. You know the drill, or maybe you don't. I'll ask you how long you've been playing together, influences, some stuff about the video and otherwise we'll just have some fun. Get you to play some songs. How's that sound?"

Mal nods, says it's cool.

"Right. Get comfortable. We have water, or," he raises an eyebrow. "Better stick to water. Give us a few minutes to set up. Feel free to look around."

We step out back where a few dusty cars sit next to a dumpster in a weed-riddled gravel lot. Dilapidated shelves line the back of the building. Mal chews on her thumbnail. "Damn, I want a smoke."

I ignore this. "Okay, so setlist?"

She pivots and pats her pockets. I laugh. "I thought you quit smoking."

"I did quit." She spins on the gravel "All I said was I *wanted* a smoke; it doesn't mean I'm not quit."

"Not quit?"

It's a sure sign Mal 's coming apart at the seams when she loses her grip on grammar. She gets back to her thumb. "Shut up, you know what I mean." Another go at her pockets. "Shoot, where did I put that setlist?"

"The one you never made?"

She shoves me and I can't help cracking up. "Okay, setlist or not, don't say, *Oh That's Nice.*"

"Oh." She starts singing the chorus, poking me in the chest. "That's Nice. Oh yeah? That's nice."

I shake my head, laughing. She keeps chanting *That's Nice* until I hold my hands up in surrender. Then, because I have to ask. "But seriously, about your other original. Are we?"

"I mean, it's still a work in progress." She shrugs. I don't know why she seems so uncomfortable with the song now. The other night it was... incredible. Whatever, now is not the time to argue the point.

"Well, we need to put *something* together."

She shoots me a smile. "I suppose we have to do *Kiss on My List,* of course."

"You suppose?"

I kick at the gravel. Next to the dumpster sits a bowl with some cat food. I look around for strays. "You know what's funny but not funny?"

"Your face."

"That Noah named the band, and here we are going on this thing without him."

Her eyes go wide. "Why would you bring that up? You suck so bad right now."

"Yeah, but now you're not nervous."

She gives me a shove. "Well, I am, but not about the music. Look at this place. We've played some shady spots, but *this?*" she spreads her arms out. "This is all very Chernobyl."

"It is sort of like the beginning of a really bad horror movie."

"Right?"

I start doing a Frankenstein monster impression, coming at Mal. She slaps my chest to make me stop. I lunge for her again when the door swings open, and she falls into me and screams.

Dave looks us over and chuckles. "You kids ready?"

Inside, two camera guys anchor the host. I quickly notice how they've set Mal's and my stools closer to each other. Again, my thoughts fly to Noah.

Dave sets on his headphones. In an instant, he becomes a different person. His voice ramps up, and he transforms from bald stoner to showman. He stares at Mal from the start, which is fine with me since she's better with the small talk and the band stuff, at least until glances at me with a big smirk before she tells Dave all about how I want to sellout to Disney.

Dave turns to me with all the "Dude, how could you?" and soon I'm backpedaling, wiping my forehead and trying to explain how that's not at all my plan. Dave, Mal, and everyone else in the room finds my discomfort hilarious.

"Okay, okay," Dave says, reeling things in. "First things first. I have to ask. The Wide Awakes. Cool name, what's that all about?"

Mal looks at me in that *Should I tell him or you tell him?* Kind of way.

Dave smiles at the camera guy. "What? So is it, like, you guys are woke or something?"

"Well, I mean we are, sure. I'm Egyptian-American, so we can roll with that."

Dave raises an eyebrow. "But?"

"But," Mal glances at me. "I guess the real answer isn't so revolutionary."

"Okay," he says, all gimmie hands. "I need the real story on this. That's why we're here, isn't it?"

Mal shifts, wipes a strand of curls from her face. "Okay, fine. So, our first gig was a Saturday morning at the community center."

"Like at a farmer's market or something?"

I cut in, happy to turn things onto Mal, laughing because I remember it like it was yesterday. "Yeah. Started at 6:00 A.M. Mal couldn't stay awake."

Mal shoots me a death stare. "It was *six* in the morning. On a *Saturday*."

"Right, and you were like a zombie, so I got you that double cappuccino, from that organic lady? Remember her?"

"Yes, and that cappuccino had organic crack in it."

"I do remember the lady warned me about that."

"Well, you didn't warn *me*, now did you?"

"There was no time. You sucked it down. The next thing I knew they were calling us to the little stage—"

"And I was shaking. Like, my pulse was skyrocketing. I wanted to rip my skin off."

"You were living in fast forward."

"Then Noah, our drummer..." Mal grabs my wrist. "Shout out to Noah Connors, the best drummer in the world. We love you, Noah."

I turn to Dave. "Noah came up with the name."

Dave takes a minute, watching us with a smile. "You two have quite a rapport. It's something to watch."

I look down, Mal states the obvious. "Well, I guess now you can watch us blush."

Dave nods, still smiling. "Which brings us to the video."

"The video? What video?"

He turns to me. "She's good! You're good. So, I'm sure you guys have kept track of how the vid is doing. This thing is getting massive hits, and um…" he smirks, "…comments."

Mal shrugs, grins at me. "We hadn't noticed."

"Right." He shifts in his stool. "Well, I love it, and whatever drunk filmed this thing managed to get a great angle. People pay for videos like this. It's remarkable. None of it was planned?"

"Nope." Mal coughs and glances at me. I think back to Noah handing me the guitar. "None of it. It was completely spontaneous."

"Very cool. Now here we are," he says, smiling. And right then, it's clear this dude is messing with us hardcore.

Mal suspects it too, but she's throwing on the high-wattage smile, and her voice is husky yet smooth and cracking in perfect places. I'm relieved when Dave lets the moment pass. He claps his hands together. "Are you ready to play it now, here for us?"

Of all the times I've dreamed about playing for people, when I thought about mosh pits, the club scene, the mohawks and leather jackets, or I saw myself in front of adoring fans, it was never once as half of a Hall and Oates cover band.

But as Mal sways in her stool, closing her eyes as I strum out the rhythm, putting a slightly ska kind of riff to the beat, it's exactly what I've become.

"Your kiss…" Mal smiles at me when she sings it. And it should be fun and cheesy and ironic, but now this stupid song means something to me. How Mal has left her hair all over the place, and she's sort of brushing up against me. Something about her eyes reminds me of autumn, the flecks of gold, the yellows and oranges within the not-quite-green sort of hazel.

I go into autopilot, playing along, but my mind is back to the basement. How we "accidently" kissed in celebration. The shock on her face as she pulled away, as I could still feel her lips on mine. How she decides we can't. How I have to go along with it, when all I want to do is kiss her again.

The next thing I know, Dave is clapping, laughing it up. "That was amazing, absolutely amazing. I love what I'm seeing between the two of you. You guys need your own podcast."

Mal laughs. I strum something on the guitar and look off. Because this is fun, right? Pretending not to be in love with your best friend? Having it recorded and aired for anyone to see? Yep, awesome.

As though feeling my discomfort, Dave narrows in on me. "So Myles. How long you been playing guitar""

"About five years, maybe?"

"Did you take lessons?"

"Mostly just stuff on YouTube."

"YouTube, this kid says. I love it. Were your parents musicians? What do they think of all this?"

It's funny how ill-prepared I am for such a simple question. Mal squirms, cuts a glance at me. I nod along. "Well, yeah. They were musicians."

Mal's knee bumps mine. "Let's do another song."

Dave smiles at her. "Well, all right. Let's!"

Maybe it's all the parent talk, or the discomfort, or maybe I'm trying to prove something to Mal. It could be I'm simply determined to embarrass myself for an audience. But I strum into *Where We End*, the song from the other day. Mal's eyes widen but I keep going with it. If Dave thinks we're a couple, I'm happy to play the role.

I keep at it, and left without a choice, Mal wipes her hair away and drops her head as she moves with the melody. When she sings it, it's great and all, but it's for show, not real like it was at the market. I slow it down, trying to unearth the magic again, until she realizes I'm not going to stop unless she sings it the way she did the first time.

Finally, as though accepting the challenge, Mal flings her whole self into the song, pushing her voice to a breaking point as she does this humming thing I haven't heard her do before. She rises to a crescendo at the chorus, and for the next few minutes it's like we leave the room.

Then I stop. She stops. And it's gone.

"Well, all right, that was… you two really have some range."

Mal and I sit there, quietly, until Dave moves on. "So, how long have you two been together?"

Gulp. "What?" We turn to each other. "Huh?" I cough. "No we're just.."

Mal shakes her head, gestures to the air between us. "Oh we're… we're not, you know…"

Dave chuckles and glances back at the crew. All of them yukking it up. The producer lady is looking at us as though we're a box of puppies. Dave clarifies: "I'm speaking musically, of course."

Everyone gets a big laugh at our expense. Mal runs her hand through her hair and laughs, revealing her perfect teeth. "How long has it been? Almost two years?"

I nod. "It was art class, remember? You had on that *Art of Noise* shirt, and I asked you about your favorite song. We realized how we both liked the same stuff. You painted that picture of the mountains, with the sunset, remember?"

Mal's lips part with her smile. She nods. "I remember."

The rest of the podcast is mostly just talking. It's actually easy to forget about everything with Mal, especially when we're chatting about old times and great music. Eventually, we get through one last song. Then it's a wrap.

Afterwards, I pack up. The crew breaks for lunch as Dave follows me out of the studio. "You okay, my man?"

"Huh? Yeah, I'm good. Thanks."

He nods and pats me on the back. "I think we have some good stuff."

I nod, without a clue of what to say. Dave glances back to Mal and the studio crew as he walks me out. "The two of you have quite a connection."

"Oh…" I squint into the early afternoon sun. "Yeah, but…"

Dave nods with a laugh. "I get it, man. And that sucks. I feel for you."

Before I can get anything out of my mouth, he pats my back and heads off. I pack up the Honda, and by the time Mal comes out with

Dave and the crew, it's like they've all known each other for years. They're telling her how awesome she is, and she smiles as she soaks it up, all this praise. When she catches my eye, she shoots me a wink.

I only wish I knew what is real and what is show anymore.

13

Noah is not answering texts, PM's, calls, or, as I found out the other day, unsolicited visits. I'm not sure what's going on, but with a gig coming up—an outdoor, end-of-summer kind of thing—we're going to need our drummer. It's not a two-person job.

On the way home from Ripcast, I drive while Mal unleashes a barrage of text messages his way. She hits him up on Facebook, but that's about as far as Mal's social media prowess allows. So she goes old school, leaving voice messages.

First: *"Hello, Noah? Your warranty on your car is about to expire. We have tried to reach you regarding this matter several times. This is your final notice. Press two to be removed from our calling list."*

Then: *"Hello, Noah. This is your lucky day! You've been selected to receive not one, but two bandmates for tomorrow night's show."*

And: *"Hi Noah, it's me. You know, like, your favorite groupie. Hope to see you tomorrow. Call me back, Byeeee."*

"That last one should do it."

Mal nods. "I think so."

It's fun, but the stakes are too high for me. I can't lose Noah to our little pretend couple duo act. He's more than a drummer to me. I have to make this work.

Mal tries Noah two more times as we near town, and then she goes through her phone, talking about some guy she knows who could sit in if Noah's continues to be a jerk. It's more than I can take, the thought of actually replacing Noah, so I blurt out an idea I've been mulling over.

"What about a second video?"

She drops the phone to her lap. "Explain."

"We do another silly video, but this time with all three of us."

"You're suggesting..." She looks out the window, then turns back to me, fighting off a smirk. "Is this like trying to save a relationship by having another baby? That sort of thing? I hear it always works out."

"No, I... *what?*"

She takes the deepest of breaths, then shrugs. "You know, what could it hurt?"

She types on the phone. I'm thinking maybe it wasn't the best idea. "It was just a thought. I'm not saying he'd—"

Her phone vibrates. She looks down to it then smiles at me. "He's in." Her phone buzzes again, and she laughs. "Wow, he's like, really in."

We make plans to do another video around lunch tomorrow. Mal is laughing about what Noah will wear, but I've stopped listening as we pull up to my house because the station wagon's doors are open, and all the floormats are out.

Mal's eyes go wide. "What is he doing?"

No clue. I'm the one who cleans the cars, but sure enough, Hank pops up. One look at his fat, sweaty face makes me want to shrink into the seat. My throat dries up, and it feels like two skillets are banging together in my chest. Still, I suck it up for Mal's sake and gather my things. The thought of confronting Hank with Mal around sends a knifing pain between my eyes.

I turn to grab my trash from the backseat, doing my best to keep my voice steady. "I'll call you later about the drummer situation."

Hank waves me over. Mal glares at him through the windshield. "I'm not leaving."

"Mal, please."

She moves for her door, but I set my hand on her arm. "Mal," I say, too forcefully. I shake my head. She shakes her head back, making no effort to hide her anger.

"Fuck this. What's his deal?"

As I get my guitar case from the trunk, a queasy fear envelops me. My legs have turned rubbery from sitting. I don't like Mal being here.

Apparently, Hank doesn't like it either. He stands up straight, his face maroon, his eyes wide and white as he points off to the road. "Tell your friend to go home, Myles. You got some explaining to do."

Mal squirms, glaring at Hank with what can only be described as revulsion. Her brow furrowed, eyes hardened, her lips puckered like she'd rather spit than smile. But whatever he does to me, I have to keep her in the car. I blink my eyes hard. I have to keep her away from him. I take a deep breath to keep my voice low but fail to sound as confident as I want to be. "Mal, please?"

She turns her disgust to me, sighs, then shakes her head. "Fine."

She gets out, slams the passenger door and tromps around the car. I'm about to say something about how I'll be okay when she stops suddenly and launches into me for a hug. She pulls me tight, so her lips brush my ear. "Call me if you need me, okay?"

I promise her I will, when all I want to do is hop in with her and drive back to Richmond. Drive anywhere. She still has my arm when Hank barks again for me to get over here.

Mal lets me go and gets in the car, her eyes caught somewhere between a plea and a glare. I nod again as she backs out and starts off. Then I turn to face Hank, who starts for me. "That girl could use a lesson in respect."

He waits for me to defend her. Instead, I turn to Barbara, all the doors open, floormats on the driveway. "What's going on?"

"I'll ask the questions here, got it? One, this is Nan's car, not yours."

"Okay."

"The car's filthy and the gas gauge is on E." He brushes past me to the back of the car, leaning in and producing a can of beer from the other night. *Damn, I forgot all about it.* "And then there's this. You want to tell me why you've got booze in here?"

"Oh, right. That's—"

Hank thrusts the can at me. "Illegal, is what it is. You're underage. It's bad enough you go all over the place, playing this garbage with girls like that, but—"

All over the place? Garbage. But wait, hold up. "Girls like that?"

"Yes," he says, tossing the beer to the yard. He edges closer, throwing his girth around, clearly satisfied now that he's pissed me off. "Girls like *that*. Drinking and driving."

"No one is drinking and driving. It's *a* beer someone offered me after a show. I didn't take it."

"You driving around with a bunch of drunks in your Nan's car?" He's in my face now, the familiar glare, his harsh, disgusting breaths, the dirty pores on his pink sponge of a nose. "You need to shut your mouth and listen to me. I'm not done. You still haven't paid the insurance, either. Get in the living room. Now."

I step back and glance at the thick, scarred leather of his belt. I shake my head. "I'm not doing this."

"You will do as you're told." He grabs me by the shoulder, but I shrug him off. A flash of surprise registers on his face before he recovers. He grits his teeth and lunges for me, wrapping me up in a bear hug. My guitar falls with a thump. With a grunt, his arm slides around my throat.

"This is what I said would happen," he says, huffing in my ear. "You are undisciplined and behaving like a child. So I'll treat you like one."

The more I fight it, the more he squeezes. My breaths go short. It's been over a year since this happened but seeing my guitar case on the ground reminds me of my bike when I was ten. I fight one last urge to kick him, hit him, to free myself, but why? What's the point? He'll only make it worse for me.

The fight drains from my limbs. His face is flushed, but I can see the satisfaction in his eyes. A bead of sweat forms on his forehead, and flecks of spittle dot his lips.

He shoves me inside. Hank is strong, so it's easier to let him pull and jerk and grunt and let the door slam shut. He throws me to the floor, heaving, gasping for breath. I've been here before. Too many times. It's easier to curl up and go away in my head.

Not a word from Nan in the kitchen. As the belt comes off, I find myself thinking of Mal's singing, and the richness of her voice carries me away as Hank talks discipline. Even though the rule is to wait. Not to punish while angry. No impulsive discipline. But Hank is angry. He's panting with a wild look in his eyes. There will be no waiting today.

The rattle of the buckle jostles my memories, along with Hank's heavy wheezing, and as I remove my shirt, four months away from my eighteenth birthday—four months away from leaving and never coming back—I feel bad for the boy I used to be. The one who had no idea what was going to happen that first time the buckle jangled. Not until the leather snapped on his back and shattered any misbeliefs he had about happiness.

Hank raises the belt. And I no longer want to run. Not to the pity of Mal's house, where her family will regard me with sad faces, drawn eyes, and solemn prayers. Not to Noah, who won't answer me. This is mine and mine alone. It's not fair to bring them into this. With Nan in the other room, doing nothing—she will always do nothing—there is no one else left.

The jolt of leather on skin is harsher than I remember. I gasp, a silent cry as I open my mouth to call out before it returns. Another strike, this time with a newfound fury. The searing burn of broken skin accompanies Hank preaching of responsibility. The sins of music, of drinking, how I'm going against God. I bite down against it, force myself numb, to feel the pain differently. Each one brings me closer to a conclusion, the end of a lesson. It can only get better from here. I'll get through this and heal.

Four times it comes down before he hobbles off, out of breath and wiping his forehead. He explains to Nan, as always, the righteous work he's done. How his father used the belt to instill values. And yeah, I hate Hank, I'll always hate Hank, but today I turn my anger on Sunglasses for leaving that beer in the car. For leaving me with this.

Nan stays put as I crawl to the couch and wipe my face with my shirt. I refuse to lie crumpled on the floor. I blink, and a sob spills out. But I catch it. I catch it and walk out to the lawn where I retrieve my guitar with trembling hands. For all the preaching Hank gave me about music, he doesn't say a word when I bring it into the house and shuffle off to my room. It's just how it works around here.

I crash on my bed, lying on my stomach as the sting screams out on my back. I wipe my eyes. Only four months, if I can make it. I don't care about the money, only the time. Four months. I'll walk out that door and never return. Four months. The tears won't stop.

It's been a while since I've been to this state of nothingness where I stay for an hour, maybe longer. Until Hank opens without knocking and pokes his face in my room. He hasn't come to make amends. I know better than that. Years of welts, bruises, and abrasions have come and gone. The white scar on my left eyebrow I see every time I look in the mirror is an everyday reminder. An apology is only expected from me.

He levels a finger at me. "You aren't to take the car. You aren't to leave this house, except for work. And I want to have a talk about work real soon. Am I clear?"

Still on my stomach, I stare at the headboard where I know every knot and swirl in the wood grain. There is nothing to do but say "Yes," but it's not enough to make him shut the door. He wants more. He wants to break me completely.

"Do you understand why you were disciplined?'

Disciplined. Beaten. What's it matter? When I was eleven it was easy to understand. I'd done something wrong and deserved punishment. He was correcting me. Yet at some point, after all the bruises and cuts and possible fractures, I began to see not a man but a monster at the door. A monster who uses religion so that he can sleep with a clean conscious. I'm not giving him that any longer.

"Myles, you hear me?"

He used to tell me how much worse I would have it if it weren't for him and Nan, how bad things would've been for me had I gone to foster care with drug addicts or bad people. But the worst person I've ever known stands in my doorway, demanding an apology.

I turn my head, but the slightest twist sends a voltage of pain down my back. I hate how vulnerable he makes me feel, as though he's only peeking in to admire what he's done to me. I hold my face without expression, giving him nothing. "No, I don't understand. I wasn't drinking and driving. I wasn't drinking period. Someone offered me a beer and I said no. They set it in the car. That's it."

His eyes narrow, jaw tightening as he regards me as though I am a child incapable of understanding. "Myles, you shouldn't be putting yourself in places where this is happening."

One time I reached out to my aunt, to see if she had heard from my mother. I was thirteen, and I called her up in Oregon. I asked if I could come out to visit. Stay. Maybe live. She let me down easy.

Hank's nasally breathing awaits. He shifts at the door. "Understood?"

I turn to sit up, but it hurts like hell. Not that I'm going to show him that. I keep my gaze at the window, to trees, to an escape.

"Understood."

He grumbles, agreeing to our truce, and then he shuts the door and walks across the tiny hallway to his bedroom. I only stare at the window. My only way out.

Four months. Because anywhere is better than this.

14

THE PAIN SUBSIDES, OR AT LEAST I GET USED TO IT. IT flares up, angry and stinging as I climb through the window, but it's worth the effort. The fresh air feels good on my face as I start up the road on foot. The neighbor's yappy little dog barks from the window across the street. It's only nine and still warm out, and although I have nowhere to go, it feels better to move than to lie on my bed and soak in misery.

Some nights, it feels like I can walk forever, as I stuff my earbuds in and crank up a playlist. If I kept walking or hitchhiked, it would solve so many problems, maybe more than it would pose. Even dropping out would solve living with Hank. I've thought of everything: military, apprenticeships, even getting a fake ID so I can play bars.

Winding around the side streets, then out to the newer subdivisions, these escape routes float around my head. But I like working with Mr. Irvin. And there's the band. This crazy video. Ripcast. Mal's voice in my head, like a warm blanket around my shoulders, brushing my cheek. Maybe it's what carries my feet for miles. All the way to her house.

Tucked away from the wide streets and well-groomed yards, the

Kamel's house sits like a mirage. Mal's bedroom light is on. The Kamels wouldn't mind too much if I knocked on their door this late at night, but I'd rather not wake them, rather they not see me like this because I'm not quite sure I can hide what I'm feeling. I walk to the side, beneath the crepe myrtles and over the mulch beds, around the prickly rose bush to her light.

Two taps on the glass. Inside I catch the hum of music, the lilt of Mal's voice as she croons along. My problems evaporate. I smile, filled with hope as I tap again, and then once more, until there's some movement. The curtain moves, and two big, beautiful eyes greet my face.

She unlocks the window, lifts it up and places a hand to her chest. "What happened?"

"Hey." Something about the way she's watching me makes me look away. I shrug. "I'm okay. I just wanted to talk to you."

When I glance up, her eyes soften, and she checks over her shoulder before she nods. "Do you want me to come outside?"

She looks over her shoulder and then to me. "You know what?" She opens the window higher and laughs. "Just climb in."

"For real?" I wasn't expecting it, but I nod quickly. "Okay."

It's all I can do not to scream out in pain as I crawl in, but I'm able to get through the window and into her room with only a wince. She stands back, watching as I get to my feet, something like a smirk on her face. She brings a finger to her lips.

"Now, now, don't wake everybody up, Charley will come in here with a new freestyle and my mom will want to feed you. And take your boots off."

I kick my boots off and sit on her bed. Mal's room is ridiculously girly. The pillows are frilly and soft, and the sight of her—a cream colored tank, shorts, her hair in a messy bun sitting precariously on one side of her head—sends my drama to the back of my brain.

Her smile disappears as she sits on the bed, legs crossed. "Please tell me you're okay. It's a bad night for me to murder Hank, but I'll do it."

I laugh. "No, it's cool. I'm fine, never been better."

"Shut up. Seriously, did he… you know?"

"Nothing major."

"Myles."

"What?"

"Stop. Are you okay?"

"It's nothing. He took the car."

"Why?" She frowns, as though she knows this isn't all, but lets it go.

I throw my hands up. "Why does he do anything he does?." I take a seat on the bed. There must've been something in my voice because she nods, as though she understands.

"Yeah." She falls beside me. It's not the first time we've sat on her bed, but it is the first time since the kiss. I can tell she's got something on her mind, but all she says is, "So the podcast comes out in two days."

"Cool."

She slaps my arm. I slap her arm and we stretch out on our backs. I'm busy trying not to stare at the curve of her collar bone, the divot where it meets the other one as her chest rises and falls, when she turns to me completely and props her head on her hand. "Myles."

A touch of her breath, the tinge of cinnamon I've come to crave. "Hmm?"

Her gaze falls to the comforter. Her fingers roam the space between us, settling on a loose thread. "You understand, right? The other day? Why I think we…"

A gust of wind leaves my lungs. I blink and nod as she flops onto her back and stares at the ceiling. "I'm serious. You mean too much to me."

My heart thumps, the welts on my back throbbing along to the beat. I force myself to sound cool, but I fail. "But shouldn't that mean…"

She closes her eyes and smiles. We both study the ceiling fan. We're enthralled with her ceiling fan. A few minutes pass before she sighs. "I'm leaving after this year."

"You are? Funny, you've never mentioned it."

"Shut up." She slaps my arm again. This time her hand stays.

"I worry about you. About what's going to happen, after next year."

I shrug off her pity. "I'll be out of Hank's house, so anything is an upgrade."

She flops back to her side and faces me, her hand resting on my arm like it's no big deal. "Well, now that we're famous it should be easier."

"We're not famous."

Her eyes widen. "Oh, really? Hang on." She twists over, grabs her phone. "Eighty-four thousand views." She scrolls down. "Eighty-four *thousand*. And a shit ton of comments."

"Eighty—"

"Four thousand. Yeah. If I'd know this was going to happen, I would have dressed better."

I glance to the phone, to the still of Mal, her face frozen in a wide-eyed gasp of surprise. No wonder this thing is piling up views. "I think you look great. You always look great."

She lowers the phone, her full lips almost pursed to a pout. She blinks her eyes slowly, deliberately. "Thanks, Myles."

We stare at each other before she shifts. "Be honest with me. Did Hank hit you?"

I take a deep breath. Back to the ceiling fan. "Come on, Mal."

She sits up and tosses the phone onto the bed. "That fat son of—"

"Mal."

"He should be arrested."

"What about Nan?"

She sets her jaw. My back screams out in pain while my chest remains warm. Her lips, the glow of the lamp off her left shoulder. She starts to reach for my hand but stops herself. "Nan was fine before he came along, right? Isn't it her house?"

"Yeah, but..." *If I leave will he start hitting her?* I don't say it, and Mal's too worked up, anyway, going on about Nan and Hank and how I'm technically still a minor and CPS should be called in and she'll call them herself if she has to and don't think she won't. We hush ourselves when we hear footsteps in the hallway, which come to a stop outside her door.

Mal's eyes widen and her mother's voice rings out on the other side of the door. "Malorie? Are you okay, sweetie?"

Mal gazes at me, her voice lower. "Sorry Mom. On the phone."

From behind the door: "Okay, just checking."

The footsteps pad down the hallway, and I shake my head at the beautiful liar in front of me. She cocks her head. "What?"

"You lied to your poor mother like that."

She levels her eyes on me. "My poor mother? Myles. Would you rather me say, 'Oh, I'm talking to the boy lying on my bed?'"

I roll my eyes. "But it's only Myles."

Her lips parts with a smile. "Oh, wow."

I turn away, like a child, wishing I could've kept my mouth shut. Mal's behind me. Gawking. I don't have to face her to see it.

"Seriously?" she asks.

I shrug. She pounces. Before I know it, she's behind me. Close. And as much as my back burns and protests, I don't dare move away. Her voice is hardly more than a breath in my ear. "You know what, you're right. Let me go out and tell her I do have a boy in my bed, but it's only Myles. She'll probably warm up some cocoa."

"Shut up."

She laughs, sets her hand on my arm, and I turn, electrified by her touch. We're against each other. She's no longer smiling, and we hold each other's eyes for ten seconds, twenty. And then she rolls off the bed, stepping away. "I should probably get some sleep."

I blink and run a hand through my hair. "Huh? Oh right. I'll go."

She watches me closely as I grab my boots and try to hide my smile. It sucks that she thinks we can't be more than friends, even though we are *something* more. But I'll take this, watching her watching me so intently as I let myself out of her window.

Because without it, I'm not sure where I'd be tonight.

15

I wake up too early for a Saturday morning. Maybe it's the stupid second video, but I can't go back to sleep. I'm not getting out of bed, though. If I do, Hank will put me to work all the earlier. Instead, I reach over to the table and grab my phone to check the video. The hits are still rolling in, closing in on a hundred thousand views and still trending upward.

I almost leave it at that, but before I set my phone back down, I sift through the comments, where Mal is the most common topic of discussion. She's incredible, she's hot, she's a star in the making. Tell me something I don't know. When I find some comments about me, I start thinking Mal was making all that stuff up in the car just to make me feel better.

This dude sucks.

GO SOLO GIRL.

Girl = amazing. Dude = meh

Did she just pick out a random guy with a guitar and tell him to play????

It keeps going. In between comments about how cute we are, I find comments about my face, my cheesing, how out of tune the guitar is. I continue past any positive comments and zero in on the hate. My eyes become filters, glossing over the love and

99

support until it catches on my lack of skills, how I strum. Someone even comments on how one of my dimples is bigger than the other.

I want to respond. I don't play acoustic oldies. I play punk. Electric. The guitar was already way out of tune. It just feels like I'm taking a beating. Then I remember Ripcast aired.

Thirty minutes pass and I'm sitting up on my bed sifting through Ripcast's social media pages. Most of the comments are about Mal again.

That chick is hot

Damn she can sing.

Look at those eyes!

I'm in love

And a few that get me smiling:

He isn't so bad, either.

Eventually, I find what I'm searching for:

Dude needs lessons

Bends are a little flat…

He should probably stop ogling the hot girl and focus on playing a little cleaner

I study each one, mentally capturing the image of the comment in my head. How to hold my guitar, what to wear, how to keep my head at the right angle. Because now we have another video to do, and I'm not feeling up to the task.

Hank bangs on the door and tells me to be up in five. I get dressed, pocket my phone, and walk out to find him in the kitchen, thus ending my streak of lucky mornings. Before I can come up with an excuse to hurry out of the house, he pats the table. "Have a seat."

Hank is always most bearable to me after the belt. It's been that way since I can remember. Maybe he feels bad, or maybe he feels his point has been made. Either way, it's not like he's ever going to apologize. But we do have to live together, which means we have to talk to each other. And that may be worse.

With a deep breath, I pour a glass of orange juice and find my place across the table from Hank. He's clean-shaven today and it makes his pink face seem chubbier. He chews with his mouth open and it's all kinds of disgusting.

"You working today?"

Hank only talks about work or God or how the country is going down the tubes because it's turned its back on work and God. Anything else is deemed unnecessary. School, music, even sports—don't get him started on the kneeling—take a backseat to this trinity of importance. You do not want to get Hank revved up on politics.

"Yeah."

"What's that?" he says, leaning in, gnashing on his bacon. He chews and chews and breathes heavily through his nose, and it's all I can do not to throw my juice at his face. I can't stand how he can do what he did and then expect me to sit here and talk to him.

I force myself to make eye contact, just for a second, before I my gaze falls back to the table. "Yep, working today."

I wish I was working. Instead, we have that stupid video to record. I want to back out, but then Noah might quit altogether.

Nan turns to me because she knows it's a lie about work. I'm off today, but I'm not going to let Hank load me down with a chore list.

He nods, using his toast to mop up the egg yolk on his plate. "Good. It will do you some good to get out and do some work today."

Nan sets a plate in front of me with an identical breakfast, but I'm no longer hungry. Hank appraises me, his gaze falling to my plate then back up. "Hair's getting long. You thinking about cutting it?"

I shake my head. "Nope."

He glares at me for a minute before getting to his feet. "Well, I'd better go. Gotta be in at eight." He drops his plate on the counter next to Nan and fixes his belt, the one that broke the skin on my back. "Remember, the car is off limits. You lost that privilege. Did you work out something with Mr. Irvin, or do you need a lift?"

I'd hike barefoot across the country on a trail of broken glass before I'd get in the car with him. "I worked something out."

He grimaces, but he can't expect I would want to spend time

with him after he beat the crap out of me. He shrugs it off. "What about the insurance?"

A blow to the gut. I grit my teeth, but let it pass. I've already made my stand with the lie about work and the hair, so I know it would only push him over the edge to argue about the insurance.

"I don't have it on me."

"You don't have any business in the car, then." He sends a warning look Nan's way before he nods, Mr. Chipper again. "Well folks, back to the grind."

Then then he's gone. And I wait for Nan to acknowledge what a big fat prick she's married to, but she simply picks up his plate to begin her daily ritual. "Myles, you'd better eat before your breakfast gets cold."

WE MEET up in the basement, and Noah's all worked up, talking a mile a minute about how we should do the video. Mal laughs, checking her phone every two-and-a-half seconds. I'm guessing she's monitoring the Ripcast site.

Noah has made some things clear. We're not doing any "soft ass, lovey dovey songs," as he calls them. I glance at Mal, who's trying hard not to laugh. Noah has certainly put some thought into this. We both shrug. Whatever it takes to keep him from playing side gigs. We decide on an original song.

With the matter settled, he breaks out a drum box thing he bought online. He sits on it and plays something that sounds like bongos. It's perfect. This way he won't overpower us with his set, and we can fit in a small place.

Mal sits back, still amused at how Noah is so worked up but trying to play it cool. She glances at me. "We could do it at the rock? At the park?"

Noah shakes his head. "No, the acoustics are going to suck. And we need a camera guy."

"I have an idea." I turn to Mal. "Is Charley at home?"

They both agree with my choice of venue. Ten minutes later we pick up Charley and head to Nan's house. With Hank pulling a twelve-hour shift, we swing open the back door of the Roadmaster. It's risky because Hank could always come home, but Mal is all about it and refuses another change of venue. She looks like she's still itching for a fight with him anyway.

We set the tailgate down and pile in the back on the outward-facing seat. Charley mans the camera, which means we get a half hour of footage of him freestyling over Noah's drumbeats.

Noah counts it down. I strum out the opening to *Can't Keep Myself*, the upbeat title track to our demo that Noah okayed. Mal shifts and turns sideways, her back against the window with one leg pulled up as she taps on her knee. I'm positioned facing out, so my legs have room.

Noah goes to work on the box, and I smile because it's good. Mal too, as she tosses her head back and belts out the opening lines.

I can't keep myself from wanting you to stay...

I can't keep myself from shoving you away...

I make a conscious effort to learn from my mistakes. Not to smile like in the last video. I settle on a half scowl while we find our groove, but each time I move my fingers or sing the chorus, I catch myself watching Mal, how she sets her head back, her voice turning me inside out.

When I flub the chord, everything stops. Mal opens her eyes. Noah straightens. Charley looks up from the camera. "What? What happened?"

"Sorry." I mumble, looking away, feeling cramped. I slide toward the bumper and off the edge of the car. Noah mutters something about the basement under his breath, shaking his head. "I just need a sec."

Mal nods. "It's cool." She sets her head against the backseat, her eyes trailing me. I need some air. I set the guitar down and walk into the yard.

Noah goes over the drum pattern with Mal as I roam off past Charley, who's fiddling with the camera.

It's too late. I can't delete the comments from my memory. About how I play. How Mal can do better. The way I look at her. Mal calls them haters, but every comment I read about how the hot girl should ditch the guitarist knocks me down a notch. I can't get it out of my head. Maybe because it's true.

If I'm not good enough, what else do I have? This is it for me. This band, Noah, and the girl I love. Any one of them could take it all away whenever they wanted. Before, a day was a day, something to slog through. Whatever happened down that road, good or bad, was part of the ride, like an exit or offramp. I'd figure it out when I got there.

Now, everything is here, right now. Thousands of people judge my entire life based on a single video clip. Every note I play will be screened and scrutinized. It's not why I play music.

I wipe my face, shaking it off. Noah howls in the car, and I smile despite myself. Maybe I do suck. Maybe this house in front of me holds my darkest moments. But I've survived that, it hasn't beaten me yet. In the car sits everything good thing in my life—the only good, really. If I can't get it together for them, what hope is there for me?

When I climb back into the car, Noah and Mal are laughing at Charley's dance moves. They stop suddenly as I grab my guitar by the neck.

"You okay now?" Noah asks, looking up.

"Yep, fine." I tousle his hair, and he jerks away. I laugh, then lower my head and settle in near the side window, my left leg dangling off the bumper. "Let's do it."

Mal shoots me a quick smile, her wide, glimmering eyes bringing me in. She nudges my leg with her foot. It's all it takes.

We do the song. I push back the likes and dislikes, the comments and everything else. This time, I don't mess up and we get it right. It's okay, not bad, but it feels too planned. We're acting. But Noah is happy with it, probably because he was so good on his beatbox, as he calls it.

Back in the Honda, Charley talks about his own new songs the whole way home. Noah goes along with it, and for a bit it's like old times again. We pull up to Noah's house, and he taps his phone. "I'll go upload this, pronto. We should be viral by tonight."

Mal leans over me, toward the back. "I wouldn't get your hopes up."

"Shit, if that Hall and Oates cover got 100,000 views, this should be good for a mil, at least."

Mal slaps at his legs. "Language."

Charley looks to Noah with stars in his eyes. "We should do one for my song."

Complete silence follows. Noah chuckles. "Yeah, sure. Maybe next time, right?"

Charley smiles. "Cool."

Noah grabs his box and climbs out. "See you, losers."

We talk about practice and the upcoming show until we get to Mal's, where Charley leaps out to go check on the video. Mal turns to me.

"I feel like we did our good deed for the day."

"For the month. Noah seemed cool."

Mal nods, glances out the window. An awkward silence falls between us until she turns to me again. "How are you?"

"I'm fine."

"What happened back there?"

I sit back. "This isn't how I expected things to happen, with the videos and stuff. I mean, it's cool, I guess. I don't know. I like shows."

She nods. "Me too."

She's got something else on her mind. I'm thinking maybe it's about us when she blows a strand of hair from her face. "Myles, the other night, when you came to my house."

Oh, that. "Yeah, sorry. Did I step on a rose bush?"

"No, but you looked really scared."

I sit my head back. She starts to take my hand like she always used to, then stops short—another casualty of the kiss. She frowns. "Would you tell me if it got too bad?"

"Yes, but it's fine. I'm good. Really." I sit back, not wanting to tell her but unable to stop the words. "I watched Ripcast." Her face brightens, until I add, "And I've been reading the comments on the other one."

"Myles."

"Like, *all* of them."

"Myles, no."

"Sorry, but it's there, and I was only going to read a few. Then, I mean damn, it's clear that—"

"That people suck and have no idea what they're talking about?" She pulls her hair back with both hands and clasps them behind her neck. "Myles. You can't do this to yourself. You can't let a few idiots who've never picked up an instrument decide this for you."

I gaze out the window, but Mal isn't going to let it go. She lowers her voice. "And more importantly, you can't let Hank decide, either. I'm more worried about what's happening at home than in the comment section, okay?"

"Thanks, Mal. But I got it, okay? Trust me, I hate Hank more than anyone, but I can deal with him."

"Really? Because by the looks of things, I'm not so sure."

"Wow."

She sits back and exhales. I do the same.

"It's hard to explain," I say. "Nan tries. She's been through a lot."

Mal throws her hands in her lap. "Amazing. Your grandmother's husband beats the shit out of you, and you're worried about dear old Nan."

I let out a sigh, thrown by her concern. Is it concern for a friend or something more? Either way, I want out of this conversation. Mal can sense it because she sits up suddenly.

"I'm sorry I care, Myles."

She starts the car and drives me home.

16

T HE SECOND VIDEO DOESN'T GAIN MUCH TRACTION. Noah isn't taking it well.

"This sucks," he says, scrolling down his phone. "'*They are so cute together.*' Ugh."

It's only the two of us in the basement. I'm trying to smooth things over, but I'm stressing about the insurance money I owe Hank. It's not helping my savings, which is not helping my plan, which is not helping my mood. The welts on my back sting like hell. It's all I can do to shrug and grab another handful of Chex-Mix.

"It's got like, what? Two hundred views? That's not so bad."

He levels a glare on me. "Do not mess with me right now."

I stuff the Chex-Mix in my mouth and throw my hands up. I can't help my smiling. Views or not, the video seems to have served its purpose. At least that's what I'm thinking until Noah sets the phone down. "You remember when we started this band?"

"Yeah." Of course, I remember. Two summers ago. I think back to how badly we sucked, how much fun it was, how far we've come. Noah nudges me along.

"Do you remember the pact?"

"Hmm, I don't recall any pact."

"The Noah/Myles Executive Pact?"

"I definitely would have remembered that."

Noah scrambles to his feet, pacing around with his drumsticks. He points one at me. "Well, let me give you a refresher. We agreed that we would keep it real. We'd play our kind of music and never go on some sellout-type shit."

"We've got the Richland Hills show tomorrow. I think it's safe to say we've already done the selling out."

"Oh, we'll fit right in." He shakes his head. "You already show up at our gigs dressed like a nerd. You and Mal went viral playing Hall and Oates. Seriously."

So much for Noah being cool. I study his face to see whether he's kidding or not. "Should I run out and get a Mohawk? Wear a dog collar? I'll do it if it's what you want. And the first video was *a joke*, okay? Do I need to remind you who recorded and posted that video?"

"You need a dog collar, for that leash Mal's got you on. The two of you are viral sweethearts, and I hate it, just so you know. You're all hung up on her. Are you going to tell me what happened?"

I take a breath. Noah does the same. "Come on man. Let's hear it."

I roll my eyes. But he knows something's up, so I gather my thoughts. I'm tired of fighting with him. I just want things to be tight between us again, so I set my hands on my head and let them slide down to my neck. "That night, in the basement, when you ran upstairs, Mal came back inside after talking to Dave. She was all excited about the podcast. And," I shrug, "we kissed."

His eyes go wide. "Dude! Like, kissed, or..." Noah starts making out with his hand.

"I guess something in between?"

"Man, for real?"

"For real. But that was it. Nothing else has happened. She freaked out, and then you came down. She said she doesn't want to mess up the band, or something."

"That makes two of us," he mutters.

"I'm not the one with a side gig."

Noah throws his hands up. "You and Mal *are* the side gig." He keeps poking. "And the timing is weird, you know?"

"Huh?"

"There's the video, and then she kisses you and you two go on that show. I love Mal, but it seems like she's using all this for a boost. Like, doing just enough to keep you around, bro."

"You always know what to say." I get to my feet. So much for that. Suddenly the basement feels too cramped. "I gotta go."

He flips his sticks in the air. "Where are you going?"

"Out. I'm just… I need to get out."

"Well, I drove, remember?"

"It's cool. I'll walk."

He drops the drumsticks. "Myles. Come on man, I was messing with you about Mal, but seriously, how is this supposed to work if you are all hopeless and shit?"

"I'll try my best to keep my hopelessness to myself, okay?" I hit the steps, regretting coming here and telling him what happened. I wish I was only worried about viral videos and traction. "I'll text you later or something."

Outside, the air is warm and thick. The crickets chirp, and the full moon hangs low. I'm in the mood for a long walk anyway, even if Noah's words stick in my head. They always do.

The walk helps some, but my thoughts are all jumbled when I get to the house. I go through the front door, refusing to bother with the window charade. Thankfully, all is quiet.

I find some dinner but don't eat much. In my room, I kick off my shoes and check the new video one more time. The views aren't taking off, but it's gathering comments.

They're so cute together!

Just kiss her already!

She knows what she's doing

The camera guy suxxxx!

It's like the whole world can see inside my head, or at least the 550 people who've viewed the video. I watch it again, then another time. My playing isn't terrible, but it's not great either. I'm sure it will get ripped apart like the others.

I set the phone down and find my notepad. Not much happens, only me scratching out the same words to the same dead-end song. I rip the page out, ball it up, and throw it away. I'm tired of it. I'm sick of Noah and his neediness, of Hank and how my heart races and my blood stirs when he's in the house. Even Mal, how lately it feels like I'm more her little project than anything else. I toss the pen to the floor and set my head in my hands.

My dad chose a different way to cope with band drama. With life. Chemicals did the trick for him, but it was never enough. Music or even family couldn't convince him otherwise. I find myself thinking about him, about convictions and confidence. I pick up my pen and jot down my thoughts. I crawl into my head and do my best to remember the last time I saw him.

Flipping to a new page, I scrawl "Dashboard" at the top and write out the thoughts. Maybe it's good and maybe it's terrible, but at least no one can pass judgement. And so, I keep writing.

17

I'M STILL WORKING THROUGH "DASHBOARD" THE NEXT morning at work. The day quickly turns blistering hot as the sun bakes the sky white. I'm soaked through by ten o'clock, but Mr. Irvin, in his thin button down and faded work slacks, doesn't even seem to have broken a sweat.

The movement helps my thoughts, even as the sweat stings my back, sinking into each welt. I wince every time I have to load up the wheelbarrow. Of course, the old man notices. He keeps asking me if I need a hand.

"No, I'm good," I tell him, hoping he'll turn away. He doesn't.

"You sure about that? You're walking like an old man."

I laugh. "At least I'm not slacking off like some teenager."

He smiles but keeps his eye on me. I make sure not to wince or gasp or limp no matter how much it hurts. I simply keep plugging along.

Later, as he's dropping me off at home, I get a text from Mal.

Mal: Ripcast wants us back!!!!!

Me: With Noah?

Mal: Seriously? ☹

I realize I'm smiling, more about the thought of riding up to Richmond with Mal more than the podcast itself, when Mr. Irvin watches me with a grin. "Something brighten your day?"

"Huh? Oh, it's this podcast thing. They want us to come back and play."

He nods. "I have no idea what you just said."

"It's like a radio show. An interview, we'll play some songs. It's cool, but they want us to come back on. The two of us. Not our drummer."

"You and the girl, huh?"

"Well, the drummer is not happy."

"Ah, band drama."

"And then some."

I call Mal when I get home. Sure, I could text and get the details, but I like the sound of her voice. She answers with a squeal, and I'm glad we're over whatever happened the other day in her driveway. She says we're all set for next week. Again, I think about Noah.

"So, just us?"

She sighs into the phone. "Myles, I love Noah, but I'm a little tired of the babysitting. Besides, as lead singer and the only female, I reserve the right to be drama queen of the band. You two can battle it out for second place."

"Isn't that like, perpetuating gender roles or something?"

"I can be very old-fashioned when I want to be. Now, when are you coming over?"

"Oh, um..."

"To work on a setlist for the thingy tomorrow. I've got some song ideas, and Mom's making lasagna, which is hit-or-miss, but so is Hank, I guess."

"Wow."

"Sorry. That wasn't even funny. But we have that show this weekend and a lot to do to get ready. Have *you* talked to Noah?"

"Yeah, he's..." I think back to the other day when I told him everything and it changed nothing between us. When he said Mal was in it for herself. "I don't know."

"So, you coming or what?"

"I need a ride."

After a quick shower, I throw on some shorts and a t-shirt. I leave 75 dollars on the counter for insurance, money that should be safe and sound in my account. But I need the car, and I need Hank off my ass.

I'm hardly even dried off when Mal pulls in the driveway. She's blasting the stereo, head bopping, her hands drumming on the steering wheel. I'm almost at her car when Hank's truck comes rumbling down the street.

So much for that.

He shifts and wobbles out of the car, scowling at Mal before he eyes me up and down as I stop at Mal's passenger door. I call out to him. "Going to Mal's for dinner. I left the insurance money on the counter."

"That right?" he says, fiddling with his lunchbox and coat. "Nan say that was okay?"

My shoulders drop. I was so damn close, too. Mal ignores him but speaks loud enough so that he can hear. "Is he going to be a dick? He is, isn't he?"

I can't tell if he heard what she said, but he glares at her before he nods to the yard. "I thought you were going to cut the grass?"

The grass in the yard is roughly two inches high. And here I thought the money would do the trick. I manage to keep my eyes from rolling. "Hank, I worked all day, I'll do it tomorrow."

He grins at this, swings his metal lunch box in my direction, shaking his head. "Good to hear. Join the club. But the grass can't wait. Besides, 'spose to rain tomorrow."

I sigh, he edges closer to me, and I tense up. My head begins to throb as he nods like he's relenting, doing me some sort of favor. "Get the grass cut first."

Over his shoulder, Mal watches intently, gripping the wheel like she might run him over. Hank stares at me from his place in the driveway. I can't help but think how if I hadn't showered, we would've been gone.

"Hop to it," Hank says, claiming his victory. He whistles a tune as he starts for the house.

I lean into the car. "I gotta cut the grass. It will only take a sec."

"This is what I mean," Mal says, her eyes a mix of pity and anger.

"Mal, it's just the grass."

"It's not just the grass, Myles."

"Please. I'm sorry."

She closes her eyes, the muscles in her forearm dancing as she squeezes the steering wheel. She aims a searing, laser strike stare at Hank's back before she shoves the gearshift into park. "Yeah, okay."

My fresh, clean shower melts into sweat as I zip through the cut. I bang it out in fifteen minutes while Mal sits on the hood of the car while thumbing through her phone. I know she's hoping Hank will come out so she can light into him. He doesn't.

When I finish up, I rush through the door, stripping off my shirt. I go for the fridge while Nan is at the sink. When I turn around, I catch her gaping at the purplish welts across my back. They feel better, but they must not look that way.

I gulp down the water, turn to Nan, then to Hank's fat face over at the table. "Grass is cut."

Nan's eyes dart away. I guess she figures if she doesn't see it, it didn't happen. As though I don't have that scar on my eyebrow from the wild turn of a belt buckle. I turn around to set the water in the fridge. She's still staring at the floor when she says, "Sure you don't want to eat first?"

"No thanks. Eating at Mal's."

I set off to my room, change clothes again, then attempt to scoot out as Hank and Nan are at the table. But when I go for the door, Hank calls me back. "I thought you okay'd this with Nan?"

I cast a quick glance to the counter. The money is gone. I turn to Nan, almost daring her. She nods, but that's not good enough for

Hank, who belches. He wipes his face, still chewing when he asks, "Did you trim?"

My hand is on the doorknob. I close my eyes, and it takes some slow breathing, some clenching and unclenching of my fists, before I can turn, smiling some but not too much. "Nope, I'll get right on that."

He nods and digs back into dinner. I get out the door before he can say another word. One look at Mal, and I know I'm not trimming. I'm going to escape this sad excuse for a house before it chews me up to nothing.

Mal glances up from her phone. "Oh, thank God, I was about to get into a comment war. Some asshole said I sound like Taylor Swift. I told him he would know but he... Hey, are you okay?"

She studies my face, then looks past me to the house where Hank lurks in the window. "What does he want now?"

I shrug. "Nothing.

It's what I hate, always bringing her down. Noah's house has the snacks and gadgets. Mal's house has two supportive and loving parents. My house holds nothing but a barren silence that crushes all hopes and dreams within its walls.

"This isn't normal, Myles."

What do I know about normal? I start for the passenger door. "Can we just go?"

She pockets her phone. "Yeah, yeah sure." She hurries to the driver's side, and I fall into the passenger seat. Hank steps out to the porch, calling after me. Mal looks at him, her eyes narrowing. Then she grins at me. "Can I give him the finger?"

"No." I shake my head. "Fuck him, let's go."

Her face lights up with a smile. "Yeah, fuck him. Let's go."

18

I MANAGED TO ESCAPE HANK LAST NIGHT, THEN ONCE
again this morning. My luck will run out soon, I suspect, as I throw
myself into work. I do my best to manage the pain as the sweat
soaks through my shirt and sinks into the welts. At lunch, Mr. Irvin
takes a pull from his cup of tap water. The usual playfulness is gone
from his voice. "What's going on with your back?"

With my eyes on my tray, I stuff my face so I have some time.
"Nothing. I scraped it against the wall."

"You backing into walls these days?"

I glance off, let that fall into oblivion. I don't know how much
I've let slip about Hank to Mr. Irvin, but I'm guessing it's more than
he's letting on. This is a small town, and they're around the same
age. They have a history, I've gathered, a history that Mr. Irvin's not
hiding very well as he studies my face. I look away. He moves on.

"Well, how's your love life?"

I turn back to him before I can stop the grin. "Not as good as my
work life."

He smiles, "I'm an old man, was in love once. Tell me, how's it
work these days? Got a big date tonight? You've been smiling like a
goofball when you're not wincing about your back."

"I am? Well, I hate to break it to you, but it seems I had the wrong idea about a friend. Our band has a gig tonight, though. You ought to come out and see us."

"Something other than the community market?"

I'm laughing now, because if anyone else said that, I'd think they were making fun of me. I shake my head. "Yes. But not necessarily better."

Insurance or not, the way I left with Mal the other day leaves me without the wagon. Mal has her car stuffed to the gills with equipment. Nothing from Noah yet.

"I see. The ladies like a musician, you know."

"Do they now?" I sit back and smile, look him in the eye. I'm surprised by the kindness I find in his gaze. His eyes are easy and trustworthy, like his laugh.

Mr. Irvin nods. "If I remember correctly, yes."

Now I'm the one chuckling. It's hard to feel sorry for yourself around this guy. "What if the girl is a musician as well?"

He nods. "Well, then, I suppose things should work themselves out."

MR. IRVIN PAYS me cash for the week. He takes a call and hops in the truck with a smile. There should be plenty of work coming up, he says. We got the contract for an awareness garden for a church in Town Heights. It's a big job with lots of bricks but when he mentions maybe hiring a third guy for the job, I assure him I can work full time to get it done. He smiles and says it could lead to more big jobs. I'm good to go. The more hours the better as far as I'm concerned.

On the way home, my phone buzzes with a text.

> Mal: MAJOR ANNOUNCEMENT BEFORE
> THE SHOW MY HOUSE ASAP

I text back about the car situation, only to find her waiting in her car at my house when Mr. Irvin drops me off.

She's wild eyed and bouncing. I ask about the announcement but get shushed and directed to take a shower. By six, I'm sitting on the couch in the Kamel's living room, waiting on Mal to get ready. For what, I still have no idea.

It's all kinds of awkward. Dr. Kamel is coming home this evening, which is sort of a big deal at the Kamel household. I scoot to the edge of the couch, looking around. Maybe that's the major announcement.

My phone buzzes again. Hank, just off work, has decided I need to come home and do that trimming I skipped. I pocket my phone. Hank will give up soon, anyway, after he eats some pork chops and parks his butt on the couch.

"Myles? Are you okay sweetheart?"

Mrs. Kamel is all glitzed up. Her hair shines, and she's wearing black eyeliner and a dress.

"Yes Ma'am. Thanks. Really, I can come back another time. I forgot about... everything."

"No, it is completely fine," she says with a smile. It's actually kind of adorable, the way she fidgets around, checking the windows for her husband to get home. And if I'm being honest, it's not hard to see what Mal will look like when she's older.

Mrs. Kamel's smile takes a dive as Charley enters the room wearing tapered pants that droop at the crotch. He's also got on his customary hoodie, even though it's like ninety-two degrees outside.

"Mom, are we going to that restaurant by the lake?"

"Yes, dear," she says with a smile. "Now will you get dressed, please?"

He throws his arms wide, lowers his head. "I *am* dressed."

She shakes her head and points to his room. "Go."

He looks at me. I shrug. Mrs. Kamel watches him retreat as Mal's door opens and she steps out of her room.

I'm expecting the Mal I know best, maybe a faded NASA shirt, jeans, and her favorite pair of Vans. Instead, it's a sleeveless navy blue dress that hugs her waist and stops at her knees. I realize I'm staring. Like, really staring.

She stops, leans against the wall, and bends her knee to fix her shoe. "I know, right. Sorry," she says, blowing a strand of hair from her face. I guess she thinks I'm shocked at how formally she's dressed, and I am, only for entirely different reasons than she suspects. Mal's beauty kills me a little bit on a daily basis. This dress is burying me completely.

Mrs. Kamel smiles at Mal and gushes. "Sweetie, you look nice."

Nice. Her hair is swept back but rebelling. The tangle falls back to her cheek. She smiles at me and closes her eyes, tucking the strand away. She's got some eyeshadow on, and she doesn't look nice; she looks fascinating. Again, I remind myself to stop staring.

Mal walks over and fiddles with her hands. "I thought you could come to dinner with us before the show. Is that cool?"

"Oh." I swallow whatever I'm about to say. Mrs. Kamel smiles.

"Yes, of course."

Now I'm feeling like Charley. My thin V-neck tee, faded jeans, and old running shoes won't cut it. I hold up my hands. "I'm kind of underdressed."

"Here, you can borrow a button down," Mrs. Kamel says. Then she's off, quickly pacing toward the back of the house.

Mal grins, shaking her head. "Because my dad's shirts will totally fit you."

Mal walks over and sits a space apart from me. I can't help blurting out my thoughts. "You look..." I nod several times. "Really nice."

"Oh." She does some exaggerated nodding, making fun of me. "Thanks."

This is the part where she tells me what's going on. But she doesn't. She shakes her head with a smile, and we sit side by side without saying a word. She's tapping her foot, and there's a perma-grin to her face, but when I turn to her, she shifts sideways and props her head on her arm.

"We'll eat some dinner, change, then get to our show. Have you talked to Noah?"

I can't look directly at her right now because she's so full of happiness. I fiddle with my shoe. "No. So what's the news?"

"Shhhh. Nope." She rips out her phone, checks it, and then rolls her eyes. "What the hell is his problem? We did a stupid video for him. Now he's ignoring my texts on the day of the show *he* booked us?"

"He'll be there. It's probably something with his parents."

"All the more reason to have your friends around," she says, tapping furiously into her phone. She mutters a string of curse words. "There," she says. "That ought to do the trick."

"He'll show. I know he will."

"Yes, or we'll borrow a drummer. We'll beg, plead, and take a hostage if we have to. I'm not letting this ruin the major announcement."

I'm laughing because, even all dressed up, she's still the same old Mal. "Are you going to tell me or not?"

She pops up with a grin. Mrs. Kamel walks in with three shirts. "One of these, maybe?" She holds up the first one. "I think this blue one will bring out your eyes."

Mal narrows her gaze. "Mom, no hitting on Myles."

Mrs. Kamel laughs. I raise my brow at Mal before I thank Mrs. Kamel for the shirt. In the bathroom, I peel off my t-shirt, avoiding the guy in the mirror as I slip on the button down. It fits, mostly, a little tight around the shoulders and the cuffs stop about two inches short of my wrists. I roll up the sleeves, run a hand through my hair and try not to wonder what the hell I'm doing.

I ran into Charley on the way out. He gestured to my shirt. "They got you too, huh?"

He's found a red polo shirt to go with his tapered pants. Mrs. Kamel doesn't exactly seem pleased, but she knows to pick her battles.

Mal smirks. Mrs. Kamel nods. "Very nice. You look handsome, Myles."

Mal gives me a once over. "You look like you stepped out of Old Navy ad."

Charles finds this hilarious. I shrug and make my way for the couch when Mrs. Kamel checks her phone. "Well, we should go."

A BLAST of Blink 182 as Mal starts the car. She throws an arm around my seat as we back out, sending a breeze of melon my way as we start off, following Mrs. Kamel's Volvo up the street.

Mal turns the volume down. "Sorry I made you come and be lame with me. I promise my major announcement will be well worth it. But I sort of want Noah around for it. Even if he is being a snot."

I shake my head, fiddle with the rolls of my sleeves, making sure they're even. "Can we just call it the announcement now? You've sort of made it clear that it's major."

"Nope. It's a major announcement through and through."

"Okay. I didn't have anything else going on, really."

I check my phone for any missed texts from Noah. Mal perks up like she's remembered something. "No plans? Oh wait, is this okay with Jada?"

"What?" I stop fiddling. She's in a mood tonight, her tight smile bursting at the seams. She raises her brow with the question, lifting her hands from the steering wheel.

"I mean, you should probably call her and let her know you're going out to dinner with your bandmate."

So we're going to play it this way? We kissed, and then she decides we're only friends, but now she's giving me stuff about some girl I had to go out with because of Noah? Nope, not doing it. I refuse to give in. I turn my attention to the window, but it only encourages Mal to keep at it.

"Or is she cool like that? She doesn't mind you hanging with the band?" She points a finger gun at me and clicks her teeth. "That's it, isn't it?"

"Mal."

She shrugs and lifts her fingers from the steering wheel. "I'm just saying, you probably should let her know, is all."

I turn to her. She grins at me, and I reach in my pocket. "You know what?" I pull out my phone, enjoying the flicker of surprise in Mal 's face as I press a button, calling Noah because I know he won't answer.

"Jada? Hey, it's me. Yeah, I'm going to dinner with Mal and her family. Is that okay, peaches?" Noah's recorded voice fills my ear. *Noah. Leave a message, loser.* I keep going. "I'll see you then, kay?"

The phone beeps. Mal only stares straight ahead, eyes squinted. I ramp up the cheese. "No, you hang up. No, *you* hang up. No, you—"

"Oh my God!" Mal reaches over and grabs my phone. Her gaze drops to the screen, where it reads, HELL NOAH. I smile big as her shoulders fall. She tosses the phone to my lap. "Jerk."

Mal goes silent. Or maybe I can't hear her over my own laughter.

Oak Hills is settled near the lake at the base of the mountains I've hiked a million times. I've never been inside, though, and for some reason I'm a little wobbly about seeing Dr. Kamel. The guy is all success and charm. I always feel like he can smell the poor on me, sniff out Nan's house.

We spot the Kamels in the parking lot. Dr. Kamel sees us, waves, then speed walks over to Mal and wraps her up in a bear hug.

"My baby."

Dr. Kamel has been on business for two months, so it's kind of like a reunion. The guy has to be wondering what in the world I'm doing here, wearing his shirt. Thankfully, he only smiles when Mal breaks away, and he has a chance to look me over. "Myles, you keep growing, my man."

Dr. Kamel always makes a big deal about my height, even though I'm only six-foot-two. He's at least eight inches shorter than me, so I guess I seem like a giant. We shake hands. He's got hair down his forearms to his fingers, and he's got one of those power grips. Not in a macho way or anything. He's just an intense guy.

"Nice to see you again, Dr. Kamel."

"Hey, nice shirt."

"Oh." My face heats up, and Mrs. Kamel laughs. I'm about to explain when he sets his hand on my shoulder.

"Myles. Please, call me John."

"Right." I nod and smile, knowing I could never call him that after what Mal's told me. He claps his hands.

"Shall we eat? I'm starving."

We make our way to the entrance. At the door, Mal 's hand brushes mine, and I'm surprised when she takes it in hers and gives it a squeeze. Then, just as quickly as it showed up, it's gone.

The restaurant has vaulted ceilings and huge windows overlooking the lake. It's busy, with clinks and clanks and the murmur of conversation and laughter. Whenever I'm with the Kamels, I can't help thinking about Hank and Nan and how pathetic we are. If we ever went out to eat, which we wouldn't, we would go to Applebee's or Cracker Barrel, and Hank would make me pay for my meal while he slurped sweet tea and preached his greatest hits—how his father had him working at twelve years old and how I need to learn some responsibility.

Not now. I push away thoughts of Hank. I just got paid, and I'll insist on paying my way even when Dr. Kamel objects.

The host shows us to the table. The lounge is busy, and I'm probably being overly sensitive, but I feel like the Kamels get a lot of attention. Maybe it's because they look Middle Eastern. Maybe because I'm with them. Or maybe it's all in my head.

Dr. Kamel takes a seat and regards his family with a broad smile. His gaze seems to capture the room. Again, I think of that day at the rock, when Mal told me their story, of how Mr. Kamel came over in the nineties when they were only slightly older than us. How he met Mrs. Kamel in med school, and they fell in love. He's talked some about it, fleeing from a crisis, arriving here with nothing more than hopes and dreams. What I like best about him is his unwavering support of his family. It's why my smile widens when he clasps his hands and looks to his son—a portrait of America.

"So, Charley, how is your music thing coming along?"

Charley's cheeks go aflame. "Dad, come on. This is embarrassing."

Dr. Kamel grins. A waiter arrives, and we order drinks. Water for me and wine for the parents. He lets his son off the hook, turning his gentle eyes on us. "And you two. How's the music? I hear there is big news?"

Mal smiles, her eyes wide and bright. "Yes. Well, as you know, our video sort of broke the internet."

I laugh. "I don't think it broke anything."

She shushes me, rolls out her silverware, and places it before her with a little smile. "Now, this podcast—Myles and me—we're kind of killing it, really." she says winking at me. "Even if my guitarist can't keep a setlist. But there's something else," she says with a grin.

"Who needs an internship when there's so much fortune and fame, huh?" Dr. Kamel says, jokingly, but Mal's face tightens. I remember what she said at the bridge, about not wanting to be like them. Still, there's something in the way her parents look at her with such pride and support that judders in my chest. A tiny, invisible sledgehammer knocks me around until I scoot my chair back, rattling the drinks on the table. "I need to, um… Excuse me."

Everyone looks up. "I'm, sorry. I just…" I point to where we came in, then make a line for the front, hoping the bathrooms are there.

In the restroom, I splash some water on my face, cursing myself for falling apart. For being here at all. The Kamels are so loving and supportive, and everything is always smiles and happiness. The way Dr. Kamel's face crinkles as he smiles at his family, how he would never hit Charley with a belt in the name of discipline or religion. I can handle the horrible things in the world better than the good. The bad things I can grit my teeth and absorb. The good things, these little beautiful moments, punch me in the gut and fold me over, leaving me gasping for air.

I'm wondering what my dad would think of me when my phone buzzes in my pocket. A message.

Noah: WTF was that VM?

THE NEXT THING I KNOW, I'm standing in front of the mirror laughing as a man enters and heads for the stall. He shoots me a funny look and then shuts and locks the stall door.

Outside the bathroom, I wipe my face and get myself together.

Me: I'll tell you at the show

Noah: K

I pocket my phone. Noah is coming. I'm having dinner with the best family in the world. Mal is my bandmate, my friend, and things could be worse—way worse. I scrape and claw and pull myself from the deep, dark pity well. I won't be a sap through dinner. Sure, Hank sucks and so does my life, but the one bright spot is sitting in the middle of the room wearing a dress that shimmers when she walks. When she turns her head and sees me coming, her face lit up with a smile. I refuse to let Hank steal the eruption of fireworks in my chest.

I refuse to let anything else matter.

19

After dinner, Mal rushes off to the bathroom to change clothes. I hang back and thank Mr. Kamel again for dinner as he refused my numerous attempts to pay for my meal. Mrs. Kamel tells me it was a pleasure. Charley gives me dap.

When they're gone, Mal reappears in a striped shirt, exposed midriff, and customary ripped jeans. It isn't until she looks down that I see she still has on her pointy little dress shoes.

She throws her hands out. "I forgot my Vans."

"I like it." The dinner with her family, the dress, the evening sun, again I have to remind myself that this is not a date.

Mal frowns at me, and I laugh as she stands before me with her eyeliner and mascara, all set for the stage but clutching a dinner dress. She's catching attention from all angles. I mean, yeah, she's gorgeous, but she's a gorgeous wreck.

I tell her about Noah as we get to the car. She turns to me, her cheeks flushed from the evening sun caught between mountain peaks. "Now for you," she says. "Please, no more Old Navy boy. I can't deal."

I glance down. "What? I sort of like it. And it goes with your shoes."

She purses her lips. "So funny, Myles."

I glance around, to the hikers taking an evening stroll, then back to Mal. "You want me to change here?"

She shrugs. "I'll turn the other way, you prude. Or you can march back to the bathroom and let them stare at *you* this time."

Mal makes a show of shifting to her window. "I'm not sure I can hold this any longer. This is big news. Huge, really. I was about to slip and say something at the table when you bolted. Are you okay?"

"I'm great. Now what is the news?" I say, unbuttoning Dr. Kamel's shirt. I ease my way out of it, one sleeve at a time, laughing at how Mal shields her eyes.

"Well, okay hurry up. I have to see your face."

I bend down to snatch my V-neck on the floorboard, and Mal lets out a gasp. I bolt upright, fiddling with the shirt, but it's too late. Mal's hand covers her mouth, her eyes already pooling with tears. "Myles."

I shake my head and quickly throw my arms through the shirt, yanking it down so hard the stitching tears. "It's fine, okay?" I hate the way she's staring at me, mascara streaming down her cheek. I sigh. "Mal? Come on. It looks worse than it feels. What's the big news?"

She wipes her face, her shock quickly turning to rage. "How are you letting him do this? What's it going to take, Myles?"

Five minutes ago, I thought this felt like a date. Now, I gaze out to the pine trees, hating myself for ruining the evening. I force myself not to give in to the wet burn in my eyes. Not to sit here and cry with her or come up with an answer for why I'm "letting" this happen.

"Myles." Her voice breaks as she shakes her head. "This isn't okay. You know that, right?"

I turn to her, her father's wrinkled shirt in my grasp. My voice is only a weak, pleading whisper. "It's just a few more months. Okay?"

She stares at me, searching my eyes for an explanation. I beg her to drive, and eventually she nods and wipes her face. It's not the way I wanted to go to the show, but right now my hands are shaking as she starts the car.

She drives maybe ten feet before she stops again. I sigh, about to beg her to let it go because I can't sit here and cry with her right now, when she squeezes her eyes shut and sniffles. She studies her hands on the steering wheel before she turns to me, her voice a raspy whisper.

"We got a spot on the Warped Tour."

"What? Is that the..." I try to process what she's telling me, but she's still leaking tears and I'm not sure why she's chosen this moment to let it go.

She nods, but her smile falls flat. "It's part of a new promotion they're doing. One stop, a side stage in Charlotte. Someone with the tour saw our videos. All of them. Apparently, we rock."

New tears stream down her cheeks. I blink away my own tears, still clutching her father's shirt in my hands. She tosses her hands in her lap, her wet eyes roaming over me. "I'm telling you this now because you need to believe this can happen. You need to see what you're capable of being so you can get the hell out of that house. If you don't, you'll never see it, Myles. Ever."

"When did you find this out?" A laugh escapes my throat. My head spins as the welts, the fear, the embarrassment, and the truth in what she's saying fight for position inside of me.

"Earlier, when I texted you." Her lips curl into a small smile. I set my hands to my face.

"Holy shit." I allow myself to smile. Mal gushes with a laugh, but her eyes tell a different story.

"Yeah, well." She eyes the clock. "This isn't how I wanted to do this, but we need to go." She sets her hand on mine. "I'm not done talking about the other thing."

I look down to our hands. It already feels like I've ruined everything. The night, the show, the news. All of it.

It's about a 30-mile ride out to The Hills, which should be plenty of time for Mal and me to turn the music up and laugh and dance and scream in celebration. Instead, it's only the wind screaming through her cracked window and her occasional sniffle, a crushing reminder that nothing will ever be like it was between us.

I knew the welts on my back were bad this time but seeing it through Mal's eyes makes it hurt worse. She sets her jaw and gazes ahead, her eyes glossy and glazed. Every time she turns to speak, I look the other way.

We take our exit off the highway. The roads widen as bright white sidewalks appear, adorned with wrought iron lampposts. A sign surrounded by wildflowers announces we're entering Richland Hills. A suburban dream, the park is full of soccer fields lined with lacrosse markings, baseball diamonds, and clean playgrounds with rounded rubber edges and dotted with precise, perfect landscaping. Near the picnic area is an outdoor pavilion, and tonight's End of Summer Bash is already in full swing. The parking lot is full of SUVs, but luckily, we're waved through. Perks of being in a band.

The pavilion is packed. Beach balls and blankets. Moms dance, bopping babies around as the dads hang near the smoke coming off the grills. If we ever consider ourselves to be hardcore, all we'd have to do is come out to the Hills to lose credibility. But at this point, a gig is a gig, and we're slated at 8:30, almost primetime. We'll take it, even if our preshow magic is all but gone.

Mal pulls up to the back and kills the engine. She turns to me, the dusky amber sun hanging over the back door on her back. She takes my hand. "I know you don't want to talk about it. But maybe later, okay?"

"Thanks." I give her my best smile. "Mal. The Warped Tour."

She smiles back at me, a little forced but it works. "I know, right?"

I open the door, get out, move the seat up, and grab my guitar. "Noah's going to lose his shit."

She stops, the smile now real and growing. "Okay but let me tell him, all right?"

We lug our guitars around a dugout to where the trucks and trailers are parked in the grass behind the pavilion. Some roadies hanging around, security guards, and volunteers with EVENT

STAFF shirts. I'm already working on a setlist for the tour when Noah calls out. "What's up, kids?"

He leans against a van parked in the shade. I shoot Mal a wary look, but she only gives me a devilish smile. "This ought to be good."

We head for the van, where the driver side and passenger side doors open, and our favorite twins hop out. My jaw drops. Mal, still smiling and ready to blurt out the news, stops cold and scoffs. "You have got to be kidding me."

Daris and Dorin, the exchange kids from Romania, gather around Noah. We've met a couple of times at the warehouse. Both tall and pasty, they have matching sheared hair and leather jackets. Noah nods at them, then us. "I believe everyone's met, right?"

I glance at Mal as we set down our things. Daris ducks over and slaps my hand. Dorin nods. They aren't actually twins, but they're close to it. I think Daris recently graduated and Dorin is in our year, or the other way around. Either way, I knew it.

Mal ignores them. "What's going on, Noah?" I can hear the defeat in her voice. Between what happened in the restaurant parking lot and whatever is happening here, it's draining all the magic out of her major announcement.

Noah kicks off the van. "Hey Mal. Looking sharp." He has that same fake smile plastered to his face, the one from his house that day I stopped over. "Nice shoes."

Mal 's jaw tightens. She cuts her eyes to me. Noah watches us closely, before clasping his hands together. "Well, here we are. There's been a slight change of plans."

Mal, glancing at the stage, where a ten-member funk band has the crowd bouncing, takes a minute before she jerks her head to him. *"What?"*

Dorin gives Mal a onceover and smiles. Noah shrugs and motions to Darin and Dorin as he whips out his drumsticks. "We're going on first. We'll do a couple of songs and then—"

"No." Mal glares at him.

Noah spins around. "You're not the only one in this band, Mal."

I sigh. This is the last thing we need right now. "Come on, Noah. What are you doing? We need to get out there."

Noah takes a step towards us. "What's the big deal? You guys are doing side gigs." He gestures to the brothers. "Why can't the guys and I go up there and do a few songs?"

He's flushed and messy, and there's a dangerous glint in his glossy eyes. I glance at Mal. Behind her, a funk band launches into a Parliament song. The crowd erupts. We need to get going because this thing is moving fast. Ten bands, twenty minutes apiece. That's the deal. We're next.

"What exactly are you proposing? We let *them* play with us?" Mal asks, saying *them* as though she's referring to mucus discharge. But Noah, with the element of surprise in his favor, shakes his head furiously.

"Nope. Better. I take my new band up there, play a couple songs. Then I leave my kit up, and we do our thing after."

"Excuse me? *New band.*" Mal rolls her eyes. "Pfft. No."

It kills me to hear him say it. But the way he's acting, arguing with him will only turn him away. Besides, my curiosity wins out. I turn to Mal. "Hang on." Then to Noah, "Does your new band have a name?"

His smirk drops as he glances at Daris and Dorin. They nod. Noah doesn't seem so sure. Mal cocks her head. "Well, spill it."

"Bromania, for now. I mean, we're—"

Mal's eyes widen as she busts out laughing. I snort, but I'm too preoccupied with the thought of Noah playing with these guys. Mal nearly tears my arm off, cracking up so hard we almost don't hear Noah say, "It's a working title. We're going to change it."

She loses it all over again, stumbles, folds over, and then gets herself upright. She shakes her head but then crashes into me again. She smacks my chest, her smile so wide she can hardly speak.

"Change it. Change it right now. To *anything*." She throws her hand out. "Name your band Bird Poo but not *Bromania!*." She collapses again, but I manage to catch her in my arms. We're convulsing when Noah turns to the brothers and gestures toward us.

"This is what I was talking about. I make them famous, and they don't take me seriously."

Mal breaks free, catching her breath and wiping the tears from her eyes, happy tears now, her voice cracking with hysterics. "Oh, Noah." She spreads her arms. "Come on. You know we love you." She dabs her left eye. "Oh man, I needed that."

The funk band does their thing, and over the next ten minutes we relent, because, whatever. We hash out a deal. Bromania, or Bird Poo, can do two songs and then Dewey and Stewie, as Mal calls them, can get off the stage so The Wide Awakes can whip through three or four of our own songs.

"Okay, but no love songs."

Mal 's eyes widen. "No one said anything about love songs."

Noah points a drumstick at me. "Yeah okay, Hall and Oates."

Mal clears her throat but only manages to glare at him. Then she turns to me. "Myles, did you bring a guitar to that party? Did you offer to play music for beer?"

I can't answer. It's like I'm living out my worst fear—the band breaking up—right now, minutes before we're supposed to go on.

Noah's mouth twists slowly, and I'm thinking he might come to his senses. Instead, he shakes his head and mumbles, "This is bullshit."

He stomps off. I look at Mal then rush to catch up to Noah. "Hey, man. Hey." I set a hand on Noah's shoulder, and he spins around.

"What?"

"What the hell is wrong with you?"

"With me?" He gets right in my face. "What's wrong with *me*?"

"Yeah," I say, stepping back, losing my nerve. Noah's a force, and he's got all the answers and reasons, and I can't think fast enough to keep up with him.

"Oh, I don't know. I basically started this band, did all the work, promotion, booking, socials, *everything*. And you and Mal land ass backwards into a video that gets over a hundred and fifty thousand views. Then you go on a major podcast as The Wide Awakes. Hmm, so where does this leave me?"

"First, you and I *both* started this band."

"That's right. We did, and now we have our shooting star for a singer." He laughs, bitterly. "She's going to rip you apart, dude. I wish you'd listen to me."

The crowd applauds as the funk band comes off the stage. The emcee takes the mic and plugs sponsors. I look down, away from his eyes.

"Can't we work this out later? The three of us?"

"Sure, but I'm still going to do my thing first."

There's no time. We need to get out there. "Do you at least know the setlist?"

He nods. *"My Reputation, Breaking You, Can't Keep Myself.* Then you'll pull some corny shit out of your butt. Blah de dah dah dah. Sound about right?"

"When did you become such an asshole?"

He leans close. A sting of his bourbon breath hits me in the eyes. "When you chose Mal over me. That's when."

"Noah." I call after him. But he throws his sticks in the air as he storms off.

Mal comes up beside me, our shoulders touching. "What's his deal?"

I look at her, then back to Noah, as I attempt to make sense of whatever is happening. For two years the band is all I had to keep me going. Practice, shows, our hopes and dreams. Now it's all coming undone. No matter what I do, someone's always walking away from me.

20

Bromania is terrible.

The emcee mistakenly introduces them as The Wide Awakes, and from the start it's a massacre. The brothers duel it out on guitar. There is no rhythm or bass, and Noah, who has assumed lead vocals from his kit, is left free to bash away and scream. Unpleasant is putting it nicely.

The funk band, fresh off stage, gawks the way bystanders might watch a train derail in slow motion. Moms cover babies' ears. Everyone in the park takes a collective ten steps back. Then twenty more.

Mal grabs my arms and digs in. It was all funny before: the band name, Noah's little tantrum, the silliness of it all. Now it's just bad. Mal bites her lip, her brow wrinkled. Fear is in the air. We're both left wondering what's going on.

They thrash away, eventually grinding down to an unceremonious halt. When it ends, the amps screeching with feedback, there's some scattered applause—more because they've finished than because of what they've accomplished. Daris and Dorin actually bow, their matching leather collars flopping over their sweaty necks.

Mal frees me from her clutches as the emcee comes out to survey the stage for damage.

"Well, okay, that was, that was something. Give it up for..." The emcee, with his tucked in Polo and Sperries without socks, turns to Noah, who's still on his stool. The guy says something to Noah, and he nods. The emcee smiles awkwardly. "Give it up for Bird... Poo."

Noah won't look at Mal or me as we take the stage to set up. Sitting on his stool, Noah's splotchy cheeks and defiant eyes settle over the crowd, and he seems pleased with himself. Now we get to go on.

It's all a mess. Mal keeps glancing at me, a continuation of what's she's done since the parking lot at the restaurant, and I suspect Noah is confusing Mal's pity for something it's not. Not only that, but he's still buzzing, although maybe it's worn off after his warm-up set. I'm only hoping we can get through this without an onstage brawl.

The audience, at least those who remain near the stage, look on, whispering and frowning, arms crossed and heads shaking until Mal flips the switch and turns on the charm. She has a way of drawing a crowd, bringing them in, and it's working. Besides, there's some big Jimmy Buffet-type guy headlining the show, and people want to stick around for that. There's nothing glamorous about this gig, but it's what we do. We power through it because we love the music.

The emcee guy looks us over and says, "There was a bit of confusion on our end. Anyway, if you've been on TikTok lately, maybe you've seen these two. Ladies and gentlemen, The Wide Awakes!"

We dive into *Bad Reputation*. It's fast and loud and Mal carries us away. She bops, hair bouncing as her voice breaks in all the right places. I play fast and it feels good with Noah behind me bashing away.

Mal's energy could power the streetlights. She bops her head and calls out to no one in particular before she flails her arms, and somehow, it's all in rhythm and perfect. Moms set their kids down and make their way back toward the stage. The middle school girls scream and want to be her. The boys are staring. For a few minutes, onstage, the three of us are one again.

Mal skips across stage, her bass swinging as Noah finds the beat. *Bad Reputation* hardly ends as we blast into *Breaking You* by Party Trash. I fall into the rhythm, and it's easy to leave all that stuff Noah said behind. To forget about my back and Mal's face when she saw it. We just play.

I forget about the crowd, leave behind the comments, worry and pain and instead float to the small, dingy kitchen, where my dad plays and sings without worry. My mom exhales a cloud of smoke towards the yellowish peeling plaster on the ceiling. They're happy in that flash of memory as I spin around and around between them.

My eyes open. Mal, her hair in her face, glances at me with a question in her eyes: *Are you okay?* I nod and smile, and she winks. Warmth floods my chest. One last lick on the guitar rings out as Noah bashes away to the end of the song where we're met with a chorus of applause.

I smile. Because it is enough for me. The sweat covers the goosebumps on my arms. It's what I love about music, how the emotions can take over your body until it's too confused to think. How I'm both hot and cold and completely in love, but still sad that it has to end. It's so good I want to cry with the laughter.

When we come to a stop, the emcee starts up the steps, and we realize our set is over much too soon, thanks to Bromania. I'm still glad we managed to salvage what was left of the crowd after Daris and Dorin did their dueling chainsaw routine. As the emcee makes his way back to the stage, someone in the front row calls out, "Sing *Kiss on My List!*"

Mal turns to me, both hands on the mic stand. She drops her head, then shrugs with a smile. I shrug back, and Noah's cussing about it, knocking on his kick drum to prove his displeasure.

I'm not sure where this is going until Mal looks them over with a bratty smile, then turns to me and does the boxer fist motion the way she did at the bridge that day. I start cracking up. We make a decision together without saying a word.

With a smile I crank up the distortion. Mal nods gleefully as I scratch out the chords fast and messy until it's more of ska version of this cheesy song that has come to rule our lives. Mal's eyes light up, and it isn't long before Noah realizes what is happening and goes ape on the drums.

Mal heats up the bassline. The emcee staggers backward like he's been stung by a bee as Mal tilts her head at him and sticks out her tongue. She lets go with a scream, and we bang out "Your Kiss, My Fist."

It's all blurs together. The emcee turns around wildly, like he wants someone to pull the plug on our set, but it's too late. The soccer moms and dads are all wide eyed and fascinated, and it's hard to tell if it's because Mal is so charismatic despite herself, or if anything sounds terrific after Bird Poo.

Mal hops about the stage, skip stomping and not so much singing but screaming out the lyrics, cutting verses and rehashing it until it's no longer a cover but our own thing. I don't fight it a bit this time. I sing back-up, and for a minute, it's like old times again. It's not me and Mal against Noah. It's simply the three of us rocking out to music we love.

For about two minutes, everything is great. Mal shoves the song into these people's faces right up until we're chanting, "Your *kiss, my fist, your kiss, my fist,*" and the crowd realizes the joke was on them all along.

We crash to a halt, and the emcee trots up to the stage in a hurry. He's at once both uptight and casual, and judging by look on his face, he wants to kill us. He snatches the mic and shoots us a quick stare down as Mal relinquishes her place. "All right, all right. The Wide Awakes. That was, well… that was something."

Later, as the Jimmy Buffett cover guys take the stage to set up, we catch our breath at the van. Mal leans against the van with a post-show smile. Daris recorded our set, and they're playing it back on his phone. We're cracking up about *Your Kiss, My Fist,* which Mal says she never actually planned on playing until I started with the chords.

Noah seems to be sobering up, not being such a jerk anymore. He has almost returned to his old self as he laughs about how we actually did the song and how the emcee dude freaked onstage.

It lasts for maybe five minutes. Then Mal, figuring it's finally the right time, pushes off the van and sort of dances over to us. I'm watching Noah closely because I don't want to miss his face when she spills the news. "So, Noah."

I force myself not to cheese. Mal catches my eye and winks before she turns back to Noah, biting down on a smile. "I got another call today."

Somewhere between *I* and *call*, Noah's face twists. Just like that, everything goes off the rails. Noah starts clapping. "Oh yay. Let me guess, *Malorie* got an agent."

Mal's big, playful smile deflates. "What? No. I—"

Noah wipes his nose. "Hey, I wanted to ask about *Breaking You*. Kind of a fitting choice, huh?"

Our little balloon of comradery sets off into the sky and out of sight. Mal's eyes narrow. Her smile goes tight.

"What are you talking about, Noah?"

Noah sets his hands behind his head, revealing two matching pit stains. He smiles broadly. "Oh, I don't know, the lyrics, for one. *Boys are easy to break?*" He brings his hands together with another clap. "Sort of transparent. I mean, this is all working out for you."

She throws a death glare at him for a full five seconds. Daris and Dorin cut the snickering. Noah glances at them, chuckles, then smirks at Mal again. "I mean, right?"

Mal studies him before she turns her attention to the brothers. "Do either of you have a cigarette?"

I'm about to say something, but it's not the time. Daris, I think, pulls out a pack of Marlboro Reds and hands it to her. Noah looks around, still with that dickhead smile, as Daris flicks his lighter. Mal lights the smoke, stifles a cough, then gestures with the cigarette like an old timey movie star. "Noah, I've liked Party Trash since I was like twelve years old."

He starts to argue the point, but Mal steps forward. "We've done that song twenty or thirty times. But now," she blows smoke in his face, turns around to her audience, her voice gaining traction as Noah backs away, coughing. "Now Noah has a problem with the setlist."

Noah cuts his eyes my way, like I'm to blame for Mal's attitude, her smoking, her putting him on blast in front of two snickering Romanians. But damn, he did that to himself. I'm about to blurt out the news myself just to fix things when he shakes it off and goes on the attack.

"You're full of shit. You're in this for you and you're using this video—and Myles—to get there."

Mal closes the space between them, aiming the cigarette at his face. "You recorded the video, Noah! Not me or Myles or anyone else. Just. You. Why is this so hard for you to understand?"

The yelling rakes my spine. Noah rolls his eyes. I bow my head, tired of watching everything I love collapse and fold and destroy itself as Mal's voice breaks completely apart.

"You know what, Noah? Fuck you." Her fingers tremble as she sucks on the cigarette, tears spilling from her eyes down her cheeks. I'm about to step in when she plucks the cigarette at him. It hits him in the chest with a spark and he jumps back.

"What the hell?"

She stares him down. "I'm so sick of you." She spins on her heels, but she's not through with him. Her face, everything she's been holding in today, comes apart with her voice. "Oh, and guess what? The call I got? It was the Warped Tour, you selfish asshole."

Noah's head springs up, his voice suddenly clear and sober. "What are you talking about, Mal?"

She squints though the tears, her chin quivering. She nods twice, like she's trying to smile but her lips forgot how. "Yeah. They want us for a stop on the tour. *All* of us."

Noah's mouth hangs open. "What?"

"Surprise," she whispers, raising her shoulders only to let them drop. She closes her eyes, looks at me, and shrugs again. "I can't, Myles. I'm done."

Mal drops her head and turns away, slinking off toward the trailers in the back. Noah stands there, wide-eyed and gaping, wiping at his chest. Daris and Dorin straighten, staring at each other.

It sucks that she was crying both times she delivered the news that she couldn't wait to share with us. Now it's gone, all of it, her giddiness, the surprise, our chance to do what we've only dreamed about. It's all undone. And the one who usually puts us back together is walking off, done with us all.

I stand there, still holding my breath. Noah almost looks like he wants to cry. "Shit man. I didn't know."

I look back at Mal as she storms off, grabbing at her waist, hugging herself. I'm about to go running after her when I catch an almost imperceptible shake of her head.

Instead, I leave her alone with her thoughts.

I'm sitting on some railroad ties near the concession stand when Mal returns. She plops down beside me, crosses her legs, and gazes out towards the show. I resist the urge to put my arm around her.

"Hey. You okay?"

She shrugs. "I could ask you that."

Her eyes are puffy, too much crying for one day. But I let it pass. Some strollers roll past us, kids with face paint and balloons. I sit back as echoes of *Margaritaville* fill the park. "Well, this is rock bottom, I suppose."

She doesn't respond, only stares off at nothing.

"What just happened?" I ask her, as she leans her shoulder into mine. I lower my head to find her eyes. "I mean, I'm still sort of stunned. About a lot of things, but especially the Warped Tour. Is this a dream?"

Mal laughs despite herself. She sniffles, turns to me, and wipes her hair from her face. Her shiny eyes reflect the glow of the waning sun. "Well, I got a call this morning and it *was* a dream come true. Now I'm here."

"We're going to have to figure this out," I say, meaning so many things, but starting with the band.

She sighs. "I'm just so sick of him acting like this."

"Me too."

We sit for a minute, listening to the music, until Mal pops up again. "You know, the community market might have been bad, but this," she motions to the stage where four guys in Hawaiian shirts strum along. "I mean, this is bad."

"Bromania bad?"

She nods, buries her head into my chest, then looks up to face me head on. "Bird Poo bad."

"Mmm, that's bad," I say without much thought, falling into the moment as Mal shifts closer.

"Myles."

"Mal."

I set my arm around her, trying to think of something to make this better when she looks up to me. "You don't believe that, do you? What Noah was saying?"

Before I can answer, there's a crunch of gravel behind us. Noah plops down on my other side and gazes out to the stage. He sighs. "This song sucks so bad."

Mal's body goes tense before she breaks off from me. She sits back, staring straight ahead again, and crosses her legs. "You know what else sucks?"

Noah drops his head. "Me. I suck." He gazes past me. "Mal, what can I say? I'm sorry."

She sniffles, throws her hair back. "You should be."

Noah leans over me. "Okay, and you have every right to be pissed right now, but y'all need to look at this from where I am. You hook up in my basement, go off on your own, and now I'm always finding the two of you stuck to each other." He looks at me, as though I'm the translator. "I mean Myles, I get it, okay? Mal's hot or whatever, but come on. If I'm sticking it out with the two of you, it can't be like this. We're a team, right?"

Mal finally blinks. Her eyes gloss over me. I think she's going to be upset I told Noah about the kiss, but she only nods at him. "Gee, Noah, thanks for talking about me like I'm not here." She turns to me. "He thinks I'm hot," she shrugs. *"Or whatever."*

I raise my eyebrows. Mal gets back to glaring at Noah. "What are you even saying right now?"

Noah shrugs. "I'm saying that I'm just as much a part of this band as the two of you are."

He starts up about the video all over again, and while there's so much I need to talk to Mal about, right now we have to fix this. The three of us.

Mal leaps to her feet. She wipes her eyes. "No one is saying you're not. This is the biggest thing that's ever happened to us, and we should be celebrating. But no, we're doing this," she says, throwing her arms out.

"Well maybe if you had led with the news…" Noah says as he and I stand. I'm stuck between them all over again.

"Look, Mal's right. We should be celebrating." I turn to Noah. "We're *all* in this band. No one's quitting. And we're doing the tour, right?"

I take a step back so it's more like a triangle instead of me being some sort of buffer. As we face each other, breathing and fuming and lost in our own arguments, I'm thinking, *this is it,* when Noah smiles at Mal. "Hell yeah, we're doing the tour. Right, Mal?"

Mal nods, rolling her eyes to fight off a smile. "Sorry I threw a cigarette at you."

Noah looks down at his shirt then smiles. "It's cool. I've been hit with worse." He gestures to the stage, where the lead singer mangles a Jamaican accent. "That drummer is falling asleep at the wheel. This is depressing."

Mal nods. "I need to go somewhere. I don't want to go home. Charley will make me listen to a new beat."

Noah shakes his head at the stage again, the packed crowd eating it up. He smiles at us. "We could hit the basement. My mom went shopping, so there's all kinds of grub."

I smile at Mal and she blinks. "Sounds good."

Noah gets to his feet and dusts himself off. "Okay, Mal. Tell me about the Warped Tour."

21

MAL AND I TAKE A DRIVE OUT TO THE PARKWAY ON Sunday. We work on a few songs and arrangements, and she spends a lot of time not taking calls, not answering text messages, and badgering me to make a "plan of action" to get out of the house.

It's around six that evening when we pull into the Kamels' driveway. She kills the engine and gives it one last go. "You don't even know how much you need this, Myles. You deserve so much better."

It's the last thing I want to think about right now, especially with the tour happening. I take a deep breath and wipe the back of my neck. I'm covered in sweat all over again. "I really don't know, Mal."

She stares at me for a while, the fight swimming in her eyes before she lets it go. We talk more about songs. Since the video, and now the tour, everything is more urgent. Mal is more motivated than usual, and I'm having a tough time keeping up.

The focus is to put together an official EP. *Can't Keep Myself* will be the title track, along with four other originals and a couple cover songs.

"We need to run this track list by Noah," I say.

"I know. We will, but you know he'll find something he doesn't

145

like about it." She frowns. "I feel like it's missing something, though. Maybe one more song."

While the Warped Tour kept us together, and our little huddle helped, Noah still doesn't exactly seem eager to hang with us.

Mal invites me inside for dinner with a slap on my leg. "Well, the only thing that will make you feel better is an Egyptian woman's Italian cooking. Come on, let's eat."

The Kamels' place takes on a totally different vibe when Dr. Kamel is around. He's not strict, but there's a certain order to the house. Charley isn't dancing around with his iPad. Mrs. Kamel floats around with a grin stuck to her face. The house always smells like food.

Dr. Kamel is setting the dinner table as we walk in. "Well, hello, Myles. Good to see you again."

I nod. The air conditioning feels good after a day in the heat. "Yes sir, it is. Anything I can do to help?"

Mal snorts. I catch her smirking at me as I look around for something to do. Dr. Kamel smiles. "No sir. You are a guest in my house."

We settle in the den. Mal keeps sneaking looks my way, and again I find myself in this unchartered territory. We can't be together, but it feels like we're more than friends. The day has been filled with these little sideways glances and quick touches, quiet pauses in conversation before she laughs it off.

At the same time, it feels good to be at her house with her family. It's more like last year, when I knew I had no chance with Mal. Before the kiss in Noah's basement. It's the kiss on my mind when she asks what I'm thinking about.

"Avocados," I say with a shrug.

Mal laughs and I sigh, turning to her and facing her head on. She's half smiling, and for the millionth time, I want to ask her if it meant anything at all. As she stares back at me with wide, intense eyes, it almost feels like she might tell me, until Charley sticks his head in the room.

"Dinner, nerds."

He lingers in the doorway, smirking at us before Mal shoos him off. Then she turns back to me and shakes her head with a smile. "Well, let's go hang with the fam."

We take our seats at the handcrafted wooden table, surrounded by family pictures. Mrs. Kamel smiles, happy to have her family together. Charley is smiling too, but it's more of a smirk. I'm wondering what he might say as Mal digs through her salad, gobbling up all the cherry tomatoes because she can't help herself.

Dr. Kamel clasps his hands together. "Tell me about this tour, Malorie. How warped is it?"

Mal rolls her eyes at Dr. Kamel's dad joke. "Sure. So we get to play the Charlotte stop the night The Finnegens are headlining."

I turn to Mal. "The Finnegens? You didn't tell me that."

Her smile reaches her eyes. "Just found out."

"Noah's going to freak."

"Oh, freak he has. He's the one who told me."

Dr. Kamel goes for the bread. "Do you have a chaperone?"

Mal takes her fork. "Working on it."

"And this is because of the video? The one that broke things?"

Mal laughs. She moves her salad around with her fork. "Yeah, I guess you could say that started it all."

"I'll say," Mrs. Kamel smiles at her husband. Something's up.

Mal sets down her fork. "What does that mean?"

Dr. Kamel serves up the steaming squares of lasagna. "I got a call from a program director at WGBT today."

"Are you going to be on the news, Dad?" Mal asks.

He shakes his head. "They called for you."

Mal and I look up in unison. Mal laughs. "What?"

"Yes, they want to talk to you two." Dr Kamel passes the dish. "I watched the video, and I can see why," he says, setting his napkin on his lap.

Charley snickers. "Did you read the comments?"

I did. All I'm thinking about are the ones I read last night.

Dude sucks

What is he doing?

But I can tell Charley means the ones about us. My face flashes hot. Mal's blushing too. "Some things are better not seen."

Dr. Kamel smiles at Mrs. Kamel. "I should know what my only daughter is doing out there, no? Besides, I think it's cute, the two of you. You do really well together. Playing together, I mean."

More giggling from Charley. Mal sends a warning glare across the table. Mrs. Kamel chides her husband playfully. "Jahi. You're embarrassing them."

He nods. "Well, it's awfully fun, dear."

The lasagna comes my way. I scoop some out and keep my head down. Mal pops a tomato into her mouth. "What does WGBT want to talk to us about?"

"It sounds like they want to do a story on you two."

Charley pipes up. "While we're on the topic of viral videos, why hasn't the video I recorded taken off?"

Mal shrugs. "Who knows why anything happens, *Charles*."

"Lots of comments, though. About how..."

Mal casts daggers his way. Charley giggles into his napkin. "What? Dad already read them." His voice goes high. "*Oh, they are totally hooking up. This is the cutest. He's so in love!!! I think he wants—*"

Mal reaches over and smacks his arm. "Shut. Up!"

Mrs. Kamel sets down the lasagna dish. "Children, please. We have company."

I keep my head down, unable to face anyone. Dr. Kamel changes the subject and starts talking work and his next project while Charley sulks and Mal picks at her dinner.

"Well," declares Mr. Kamel. "I think we've succeeded in making our guest highly uncomfortable. Now, let's talk politics, shall we?"

Later, we're in the den, clicking around for a movie on Netflix when Mal 's phone starts buzzing. She types something, then sets it down and looks at me. "Dinner was fun, wasn't it?"

I laugh. "Yeah. About this thing on the news?"

Mal smiles and rolls her eyes. "You know it's going to be one of those, 'local students find internet stardom' pieces."

"We need to let Noah in on that."

Mal cocks her brow. "Hmm, nice. Distract him with the news thingy and then we sneak off and do the podcast."

"We're terrible people."

Another buzz. "But we're certainly popular." She checks it, and then turns to me, smiling and shaking her head. "Myles."

"Mal."

"Noah's going to have to get over it. Besides, he's so stoked about the Finnegens, I doubt he'll care."

We settle in for a movie, but Mal's phone continues to buzz through most of it, until near the end when she finally turns it off and stuffs it under the cushion for good measure. At some point, we fall asleep against each other. The credits are rolling when she wipes her eyes and stretches.

"Do you want to crash in the basement?"

I look toward the doorway, wondering if Mr. Kamel saw us sleeping on the couch. Then again, *it's just Myles.*

"Is it okay with your parents?"

She assures me it is, and I follow her down the steps. The Kamels' basement is plush with thick carpet, crown molding, framed pictures, and all sorts of keepsakes from Egypt within the built-in shelves. It's like a museum compared to my house.

Mal's eyes are heavy as she leads me to the sunken den and gestures toward the bathroom. "Well, here you go," she says, and starts for the stairs.

"Thanks again."

"You're welcome." She smiles, her eyes never leaving mine. Two seconds, three, four. I take a breath and she blinks. "Okay, so... yeah."

She starts up the steps, stops and turns with a sleepy smile on her face, one hand on the rail. "Goodnight."

I smile back and hook a thumb to the backdoor. "Should I leave out the back in the morning?"

She laughs. "You are to disappear at midnight."

"Wait, really?"

Mal laughs again. "You'll be fine."

She lingers for a minute, her hand on the railing, a tangle of hair in her eyes. She opens her mouth, and I hold my breath for whatever is coming. She closes her mouth, nods, then starts upstairs.

When the door shuts, I'm left standing at the bottom of the steps with a smile I can't get off my face. This was probably just another day for Mal, but after the parkway, the songs, dinner and the movie on the couch, it might have been one of the best days of my life.

I OPEN my eyes to the blinking clock, which shows 5:09 A.M. I roll over in the bed, lost in the windowless dark.

After finding my clothes, I get dressed quietly and quickly and let myself out the back where the slightest glimpse of dawn touches the horizon.

This early in the day, nothing seems real. It's a wet, dewy dreamland as the soft, fuzzy morning highlights the huge houses with arching windows and large, wrap-around decks. I'm not so worried about being seen, not at this hour, but I hurry along anyway, with my bedhead and wrinkled clothes, trudging up the lush rich lawn in dreamlike stagger. I'm still stunned as I cut over to the golf course fairway, hoping the sprinklers don't catch me.

I walk for miles in the cool gray dawn, relishing last night, eating dinner with the Kamels, falling asleep on the couch with Mal. By the time I get to the part of town that actually has convenience stores, I walk into one woozy and smiling, grab a coffee and some packaged donuts, then keep huffing it to my house, where the sky rewards me with a smooth pastel of pink and orange. For the first time in a long time, I am filled with hope.

2 2

I find my phone in my room. No harassment calls from Hank. A few texts from Noah about the gig at the warehouse. Luck is on my side. Hank's at work. An hour later Mr. Irving arrives to pick me up for work. I grab a piece of toast off the plate in the kitchen, and I'm still hanging onto how great yesterday was when Nan calls after me.

"Hank isn't pleased about you staying out all night."

My feet slide to a stop. "Well, what *does* please Hank?"

Nan sighs. As usual, I'm torn between wanting to make amends with her and hating her guts because she refuses to stand up to Hank. Then again, I fight the same battle with myself. I haven't exactly stood up to Hank, either.

I think she's going to drop it when she slides a chair under the dining table. "He's only trying to teach—"

Nope, not doing this. "Want to have another look at my back, Nan? See what it's taught me? It's taught me not to bend over or stretch too far too quickly after the welts break. It's taught me how to come up with excuses abOut what happened to my eye. You know how many doors I've walked into?"

She hangs onto the chair, mouth tight as Mr. Irvin pulls in. I give

151

her a second to respond, but she only turns away and gets back to straightening. So be it. It's sunny, and whatever powers the old house has over me don't stand a chance today. I'm not letting Hank's shadow ruin another day.

I hop in the truck, and Mr. Irvin backs out. "Where to, my young lad?"

I spot Nan, standing in the window, turning away when Mr. Irvin waves. Her wrinkled face is a sad reminder of what happens when you live with regret. Not me, not today. I pry my gaze from the window and look to my driver, whose own sad eyes are at ends with his hopeful smile. I want to make a joke and play along, but sometimes it's too hard. I throw my hands up. "Anywhere but here."

The smile falters. He nods, sets the truck in gear, and gives me a nod. "Okay. Sounds like a plan."

We head out to Town Heights to dig out the walkway for the awareness garden. It's like medicine, getting out and throwing myself into the work on a hot summer day. My hands are dried out, my shirt is drenched, and Mr. Irvin even brings me over as he mixes the mortar to show me how each brick will lend itself to the cause. The walkway has to wind around the bushes and grasses, and I'm humming to myself as I carry two bags of sand over to Mr. Irvin. He turns to me, squinting in the sun.

"How was your weekend?"

"Hmm?" Thinking of yesterday, I drop the bags and smile. "My weekend was pretty damn good."

"This have anything to do with the lead singer?"

"What?" I can't help my laugh. I know Mal doesn't want to risk it, but there's a closeness between us. I see it in her eyes and feel it on her skin. I shoot the old man a look. "Mr. Irvin, I have no idea what you're talking about."

"Malorie, right? You guys are Tick Tocking or something, you said?"

I'm dying. "Oh, right." I clap my hands together, my nails full of sand and mortar, just the way I like them. "Yes, we are definitely

Tick Tocking." I think back to Mal crying on Friday. With me in the car, with Noah after the show. "I think."

He draws the trowel across the bricks he's laid. "Well, I suppose that's good."

I smile, turning to get another load of sand. The Warped Tour. It doesn't get better than that. "It is. It's really good."

We talk about the band some. How we're putting together some songs while we've got some buzz. I tell him about the EP, the local news. How we're opening for the Finnegens. I'm a blubbering fool.

But my great mood takes a hit as the day goes on and I hear nothing from Mal. At least Noah seems more like himself again as we text back and forth about the details of the next warehouse skater show and, of course, the Warped Tour. I'm still not sure how we're going to break it to him about our return to Ripcast, but I'm hoping the local news thing will soften the blow. I tell him I'll stop by later.

I get home at five, mow the lawn, and trim without being asked so Hank doesn't start something. The whole time I'm still dreaming about the tour, about the news, about Mal. I take a shower, and I'm all set to head to Noah's to talk about the new gig when I hear the click of the recliner spring, and all that hopeful thinking goes to waste.

"In here, Myles."

I come down the hallway and find Hank taking his place at the table. Nan hovers like a picture of obedience. Hank motions to my place at the table. "Come sit with us."

I nod to the door. "I've got plans."

He's already shaking his head. "Plans can wait."

Best to get it over with. I slink into the kitchen, my hair still wet and dripping on my shirt. Nan has put together some sort of hearty casserole that promises to keep the house smelling like meat for days. I sit, and Hank takes his place. Nan quietly finds her seat, and we're all set for misery.

"Get yourself a plate," he commands.

It's a little unsettling how focused he is this evening. He isn't glazed over and tired like he usually is after work. There's a sharp gleam in his eyes, like he's looking to settle a score.

I take my plate, the faded one with the basket weave around the edges, notched and scratched from all the knives and forks over the years. I scoop up a small square of meat, like meatloaf but with beans, some sort of breading on the top. Minutes ago, my stomach was growling, but now, with whatever Hank has planned, eating seems like a very strange concept.

Hank gulps down half of his Diet Dr. Pepper, stifles a burp, looks at Nan and then to me. "I'm not going to get on your case about last night. Even though if you ever stay out all night again, you best just stay gone. You hear?"

Gladly, I think to myself as he works his jaw, breathing through his nose, waiting on my answer. I squeeze my eyes to straighten my focus, to force myself to meet his gaze. "Yeah."

"Yeah?" He turns his head to Nan, "You hear this kid?"

Nan grimaces at her plate, her many wrinkles forming roadways to her wispy gray hair. Not for the first time, I wonder if it felt like this for my dad, too. Like the house was closing in, squeezing the life out of him.

All my boldness from this morning—walking out of the Kamels' house, starting the walkway with Mr. Irvin—is a distant memory. Sunday's rush of happiness sinks into the crevices. It's just another thing Hank can rip away from my clutches anytime he wants.

He shifts in his seat, the battered wooden furniture Nan has scrubbed to the bone. The chair whines like it's going to break, but it manages to hold. "I spoke with Jeff on my way out of work. Says were going to be doing some hiring. Entry-level stuff, second shift. I told him you'd be interested."

I choke on my first bite. Coughing, it takes me a minute to get it down. I slide my chair back and stand. I need water. I need to move because my heart is flopping against my chest. I refill my cup and wash it down past the block in my throat. Hank waits patiently as I get settled, wipe my face with my napkin, and fumble over my thoughts. It's probably best to start with the obvious.

"School starts in two weeks, Hank."

"I know it does. This is a special opportunity, a foot in the door. The pay's decent, too. You could come in at five, when the first shifters are leaving. Four days a week, weekends off. Pretty cushy if you ask me."

I turn to Nan, my eyes pleading for her to say something because I'm coming undone. While I'd expected Hank to say something about me staying out, maybe another smack on the head, some yelling and shouting, I never once imagined Hank would come home and offer me a job.

He scoops out another serving of drippy casserole. I manage a breath and fight to stay calm. "I like working with Mr. Irvin."

Hanks makes a *pfft* sound, like something a kindergartener would do at the playground. He shakes his head, looking to Nan as he plops the huge glop of meat down on his plate and gets to work with his knife and fork. "I know you like piddling around with that fairy, but this is something that could help you down the road. They don't take anyone off the street, you hear me?"

Fairy? My chest tightens, fear turning to anger even as I know he's only trying to get a rise out of me. One fight at a time. Again, I try to finesse my way out of the certain hell he's proposing. "Well, thanks, but I like being outside. We just got a big contract, too. If we finish this up in time, there will be more things coming. And..."

The clownish smile on his face stops me cold. It's like he's amused by my ambition. More head shaking, more fork pointing. "Okay, a couple things here, Myles. I don't know what that man is feeding you, but you need to think bigger than farting around doing odd jobs. Two, that girl of yours comes from money. Her parents let her dance and sing because they can. They let her talk back because they think it's cute. Let her think she's important." He shoots another glance at Nan, who might as well have left the room. "I hate to be the one to break it to you, but the music thing ain't going to pay the bills, okay? I'm offering you a real-world solution."

I'm still holding my breath. He's managed to dismiss everything

I love in between bites of dinner. I start to get up. "Look Hank, I'm sorry. I can't."

"Sit down." Hank's voice booms through the kitchen.

Nan lets out a shaky groan as Hank sets his fork down. His way of telling me know he's serious. I fall back into my seat, shaking with anger and fear and confusion. Why does it have to come to this? I pinch my nose between the eyes and will away the tears.

Hank takes a few more deep breaths. "You going to work for that old man all your life? Don't tell me he's filling your head with all this music stuff, too. He of all people should know better."

"What does that mean?"

"Means he'd rather play piano than fight for his country."

"He *did* fight for his country!" My voice breaks.

"Then came home and whined about it."

I bury my head in my hands, only wanting it to end. "Why do you have to blame Mal, or Mr. Irvin?" I force myself to look up. "It's what I want. I don't want to work at Southern."

He slams his fork down. "You think you're better than me?"

I can't. I throw my head back, look down to Nan. "Jesus Christ. Do I really need to sit here for this?"

Hank fumbles his napkin as he leaps out of his chair. The floor bangs with his steps as he leans in and lays a meaty finger in my face. "Boy, you will not take the Lord's name in vain in my house. You've got a lot to learn about respect. You hear me?"

I turn to Nan, even as I already know she'll never do more than say, *Hank*, in that way of hers. Tonight, I don't even get that. She sits silently at the table, her mouth a tight, straight line as Hank decides how he'll punish me this time.

There's nothing left to do but get it done with. "I'll think about it."

He stands over me, panting through his nose, anger rolling off his skin like heat on asphalt. His eyes have that violent glint to them, the shine they get when he reaches for his belt. "This is an opportunity. I'm trying to help you along."

"Well thanks, but again, like I said…"

White sparks explode on the left side of my face. My head snaps back like it's come unhinged from my neck. A bolt of pain flushes down my cheek. Nan gasps, and it takes me a second to cover myself, to whimper and scoot back and realize it wasn't a slap this time but an actual punch.

My ear rings. My eye feels hot and wobbly. I push it away, fighting off the alarms as I steel myself to hold it and look directly at my attacker. But I can't last. My blurry gaze skips across the table to the crooked pictures of flowerpots and farm scenes that take up the wall.

Hank turns for the window in the living room and gazes out as though he's talking to God himself. "You think I wanted to do that?"

I keep myself from slouching, from wiping the tears leaking out of my eye, blurring everything around me. *Yes, Hank. I do.*

He returns to the table, rubbing his knuckles. Before he can look away, I catch something new in his eyes. Surprise. Shame. Regret. It's hard to tell, but as my eye pools with tears and a throbbing puffiness grows on my cheek, Hank only looms over me as though he's waiting for an apology.

The side of my face feels like it's been hit by a hot iron. I don't dare touch it. I don't move. Hank makes a fist and I brace myself, still as a statue. But something tells me he's not going to hit me again tonight. And he doesn't. He only stands over me, catching his breath, until finally, he shakes his head and gets back to his dinner because it's getting cold.

He picks up his fork and gets to work on his plate. "Respect, Myles. You have got to learn to show some respect."

I turn to Nan, let her see the swollen lump over my eye. "May I be excused?"

She glances at Hank, her chin quivering as I pick up my dinner. At the sink, I rinse and wash my plate, then open the freezer. I find the ice pack and take a glance to the table where Hank chews, his heavy breaths straining to get through his nose.

"Grass is cut," I announce, then I walk out the door.

23

I REMEMBER ONCE MY DAD TOOK ME TO THE PARK. I WAS maybe four, and it was crowded, with kids yelling and screaming on the swings and climbing the slides. There was this little castle thing where I loved to hide. I'd crawl inside and just sit by myself. This time, when I popped up and looked over to where he'd been smoking and talking with some people, he was gone.

He wasn't anywhere. I climbed out of the castle and walked in circles, calling, "Dad? Dad?" until some of the other parents started asking me if I was okay. I ran back to the castle where after an hour or a few minutes, who really knows, I crept back out to daylight. My dad still wasn't around, but this nice lady brought me over to the bench next to her pouty little girl. The lady fed me snacks, asked what my name was and my favorite color. I stayed with her for a while.

The way she spoke to that little girl—and to me—I'd never heard someone so nice and caring. After a while, I was sort of hoping my dad wouldn't come back. Of course, I wanted him to return eventually, but my little kid brain was confused. This lady smelled like fresh laundry and had a bag full of snacks. Her shiny hair was pulled into a tight ponytail, and her clear eyes were wide with concern. I thought staying with her wouldn't be so bad.

We'd moved on from the favorite color and numbers game, and she was asking if I lived nearby when Dad finally came strutting over to the playground as though he'd been gone only few minutes, like he'd run to the car to grab something.

Myles, buddy, hey there. Sorry, I got tied up….

And that was when I lost it. All the confusion, all those jumbled feelings, the wondering, the guilt of wishing he wouldn't come back, it knocked me over. He picked me up, his breath harsh from cigarettes, his stubbly cheeks scratching my face as he hugged me. I think the lady asked him where he'd been or something, but he laughed it off. My dad had a laugh for everything.

It's a weird time for that story to wash through my head as the ice pack melts and leaks and drips onto my shirt as I walk. I toss it in a trashcan on the curb as I come up on Forest Hills. My eye is thumping like crazy, but I don't feel like explaining it to Noah. I can't text Mal about this, obviously. I'm on my own.

I take a left, down the old Knotty Oak subdivision. It's like my feet know where I need to go.

Mr. Irvin's bungalow sits down the hill, buried in shade with a wrap-around deck he built himself. The porch is the feature of the house, with sprawling ferns spilling from the hanging baskets. But usually Mr. Irvin can be found in the detached garage, where the bay door is up, and I spot him outside, working on the truck.

I start down the driveway when he pops up from under the hood.

"Myles, that you?" He wipes his hands with a rag and steps away from the hood.

"I was in the neighborhood and figured I'd drop in."

He laughs, before his gaze narrows on my face, and then he's not laughing anymore. "Oh, hey. You all right, there?"

Another shrug. "Just dandy."

He nods, those old blues lingering on me. "I see."

A moment's awkwardness. A car passes up the street. Mr. Irvin motions to the garage. "Here, let me get you something."

"No. It's okay, Mr. Irvin. Don't worry about it." I try to laugh it off. "I'm going for a look here."

He doesn't laugh. "Ah, don't kid yourself. Come on." He starts for the garage.

I follow him, catching the many smells—old fires, oil and gas, bug spray. He reaches into the ancient refrigerator that's shaped like a bullet and tosses me a bag of frozen peas. "Here. It's not like I'm going to eat those."

"Thanks." I press it against my cheek, which must look worse than I thought. I haven't found the nerve to check it out yet, but if the throbbing heat is any indication, it's not pretty. It hurts to blink. The bag feels nice.

"So," he says, rocking back on his heels, looking around. "You want to tell me about it?"

Up on the street, little kids zoom by on bikes, pumping the pedals, all giggles and squeals. We watch them until they're gone. I nod to the truck, where a pan sits under the engine. "You changing the oil?"

He turns his attention to the truck. "Doing a complete flush. Transmission fluid, brakes, oil... the works," he says, trailing off. "You need me to take you somewhere? Get that looked at?"

I shake my head. We step outside and stand before the truck. To our left is a huge mound of sand and a pallet of bricks. For a while we talk about work, the awareness garden and how it's coming along. We dance around the subject of my eye, and the peas help. Soon, it's not feeling so bad, and I don't know why I say it, but, like everything else that's happened this evening, it just comes out. "You said you play piano?"

He watches me closer, his mind changing gears. "Ah, yeah. Long time ago."

"You still have one?"

"What, a piano?"

I chuckle. "No, a pile of bricks."

He looks at me for a second before a grin breaks across his face. "Actually, I do. I have both."

He invites me into the house, where he's got more than a piano. He's got a few guitars lining the walls. Nice ones, too. I'm not buying what he said about only having played a long time ago. Everything is arranged like a studio, and it's all too easy to convince him to jam.

"Do you mind?" I say, motioning to the mahogany Les Paul.

"By all means."

I set the peas to the side and carefully lift the guitar from the holder. As I get situated, he takes his place at the piano.

As soon as his fingers touch the keys, it's no longer the Mr. Irvin I know. The big mitt hands I've seen mix grout, lay bricks, and scoop dirt become delicate instruments. I set the guitar to my lap as he plays a melody that at once sounds original yet familiar. It's sad, triumphant, and powerful but gentle all at once. It sounds like something you'd hear in a dark, still theater, where no one moves or whispers so not to miss a key.

When he's finished, his shoulders slouch. He gazes at the wall, lost in thought.

I strum the guitar. "That was amazing." He smiles and closes his eyes in gratitude. "Whose song was that, anyway?" I ask, expecting him to name some fancy French composer. Instead, he looks to me thoughtfully.

"Just something that came to me."

"What? You *wrote* that?"

"You'd be amazed what comes to mind when people are shooting at you." His gaze falls to my guitar—his guitar in my hands. "Shall we jam?"

Hearing him say it, I can't help but laugh, even if it kills my face. I nod. "Yes, we shall jam."

Mr. Irvin was full of it all along. He's better than good, with an ear for anything. He can do more than play overtures on that piano, and together we come up with some Elton John-type stuff. His big, long fingers tickle away at the keys like he'd never touched a brick. We play for an hour, then two. My eye hurts like hell, swollen and hot, but the music helps, and pretty soon we're sitting around, him at the piano and me hanging onto the guitar.

I strum out *Where We End,* the song Mal came up with. Mr. Irvin loves it, and before I know it, I'm gushing about her.

"She gets this look in her eyes when I play it, with this lopsided grin. It's like she's smiling despite herself, and it makes me…" I puff out my cheeks with a wince.

He sets his head back, a faraway gaze on his face. "Yes, I remember. Joyce could always level me with her smile."

My throat tightens. He'd mentioned his wife once. I knew she'd passed away but didn't know how to approach the topic. I look around the room. Books on the shelves. Frost, Whitman, others. Poetry and music. Not a bad way to pass the time.

The next thing I know, he's hopping up and returning with another bag of frozen vegetables. From there, I tell him about the other night and how Mal's eyes make me crazy and the sound of her voice sets me at ease and stirs me up at the same time. He tells me how Joyce would sit beside him while he played piano, singing along, swaying. What he wouldn't give to feel her arm against his one more time.

I set the guitar down, staring at him and nodding. "Yeah."

After a while, he asks about the eye again, but I'm still caught up on the thing about his wife's arm brushing against his. Such a simple moment, but it's everything. He understands exactly how I feel about Mal. So I figure, what the hell?

"Hank wants me to take a job at the foundry." Mr. Irvin takes this in, listening as I unload the wreckage of my life into his living room. Maybe it's the piano or the confession of his overture, but I'm telling him more than I've told anyone. How Hank's never actually punched me until tonight. How I've got to do something.

When I force myself to finally stop talking, Mr. Irvin watches me for a minute. "You know, I went to school with Hank way back when."

"Really. How was that? Was he a dick back then too?"

Mr. Irvin chuckles. "Well, he was a lot like what you're describing."

"So, that's a yes. Hey, something I've been wondering. How come Hank didn't go to Vietnam?"

"Oh, well who knows why things work out the way they do."

I figured he'd say something like that. It isn't in Mr. Irwin's nature to gossip or talk shit, so I know that's all I'm getting. We play a few more songs until he's yawning too much to do anything else, and he says I can crash in the guest room.

Another night out of the house. Hank's going to love that. But it's going on eleven, and sleep sounds good after the night I've had. I get to my feet and thank him again. He says it's nothing, but he's wrong. He saved me tonight. Not only crashing but the playing and, the talking. I'm not sure where I'd be without it.

I start for the guest room but stop. I turn around with one more question on my mind.

"Hey, I thought you said you hadn't played in a long time?"

He gives me a smile that breaks into a yawn. "No, no. I play. I just haven't played anything worth a damn. Until you came along."

I nod. Again, my eye hurts when I smile. But it's worth it.

24

Mal's running late for practice, and Noah is in a mood. He sits at the kitchen table, sulking about our band video—which has a few thousand views but has been a total bust compared to the first one. He reads the comments in his most obnoxious, nasally voice. "*'Dude, she's so hot. Drop the losers. That guitarist is lost.'*"

Mrs. Connors ducks out of the refrigerator, she looks at me and frowns. "Myles, are you sure you're okay?" she asks for the fifth time today.

"Yeah. It's…"

"*They're so cute together.*" Noah tosses the phone on the table and sighs. "Freaking gross, man. But yeah, the eye. I know we talked about your look, but what the hell?"

He knows Hank can be a dick, but this is new territory. The punch is a first. And while the swelling has gone down somewhat, the bruise has darkened. I'm trying to think of something to say when Mal comes rushing in.

"Sorry," she says in our general direction. "Hi, Mrs. Connors."

Mal chats up Noah's mom about the tour. Mrs. Connors has agreed to be our official chaperone, which would be fun to tease Noah about if we all sat around joking together like old times. Mal

165

and Mrs. C. go on about how big this is for us, playing in Charlotte, when Mal turns and playfully smacks Noah on the arm. He smacks her back and they go on for a minute.

Then she turns to me, and everything stops.

"Oh…" She closes her eyes and deflates. She tilts her head as she starts to say something before she glances over her shoulder at Mrs. Connors and pulls it back. And that's it. She turns away, and I'm lost in the shuffle when Noah suggests we go downstairs.

I don't want sympathy for my eye, but Mal almost seems angry at me over it. She sets her jaw and ignores me. Noah makes jokes about a stain on the carpet where Daris snorted Dr. Pepper up his nose, but I'm hardly listening. Mal stays buried in her phone.

Maybe she's reading the comments, too. About dropping the losers. Once I think about it, I can't stop wondering what big news or secrets she's hiding this time. The podcast, the tour, all of it, how she's like the gatekeeper of information.

She's the one they want. We're just the supporting cast.

My amp hums as I wait for something to happen.

"Hey, shiner, want to practice?" Noah asks. Mal whirls her head to him.

"Don't—" She sucks it back in, lowers her voice. "Don't be an asshole."

"Dude, I'm kidding. Everyone okay?"

Mal sort of nods, shrugs, then glances at me again before she shakes her head and gets to her feet. "I have to go." She turns to me. "I'm sorry, okay?"

I stare at her until she finally looks directly at me, almost like it's an accident. When she does, her eyes soften as she takes me in, but then it's gone, like she's forcing herself to go through with something.

"Mal, what's up?"

She shakes her head. "Nothing Myles. I just have to go." She shakes me off and rushes up the stairs.

Noah taps on his snare. "Here we go," he says, as though the prediction he made is coming true.

When Noah and I get upstairs, Mal is already in her car, backing out of the driveway. Before she puts the car in drive, she stops, her face completely expressionless as she looks to the house. She quickly wipes her face and gets on her way.

Noah sets a hand on my shoulder. "Damn, dude. What did you do to her?"

I shake my head. "Nothing. I don't know what happened just now."

"Of course you don't. It's Mal. Your brain turns to shit every time you think about her. Come on, there's pizza in the oven."

"I know, but I thought—"

"No, my man. You were not thinking."

My insides are melting. Everything oozes and burns, and I can't hold another thought. "I should go, too."

"Go where? Home to sit in your bed and cry? Look, I'm going to tell you something I shouldn't because the best thing that could happen for everyone in this band would be for you to move on. I mean, you two... ever since that thing with the video and the basement—"

"Noah. What are you trying to say?"

Noah spits in the sink, rinses it down with the faucet and turns back to me. He throws his hands out. "This." He points out the window. "Practice. This is what I'm trying to say."

"Can we not do this right now?"

Noah sighs. We grab some pizza, and I do my best not to sulk and be hopeless. I try to hold a conversation, but all I can do is wonder about Mal. Later, as Noah gives me a ride home in his mom's Subaru, he's laughing about the Maroon 5 station she's got programmed. "Seriously, listen to this dude."

"I'd rather not."

"It's gross. I think my mom has un-motherly thoughts about him."

I gaze out at the houses as we drive off, wondering what in the hell. Noah sings along, horribly on purpose, to some monstrosity of pop.

"You're going to have to keep your shit together for the tour stop, okay? Think you can do that?"

This is where I should tell him about Mal and us going back on Ripcast, but I don't have the energy. "Yeah, I'll be fine."

"*Yeah, I'll be fine,*" he mimics. "*My name is Myles and I talk like this.*"

"Hilarious."

"And another thing, but I don't want you to freak out."

I snap out of my thoughts. "Well now I'm freaking out."

Noah sets his jaw in a way that tells me it's something more serious than I thought. "Dude, as a band we need to start preparing for life after Mal."

When he turns to me, I close my eyes. He looks back to the road. We stop at a red light. "You know what I mean, too."

As much as I've been thinking about it already, to hear Noah say it makes it feel real. Like it's not only in my head. Mal's going to leave us.

Noah talks to the windshield. "I'm not even mad at her. It was always a matter of time, and now she's getting *all kinds* of attention. Like, move-to-L.A. type buzz. I can't believe I'm the one saying it, but we can't hold her back from that."

"She didn't say that, though, did she? She hasn't said anything to me about it."

He lifts a hand from the steering wheel and shoots me a sideways look. "Of course she hasn't *said it.* But look how she blew up the other day."

"That's because you were being a dick." My mouth is dry. I clear my throat.

The light changes. He starts to say something but exhales. "Maybe so, but that's why I was jamming with the brothers. We have to keep some options open. That's all I'm saying."

I wipe my mouth and try to appear like someone who hasn't been smacked in the face several times. Noah laughs. "At least we've still got the Warped Tour, right?"

"Yeah."

It's almost funny how the tour has become our default reset.

Man, everything sucks, Mal is leaving, and I've got a side gig, but hey, the Warped Tour, right?

Noah pulls up to my house talking about Hank and telling me I ought to knock him on his ass. I'm hardly paying attention. I thank him for the ride, and he nods.

"No problem. Oh, hey, you remember those chicks from the warehouse?"

"Sure," I say to speed him along.

He shakes his head and turns off the stereo. "It's not just Mal getting attention. One of them has been texting me. Thinks you're hot. Maybe that mysterious brooding thing you've got going on is working."

I roll my eyes. It hurts, but I can't resist giving Noah a hard time. "You've been texting girls? About me?"

"What? No. I mean, it wasn't like that. I was trying to hook up with her friend, maybe the two of us could hang out again."

"I appreciate your efforts, really. And we can hang. But the last time we did this double-date thing, it didn't work out so well for me."

He sets his head back and laughs. "Worked out for me, though."

I duck out of the car and start to shut the door when he calls out. "Hey man."

I stop. "Yeah?"

"Seriously. If you need to crash, call me, okay? Mom's super chill since my dad's been out of town."

"Thanks, Noah."

"And hey, maybe I'm off about Mal. Maybe she loves the band too much to leave. Good luck tomorrow, by the way."

My eyes widen. I recover with a sigh and drop my head. "About that."

He laughs. "Dude, y'all aren't slick." He holds up his phone. "It's called the internet."

"You mad?"

"Nah. No room for drummers in there, anyway. Go do the couple act. You guys are pretty good at it. That eye, though..."

His phone lights up. He smiles.

"That the girl?"

"You know it. Sure you don't want to go?"

I turn to my house, hoping it will be a good night. A quiet night. I nod. "Nah. I'm…"

"Yeah, yeah. I'm out."

25

BEING HOW MAL BOLTED PRACTICE AND IGNORED MY texts, I'm almost surprised when she shows up to pick me up the next morning. It's around ten, and I'm a mess. I didn't sleep because I was too stressed about the band, Hank, and all that stuff Noah said about Mal. So not only do I feel like a zombie, and with the black eye, I kind of look like one too.

Mal points to a coffee, and I'm thinking it's a grand gesture of apology when she turns up the radio and backs out of the driveway.

She drives fast, like the sooner we get there, the better. I sip coffee and sneak peeks at her. Cut off shorts, faded t-shirt, messy bun. Of course she looks amazing. She glances over and catches my eyes. I still don't know what to say to change things.

We stop for gas. I offer to pump because I can't help myself. She shrugs and smiles and says all the right things, but something's off. Way off. I pump the gas and she stares at nothing.

When I get back in, she asks about the setlist. I pocket my debit card, and she looks for her bag as she bites her lip. "Why did you pay?"

I shrug. "You drove. I've got the gas."

"Oh." She frowns. "Well, thanks."

At some point, I bring up the warehouse gig on Saturday. I attempt to make some lighthearted jokes about Noah. Mal says she texted him last night and he was cool with it. I tell her about his date, but she doesn't laugh. It's not the same, and all I want is for it to be the same.

When we pull up to the studio, and she pops the trunk, I start to get out when she calls after me.

"Myles."

I stop, pivot on the gravel. She looks down, then back to me with pained eyes. "What's it going to take?"

For a second I think she's asking about us, but she means Hank. Moving out. I shrug. "Well, my back has healed up."

She nods, rubs her cheek. "I'm not laughing."

I'm not about to get into this now. I do my best to smile. "What this?" I point to my eye. "I walked into a tree."

She closes her eyes and takes a huge breath. "Let me just get this off my chest. When I see you like this, and we just go along like it's nothing? It makes me feel like an accomplice to a crime. Because that's what it is, a crime. You know that, right?"

I take a step toward her. "Is that why you left last night?"

Dave, the host dude, opens the door and waves. Mal waves back. "We can talk about it later, okay?"

I don't have an answer for her. She nods, and we start inside.

Dave greets us at the door. "My duo. How are you?"

We nod, smile, try to appear as though everything is wonderful. Dave goes on about the numbers and says we're on track to be his most popular podcast yet.

"You know the drill. Do some songs, talk some shit. We're all set up this time, so we can hop to it. Nice shiner, dude." He turns to Mal. "The boyfriend?"

Mal shakes her head. "No boyfriend."

I stare at my feet. I hate leaving things in the parking lot the way we did, even after we spent two hours together and hardly said anything at all. But it's too late now, as Dave claps his hands and says something about rock and roll. Mal sets a dazzling smile on her face and nods.

"Let's do it."

She comes alive. Flips the switch and turns it on. I've brought the electric guitar this time, hoping to change it up and maybe hide my flaws. I'm plugging in and getting things right when Dave gets creepy.

"So, Mal. You drive the boys crazy, I'll bet."

I look up. It's gross, I mean, this Dave guy has to be like forty, looking her over the way he is, saying stuff like that. Was he like that last time, or am I extra aware since what's happened with Mal and me?

Mal laughs it off, and I'm wondering if she's itching for a smoke again. Dave nods at me. "Well, you drive one of 'em crazy, that's for sure."

Back to tuning for me. Dave laughs with the crew. "Sorry, we promised we wouldn't let you guys off the hook with easy questions this time. Honestly, the two of you, it's there. The tension, the chemistry." He lowers his voice and switches to a spot on British impression. "The drama."

The lights are too hot on my face. I wipe my brow, aware that the computer guy is catching it all, live streaming our awkwardness for the world. Mal does this throaty laugh. "What's a band without drama?"

Dave sits back and slaps his leg. Seriously, the guy is enamored. I'm not doing so hot when he turns to me, still lit up and charmed by Mal as he nods his chin like we're a couple of old bros.

"Myles. Mr. Conversationalist. How's your life since all this went down? You doing okay? Getting into mosh pits, yeah?"

"Something like that. I can't complain." I'm mumbling because this is wrong. I'm totally lying and not selling it. Dave waits for me to continue, Mal turns to me with a flash of concern in her stage smile. But I can't. I'm not in the mood to do this.

When I don't say anything, Dave leans in. "Oh man. Careful

now, I'm sure the ladies don't want you messing up that face of yours, right Mals?"

Mals? Is this guy serious? I'm thinking there's no way I'm going to make it through this interview when Mal touches my arm. "I think he wears it well."

She shoots me a small smile when she says it. Dave is already smirking, ready to pounce, when Mal grabs the reins. "Can we like, do a song, or what?"

"Great. Let's do it."

I don't wait and immediately scratch out the opening to *Can't Keep Myself*, thinking we can power through and get this over with. Mal leans back, eyes closed, and it both hurts and helps, seeing her so free, without drama, without pain, without a care besides what's happening in this old wood-paneled studio. Like it used to be.

Can't keep myself from wanting you to stay
Can't keep myself from shoving you away
Maybe it's the way you let me be me
Maybe it's the way you get me to be
Maybe it's the way you live inside my head

Mal's changed the lyrics slightly, and I realize I'm playing it a bit differently. She sings out the chorus in this jaded, more powerful way than I'm expecting. Her voice breaks so perfectly, it leaves me gasping. I glance over as she pitches forward, her hair falling as she shakes the words from her head.

Can't Keep Myself

We've never played it like this—loud and powerful but somewhat stripped down at the same time. Whatever we're doing, it works, and as Mal pulls her hair back, losing everything as she belts it out in the dingy little studio, I'm only vaguely aware of Dave's Holy Crap expression. It pushes me through. I keep playing, getting into it, letting everything between us melt away.

Dave exchanges glances with the soundboard guy. Mal wipes her forehead, her shoulders sagging a little from the performance, which, is what it was, a performance.

"That was an original, yeah?" he asks, his voice more serious than I've heard it before. She nods with a small smile. "Wow, the energy there. I could feel it between you two."

It's a little cramped, as some studio people have come in the room. They whisper to each other, and the computer guy points to the screen. Someone else cups their hands to the glass and peers in through the window on the door. I'm sort of folded over my guitar. I don't have to guess what they're all thinking. It's Mal. Her voice. She's so good. Too good for me.

Dave gets back on track. We discuss the Warped Tour, how Dave knew if he got our music in the right hands, we were a lock. He asks a bunch of questions about it, and I know I should be more gracious, thank him more for this opportunity. Instead, I slog through things, letting Mal do most of the work. It's like we're playing roles, parts we've carved out for ourselves during these little podcasts. Mal, the super talented singer, the beautiful personality, and Myles, the silent grunt of a guitarist, the guy in the corner who never says much and can easily be replaced.

The more I think about it, the more I'm ready to leave. I shut down, floating through it as we dive into *Where is My Mind*, our favorite Pixies cover—fitting for me. Then Mal gushes more about the tour and how amazing it's going to be.

When it's over, Dave goes over something with a producer. He thanks Mal. He brings me in and tells me I need to loosen up on camera, that Mal is going places and I'm a damned good guitarist, but if I want to survive I need to do the other stuff. He's laughing when he says it, but he might as well be punching me in the face. I already know it's true.

I pack up, and Mal does the small talk thing. Dave name drops and talks contacts while I head to the car. What can I say? I'm not too worried about my stage presence at the moment.

After what seems like an hour, the door opens and Mal appears with Dave, still laughing and smiling and waving. Everything's all *right on* and *hell yeah* as she gets to the car and sets her things in the backseat. She settles in behind the wheel without saying a word. She turns the key, backs out, and we're on our way.

Her mouth is tight as we hit the curve of the winding drive. She looks straight ahead while I'm fighting all kinds of things in my head. Mainly, I'm stuck on the idea that Mal is "going places" while I'm staying put with Nan and Hank. I set my head to the seat, settling in for the long silence, figuring it's going to be like it was on the way up, when Mal whips the wheel and the car skids over the gravel into some bumpy construction lot with old railroad ties and pallets and tall grass growing over an oil tank.

She slides to a stop and throws herself back into the seat. "Okay, let's talk about it."

I'm struck by her question, the ferocity of her voice. "About what?"

She lets out a deep sigh, grabs the steering wheel with both hands like she wants to strangle it. The muscles in her arms flex as she leans into it, then rears back and glares at me. "Back there, what were you doing?"

I shrug.

She glares at me for a full minute before she throws her hands up. "Why did we even do this, if…?" She sighs.

"I don't know. Why did we?"

Three times she hits the steering wheel. "What is it, Myles? What do you want?"

I don't have an answer for her. She blows a strand of hair from her face and leaves it at that. I wait her out, let her simmer, until she closes her eyes and bites her lip as some of her anger melts away. "Myles."

Again, just Myles. Never anything else. I look off to the pallets and dust and wonder what they were planning on building, why it never panned out. Maybe they ran out of money, had to leave everything and bail. I feel Mal watching me, and I shrug again. "I don't know. That Dave guy is weird."

She nods, as though she figured I'd say that but knows it isn't the problem.

"You know, when we agreed to go on, it was to *talk*. That's what an interview is. Guy asks questions, and we answer. Not me. *Us*. You were just sort of sitting there, you know? You might not like Dave, and yeah, he can be sketchy, but he's the main reason we're on the tour."

I shrug again, only sort of aware that I'm acting like a five year old. Mal lifts her head toward the window, to where the old radio towers peek out from the treetops. Her voice goes soft. "Myles. You have to come out of this. You've gotta get over whatever this is."

Like I can just decide to be as good as her. Or... *over* her. It's all I can do to hold her gaze before I turn away. "That's easy for you to say."

I feel the aggravation in her sudden shift to face me head on "Let's get this out, right now. I thought we did this already with Noah, but clearly you and I still have some things to work out."

Things to work out. I shake my head. She gives it back to me. I throw my shoulders up and down. "I don't see the big deal. You were great in there. You're always great, and honestly, what does it matter? The comments, the sound techs, Dave. You're the one they want."

Her eyes close, and she sinks back in her seat, fiddling with the ring on her thumb. "Of all people, I never thought *you* would do this."

"What? Tell the truth?"

Another sigh. "Yes, Myles. I'm getting calls. Calls from agents, or people who say they're agents. From band roster people. From shady agencies who want a retainer, some legit, some sleazy. But what do I know? I can't tell the difference. I don't know who's for real or who's looking after my interests, *our* interests. I'm finding it awfully hard to navigate all this, Myles. And now you start doing this."

So it's true. She's getting calls. A cold, sharp prickle of fear rushes over my skin. I turn to Mal as she sets her fist to her mouth. I blurt it out. "Are you leaving the band?"

She turns to me in complete disbelief. I can't face her. I need to get it out, rid myself of this storm cloud I've carried in my chest since last night. "Noah thinks we should prepare for after you leave. I told him you wouldn't do that."

I stop talking because she's shaking her head. Her face reddens. She closes her eyes, and her mouth tightens. "Because Noah's been the voice of reason lately, right?"

I start to say more but she cuts me off. "You start reading fucking comments, and now you know everything, right?" Her voice is calm but quivering, the words sharp and searing. "You know everything about me now?"

"You don't exactly give us much. What else am I supposed to believe? People saw the video and reacted. I suck. I'm hopeless. I can't hold a note. It's all out there." I gesture to the windshield. Out there.

"Stop, Myles." She yells at the windshield. "Okay, just stop it. You're better than this. You're too good to do this to yourself, and I can't take it anymore, all right?"

Her voice cracks, and she turns away again. I set my hand on the door handle, ready to get out, get some air, maybe just walk for a while, when she takes my arm.

"Wait."

I stop at her touch, at the sound of her voice, a broken whisper hinging on a sob.

"I'm not leaving."

She looks down, wiping at her eyes. She throws her head back and flops her hands in her lap. Hearing her say the words out loud fills me with shame. All this attention, I thought it was everything we'd ever dreamed about. Turns out, I'm just mad at Mal for being so talented—for being wanted.

"You know, when I'm out there, or," she nods towards the building. "In there. I put up this shield. Seriously. I know it sounds dumb, but I do. I've always done it. At the warehouse, the community market, I put up a shield for protection. Whatever they want to say about me, all that rude shit about boys and gross stuff, I just let it hit the shield."

I peek over at her. Mal has always been invincible, but seeing her now, talking about some imaginary defense, her eyes wet and glossy, it takes the fight out of me.

"It doesn't sound dumb to me," I say. She turns her head to me, and I shrug. "But sometimes it seems like you have a shield up with other things, too."

Her eyes glisten. She cocks her head at me and closes her eyes. "Look, Myles, let's not complicate this even more. There are so many reasons why we can't. We made a mistake and—"

"A mistake?" I stare out to the dusty lot, pick at the fraying thread on my jeans. She keeps finding new ways to hurt me without even trying. "Wow. Sorry I'm not good at pretending or shielding or whatever."

"Myles, come on."

"Is it, though? Is this a shield, too? When we kissed?"

It comes out hard, powerful, and her eyes flash. She slams her head back into the seat. "Oh my God, Myles. This is what I mean, we can't let this get in the way of everything."

"Why? Why can't we have both?" I start to say more when I see the tears sliding down her cheeks. I look out the window, wondering how we got here at all. I take a few deep breaths to calm myself. "I'm sorry, all right? I know how you want to get away and leave and—"

She flings herself off the seat. Her face is wet and her eyes pleading. "You want too much, Myles. Okay? I can't," her eyes fill with new tears, spilling over her long eyelashes. "I can't do it. I keep telling you that. We can't do this right now. I don't want to leave the band, okay? I wish you would stop it. The basement, when we kissed it was, it was..."

"It was perfect."

She closes her eyes and more tears fight their way out. "Yeah, but..." She shakes her head, wipes her eyes with the back of her hand. "I don't even know how to put all this together. We're on the freaking Warped Tour." She grabs my hand. *"The Warped Tour.* And you're so worried about comments, and then this whole thing with… us. It's making things a little crazy, you know?"

I keep my gaze on the window. There it is again. *The tour.* The magic elixir. Only, what if it's not?

She gives my hand a squeeze. "The kiss wasn't a mistake, okay? But the other night, when I saw what Hank did to you, and then watching you go back so he can do it again?" A new tear rolls down her cheek. "You can't keep going back. You have to get out, Myles. But you won't, and I can't sit by and keep watching it happen. It hurts too much."

I close my eyes. "I really don't want to talk about Hank right now. And I can't pretend with you anymore. I can't just turn off how I feel about you." I start to say more, say it all, but I clamp my mouth shut and turn away again.

She only nods. The last thing I hear is her sniffling, a huge wet breath as she starts the car. Then the gravel crunches under the tires as we get turned around to head home.

26

After the way Mal and I left things, I probably would have lost my mind if it weren't for jamming out with Mr. Irvin after work. We get into these Elton John/Ray Charles riffs that are different than I'm used to but fun because he sings with surprising range.

We eat off the garden in the backyard, which is small but overflowing with all kinds of leafy plants bearing fruit and vegetables. It's fenced high to keep the deer away, with vines climbing up and arching over us. Mr. Irvin is a heck of a chef, and we cook veggies off the grill, something I never knew was a thing.

While Mr. Irvin has always been easy to talk to, lately it seems he's taking more interest in my life. I surprise myself by opening up, finding it sort of helps me deal with Mal. With home. We're in the kitchen cooking veggie packets after work on Wednesday when he mentions how he came home from the war and joined the protests. He'd seen enough to want to keep anyone else from going over there.

"It's when I met Joyce," he says all casual, grabbing an onion the size of a softball. He points the knife at me. "She could dice an onion like it was no one's business."

Again, I want to ask what happened, but I'm not sure how. Mr. Irvin, still dicing and cutting, casually says, "Joyce passed away years ago, complications with the baby."

It's like a sucker punch. The breath leaves my lungs as an icy chill blankets me. As much as I've been yapping, I've hardly asked about his wife. And his kid? I open my mouth to apologize, but it seems too light for the weight of the subject matter. I'm still trying to figure out what to say when he looks over his shoulder and nods that the grill should be ready.

I step out to the heat and turn the dials down on the grill. I realize it's probably why we get along so well, the loss that's bruised our souls. My parents, his wife and child. There's a sense of pain in his voice, of loss in his gentle movements. It's something I recognize.

When I get home, Hank's truck sits like a threat in the driveway. My muscles do their usual ritual as I walk into the dark, tensing at every creak on the floor as I pad to the bathroom. After a quick shower, I brush my teeth and peek out to the hallway. I've managed to avoid him since the incident in the kitchen, and I'd like to keep it that way. Then again, it's not Hank's style, lurking in the dark. He's more of a hit-you-at-the-dinner-table sort of guy.

My back no longer feels like it's on fire, and it's nice to be clean. As tired as work has made me, I'm in no mood to sleep. I'm thinking about Mr. Irvin and his wife. I find my notebook and scratch out some thoughts, stupid poems that have no chance of becoming songs. I work on something new, but my mind keeps going back to that "Dashboard" thing.

A few years back, I found a box with some of my dad's things, including a few pictures, CDs, and demos he'd made somewhere along the way. Mal had Charley put the demos on a thumb drive.

As terrible of a father he was, the guy was an excellent musician. When I turn off the light and listen to him in my earbuds beneath the hiss of background noise, I'm always taken aback by how his voice cracks so perfectly on the notes, so pained and ripped apart as he plays in some room to my mother and friends.

They must have recorded it in the living room. Sometimes I wonder where I was as they laugh and joke and clink bottles amid the murmurs of company. Mom sings along, casually, in that effortless way of hers, and I can hear the flick of a lighter as my dad takes a drag. Some scattered laughter, and then he goes back to playing.

It's crazy to think he was playing on these same two guitars I've come to call my own., I want to be different from him, but I can't help wanting to play his songs better than he played them, almost like I'm doing my best to make him love me even though it's too late.

Or maybe it's simpler than that. Maybe it's like Mr. Irvin cutting onions and thinking about his wife and child. Maybe hearing my dad sing, playing his songs, is the closest I'll ever be to him.

MR. IRVIN and I work against the clock to get the awareness garden finished in time for the big ribbon cutting ceremony. Even with a deadline looming, Mr. Irvin continues this new trend of having me do more of the skill work instead of the usual grunt work. I'm doing all right. We're still making good time.

Leaving for work, I decide today's the day I take back Barbara, but when I grab the keys, Nan looks over her shoulder. "Who said you could take the car?"

I shrug. "I need to meet Mr. Irvin. Is that okay, if I use it for work?"

"Hank isn't happy about it."

"Well, I paid him."

Nan stares at me. "Did you hear what I said?"

"Yep."

She looks away. "You know he's trying to help, right? With the job and all."

A laugh escapes before I can catch it. I'm not touching that one. I turn to leave, figuring that's it, when Nan calls after me. "Get back here, Myles."

The force in her voice stops me. Slowly, I do as she says, flinching when she reaches out and takes my chin in her strong hand. She studies my face, breathing hard through her nose before she looks at me directly in the eye. I figure she's examining my black eye, and I glance off because it's weird and because her breath smells like black coffee.

She lets me go when I pull away. "You look so much like him."

That again. I stop cold. "What?"

She simply turns and goes back to scrubbing. "Like Christopher." She shakes her head. "Sometimes I look at you and have to remind myself you're not him. That he's gone."

I tilt my head, gripping the keys. My throat closes, and I want to throw my hands up and scream at her. She's giving me nothing on my father for nine years, and now she's brought him up twice in the past few weeks.

"He was stubborn like you. He always thought he had the answer to everything. I see you out there and I just... he wasn't much older than you are now."

My feet cling to the floor. I'm heaving, fighting off all my questions about my father. I'd love to bombard her, sit her down and force her to tell me everything. But if I do that she'll simply shut down. Instead, I take a step toward her, hoping maybe she'll finally get it. "Nan, I'm not him. I may play music like he did, but you have to trust me. I have things I want to do."

"So did he. He wanted to go off to the parties, the drugs."

"No, Nan. I want to write songs, meet new people. I want to start my own business, maybe." I catch myself from yelling. My voice cracks because I want so badly to finally get through to her, make her understand. "I want to get out and make my own way, you know?"

She's back to the counter, working a spot she's probably been scrubbing for years. A spot that will never come clean the same way she will never change. After five seconds of silence I nod, realizing there will be no big breakthrough today. Still, I reach for her, touching her shoulder all the same. She tenses up when I lean over and kiss her on the cheek, recoiling with a slight gasp.

I toss the keys from one hand to the other and walk out the door.

That afternoon, I'm edging out one of the gardens when my phone starts blowing up with jumbled text messages from Noah. Each one is stranger than the last—mostly misspelled words and riddles. But there's clearly a theme to it all: I'm whipped, a sellout, a poser, and a phony. I wipe my brow and shake my head. He must be day-drinking. I need to go check on him.

Mr. Irvin assures me he's fine with me leaving, but I help him load up anyway before I go check on our drunken drummer. A quick *Find My Friends* ping gives me his location. Wonderful.

Twenty minutes later, I'm pulling up to Daris and Dorin's house, stressing about Noah and his backup plan. I follow the sound of laughter around the side of the split-level home, where I find Daris and Dorin sprawled out on lawn chairs. But no Noah. I climb the stairs to the deck and nod at the twins.

"Where's Noah?"

One of them points to the yard where, sure enough, Noah's splayed out on the grass, mumbling to the sky. I turn away as the other twin offers a half empty bottle of rum. From what Noah told me, their host parents are hardly ever home. Seems they have the run of the place.

The grass is thick and green with well-manicured trees and bushes. I nudge Noah with my shoe. "Hey man. What the hell?"

He rolls over. There's a smear of dog crap on his left elbow and a collection of mystery stains down his shirt. He looks up with a loopy squint and a droopy smile. "Ah, there you are. My favorite guy."

"Yeah, it's 5:28 in the afternoon. You wasted?"

Shaking his head. "I'm a rockstar, baby."

It's clear the Noah from the other night has clocked out. I plop down next him, but not too close, and wonder where to start. I'm thinking about my talk with Mal, my talk with Noah. How before we can even think about the tour, this band has some major hashing out to do.

Noah's still belting lyrics to a song I've never heard. He smells like a hot dumpster full of old fruit. The D brothers join in from the deck, sharing the bottle and laughing between sips, as though this is the funniest thing they've ever seen.

Noah sits up. His eyes widen then shut, and he puffs his cheeks out like he might puke. He sets a fist to his chest. "I watched your little poopcast."

"I thought you were okay with it?" He shrugs. I nudge him with my elbow. "Well, what'd you think?"

"Same, that you're whipped."

I nod. "Ah, okay."

"You can't even deny it anymore." Again he burps and gets more than he bargained for, covering his mouth until it passes. "You're whipped, and she's going to crush you to pieces." Another burp. I scoot away. "Agh. False alarm." He spits and wipes his mouth. "But the way you did the song was cool, I'll give y'all that. When did you work out the new arrangement?"

"We didn't. We just..." I shrug. "It's how it came out."

He turns to me with a hiccup. "Bullshit."

There's so much I want to tell him, about the show, how Mal's having trouble with all the new attention. But there's no point trying to talk to him like this. I look up to the bright sky and clench my jaw, wondering if things will ever be like they were.

Noah wipes his face. "Well, either way man, it's how we should do the song at the show. I mean, at least we get to do the Warped Tour. But after that..." He shrugs, picks at the grass. Something in his voice, the way he says it strikes me as prophetic. But it's not. He's drunk and feeling sorry for himself.

I'm done with being the middleman. I start to get up. "I'm not doing this right now."

He laughs. "It's all you do, bro."

"Yeah, I guess I should be over here doing *this* with you? Your backup plan, right?" I throw my back towards the twins. "Looks like a blast."

"You don't know anything about fun anymore. You don't know anything about me."

I stop. "Huh? What's that supposed to mean?" He shakes his head, looking away. I sit back down beside him. "Noah, what's up? What's going on?"

"My parents suck, man. They hate each other. My dad came home, for one night," he says, holding up a finger. "They almost killed each other. My mom accused him of having an affair. He called her a crazy bitch. It's like they truly can't stand each other, and it's not much fun to be around."

Damn. I close my eyes, try to rearrange my thoughts before I turn to him. I knew things weren't great, but I had no idea he was carrying all this with him. "Man, I'm sorry. Look…"

"Don't." He flops back down with a sigh. "Dude. I know your life at home is shit, so I'm not trying to… you know. I mean you've got your own mess. It's just… it's fine, really. My folks need to split and be done with it. but my mom won't talk about it. When Dad's gone, she goes back to acting like Betty Homemaker and pretends like everything is perfect. You've seen her. It gets old, you know?"

"Yeah."

We sit like that for a bit. If he just wants me to sit by him, that's what I'll do. But when he does want to talk, I'll be there. I need to be there for him. Just when I think he's passed out, he lets out a wet burp and sits up, wobbles, then falls back again.

"Little help?"

I laugh, hop up, and try to help Noah to his feet.

"So where am I taking you to hose you off and sober you up?"

27

I TURN MY FACE FROM THE PUTRID STENCH OF VOMIT AND liquor as I get Noah upright and lug him up the backyard. The brothers laugh it up and wish us a good time, waving and snapping pics as we hobble across the lawn. At the car, Noah doesn't put up much of a fight as I strip off his filthy shirt and place him in the back. He tells me I'm an all right guy between bursts of drunken power ballads. I do my best, but I feel terrible. I really had no idea he was so torn up about his parents.

Two minutes later, he's out cold, snoring in the backseat, a film of sweat glistening on his forehead. I'm not sure where to go. I can't take him home yet, so I drive to the mall, still thinking about the band and how I only want us to be tight again. I park and send Mal a message.

She responds quickly, demanding we stay put (Do not move!). She's on the way. Five minutes after that, she texts again, saying she needs ten minutes, max, because she's stopping to buy a Sharpie. I start to text her back but I'm laughing too hard.

I step out of the wagon as Mal comes barreling into the lot, her blue Honda speeding over the faded parking lines before it screeches

189

to a stop. I smile as she leaps from the car, music blaring as the door hangs open, her eyes brimming with mischief.

"Hey, I don't think it's a good idea to—"

She stiff arms me out of the way, rips open the backdoor, and dives in before immediately jerking away and covering her face. She drops the Sharpie, her nose wrinkled as she dry heaves.

"Arghh!" She squints at me. "What is that smell?"

"It seems our drummer has fallen into the lifestyle."

She picks up the marker and chances another peek before she looks back at me. "I don't know if I can. Did he get sick in the car? Where's his shirt?"

Now I'm leaning in, my laughter stalling out as a flash of Hank comes to mind—of him cleaning out the car, preaching about drunken teenagers. "I seriously hope he didn't."

She uncaps the Sharpie again and pinches her nose with one hand. I hold my arms out to block her, laughing. "Mal, no. I've got to take him home."

"I'll be nice," she pleads like a little girl. "Just a few penises. I mean look at that pale, bare, canvas. It's begging for it."

She confuses my laughter for a yes, but when she starts for him again, I step in front of her. She smiles, her eyes widening. "Watch it now, I'm armed."

I take her wrist. "I can't let you deface him. I have to face his mom."

"Oh please. You know his dad is at some country club. Besides, he deserves this, getting tanked with the twins."

I hesitate, thinking about what Noah said about his parents. That and it's hard to take Mal seriously the way she's scrunching up her nose, itching to draw penises on Noah's face. I smile first, then she's cracking up, and soon were falling into each other when she looks at me again and cocks her head. "Just let me do a few words and…"

I'm still holding her, our faces inches apart. It's nice to have the other day behind us, even as I'm getting lost in her eyes. She laughs it off and tries again to step around me, faking one way before we clash into each other again. Mal squeals, and soon we're wrapped up. I forget about all the stuff we did or didn't talk until I hear the squeak of the back door and what sounds like a hose pouring onto the asphalt.

We jump back, still almost hugging when Noah, looking up, eyes glassy, lets a trail of drool hang from his chin. "You both make me sick."

Mal breaks away and strolls over to him, avoiding the puddle of puke. She cocks her head and pulls Noah's head up by his hair. "You are so lucky," she says, waving the marker at him. He raises his head, wobbly, unfocused.

"I'm never drinking rum again."

Noah pukes a few more times. Mal has not only bought a Sharpie, but more thoughtfully, a bottle of water and a towel. We give him a minute to chug down some liquids and wipe himself down while we turn up the radio and hang out on the hood of the car as the sun dwindles to a soft glow.

After a while, Noah wobbles around the car, his shirt on, gripping the ends of the towel hanging over his head. Mal, talking about our upcoming warehouse gig, slides off the hood and looks him over. "You are not to have a drop before the show."

"Yes, Mommy."

She spins on her heel, like a teacher, pointing the Sharpie at him. "I'm serious. You're getting sloppy."

Noah stiffens. "What?"

"You heard me." She winks at me. We both know Noah can't take criticism. He wipes his chin again, slugs down more water, and then spits out a mouthful.

"I am not sloppy. You two are too busy doing podcasts and pretending not to like each other to notice anything, anyway."

"I thought you didn't care about the podcast," I ask him, but Mal ignores it completely.

"You've got less than two weeks to get your act together. You think you're ready for that?" She looks at him and scowls. "Not even close. That is if you're even going."

I turn to Mal with wide eyes. Noah, hunched over with his hands on his knees, looks like he might spew again. "What?"

"With Bromania doing so well, do you have time for the tour? I'm sure you guys are booked, right?"

Noah spits. "Shut up. You're the one who's leaving."

Mal's smile drops like an anvil. She looks at me, then back to him. A truck rumbles across the parking lot, hauling a dumpster to the other side of the mall. Other than that, it's only the three of us. I'm bracing myself for things to blow up like last time when Mal busts out laughing.

Noah straightens. We exchange glances. Noah fixes the sleave on his shirt. "What's so funny?"

Mal's hands fly up to her head. "Everyone seems to know exactly what I'm doing but me. And you know what else? It feels like the two people I know best almost *want* me to quit this band."

"What?" I step forward. "No we don't."

Noah joins me. "We don't want you to quit, Mal. It just seems like—"

She turns to him. "How about you let me decide? Stop assuming things, okay?" Her eyes find me. "Both of you."

Noah nods his head. "Okay. I will. But no more secrets."

"Huh?" Mal drops her hands from her head.

Noah, eyes still glossed over, nudges me. "Ripcast. The tour. The news broadcast. If you hear something, just let us know. How hard is that?"

She regards him for a minute, then looks out to the pinkish clouds over the mountains. She nods slowly. "Okay." Mal steps back. "Okay, I will."

"Thank you," Noah says.

Mal smiles.

"What?"

"Well, there is some *news*."

"See!" Noah rips the towel off his head.

I glance at Mal, and she wiggles her eyebrows. "Well, while Noah was getting tanked, I was talking to Julia Jenson down at WGBT

News. About the interview? They want to do it Friday, before we go on at the warehouse."

"Lame." Noah and I say in unison.

Noah straightens. "Like one of those local kids make it big, pieces?" He cuts a look at Mal. "Oh, wait a minute. An interview? As in..." he gestures to Mal and me. Mal shakes her head so hard her hair takes flight.

"Nope, you too, sweetheart. They want footage of us playing. You will need to be on your best behavior. Or not. I mean, it is the local news, so it's going to be cheesy."

Noah tries to hide his own cheesing. Clearly, he's thrilled about being involved. I smile at Mal because she played it just right. Noah is happy. I'm happy. And while we're all sitting around being happy, talking about the news and interviews and having a moment in the parking lot, Mal pops the top on the Sharpie and nods at me.

"Myles, grab his arms. Noah, it's best you don't try to fight it."

28

WE SET UP AT THE WAREHOUSE AROUND SIX ON FRIDAY. Soundcheck goes smoothly as skaters arrive, and we all appear to be on the same page. Noah is hyper and agreeable. Either Mal got through to him the other day, or he doesn't remember anything at all.

Even with the tour looming, the warehouse show is still a big deal. After doing Ripcast twice, surviving the debacle at Richland Hills, and landing a spot on the Warped Tour, it feels more like a final tune up before the real thing.

The plan is to do the local news interview right before we go on at eight, and Garrett, the show organizer, is expecting a few hundred people tonight. Tune up or not, thinking about all those people makes me jittery.

Garrett talks fast, checking his phone and doing eight different things at once. "Everything is legit. I've got a permit and all that. You guys might make some real cash tonight."

I cut a look to Noah, wondering if he means it or if we'll get shortchanged again. Even with all our internet fame, we're still the opening act, going on first for a three-band lineup. Garrett hits his vape. "So, Warped Tour, huh?" His gaze drops to Mal's legs, then resurfaces. "Well, just try to remember your roots when you get that deal. Oh, and try to give me a shoutout on the news, cool?"

We're in the back, behind the loading docks. I gaze out to the warehouse, where the skaters do their thing. It's way more crowded than last time, and things are getting loud. Kids keep staring at us. Yeah, Mal has promised to be more open, and I'm supposed to be shielding it all out or whatever, but it's easier said than done. I've always gotten nervous before shows, but since the video, even as I've promised to stop reading comments, I can't seem to relax and play like I used to play.

Through a cloud of vape, Garrett shoots me a quizzical glance. "You okay, dude?"

"Yeah. I'm…" I squeeze my eyes shut and force myself to smile. I catch Mal watching, and I shake my head. "I'm fine, really. I'm just…"

Mal steps forward, crossing her arms over her chest. "Myles, look at me."

I do, but it only makes it worse. All I see is what they see. Her eyes dazzle, outlined in her "warpaint eyeshadow," as Noah calls it. Her hair is pulled back, her lips full as she searches my face. She leans in closer. "Stop thinking about it and just play."

My gaze falls to my feet. I suck down a breath. "I got it. I'm good."

With an hour to kill, we grab something to eat. Noah is amped, hopping all over the place and fidgeting the way he does before a show. It's good to see him sharp and sober, how he's been since all the puking. For the first time in a while, it feels like the three of us are tight again.

We get a table and catch a few lingering stares. I push away the nerves, the doubt, the paralyzing fear creeping up my spine. I tell myself this won't be like Ripcast when I shut down. For the millionth time, I try to convince myself to get over this thing with Mal. She can have anyone she wants. Why in the world would she want me?

Noah reaches into the basket of fries, grabs a handful, and sits back with a smirk. "Well, guys, this might be the last time we slum it."

Mal rolls her eyes. "It's one date on the tour, Noah. It's awesome, but I don't think we're ready to quit the warehouse."

"Well, it could be, you never know." He drums on the table before his eyes dart past us. His smirk grows to new heights. "Oh damn. *This* should be good."

I turn to find Jada making her way over to us. Her hair is a new shiny shade of blue. She fiddles with a ring on her finger as she stops and looks us over. "Hi Noah. Hi *Myles*."

She throws a sharp look Mal's way. Her voice is stronger than I remember, and it's weird because, well, everything.

I nod. "Oh, hey Jada. How's it going?"

Mal turns to me with a conspiratorial smile. Probably because my voice is high and weird. Noah sits back, relishing in my misery.

"Good, um," she keeps looking at Mal and then me, and then back to Mal. It's getting strange, and it shouldn't be. Jada and I were forced to hang out once because of Noah, but Jada is acting like it was more as she picks at her shirt. "I texted you a few times, but I guess you've been busy."

Noah keeps chewing and smiling. I nod along like an idiot. "Yeah, we've been playing a lot."

Mal snorts, and Jada sends her a look. I wish there was a way to warn Jada to tread lightly. Mal lives for confrontation. But it's too late. Mal snorts again, and maybe it's preshow jitters, but I'm having a hard time holding back the giggles. Jada turns to her and says. "Margorie, right?"

Mal stops laughing. "That's me. Marge."

"I've heard so much about you," Jada says, glancing at me. I look for an escape route.

Mal cocks her head. "Oh, well yes. Thanks, *Jane*."

Jada blinks. Noah looks like he's watching his favorite movie. I'm fighting off the urge to bolt, but nobody at the table wants to let me go. Jada turns to me. "Well, I'll see you, Myles. Seems all your dreams have come true."

She breaks off and turns away, and then she walks off to her friends, who send glares to our table.

Mal snatches a fry. "That was weird."

"Yeah."

Mal looks at me. "All your dreams, huh?" She snorts again. My face goes hot as Noah shakes his head.

I stare him down from across the table. "Did I ever say thanks to you, for... *everything?*"

"No, but you're mighty welcome."

Mal laughs. I drum my fingers on the table. "Shouldn't we be talking about this interview?"

They both ignore me. Noah sits back, watching Jada walk off. "Wow, Myles. Kind of cute, too. Dude, only you would go out with a girl and talk about Mal. You sir, are the lamest."

Mal elbows him in the ribs. "It's *Marge*, you nerd."

"I didn't..."

Noah finds the fry he dropped and eats it. He looks over to Jada, who is being consoled by a girl with a mohawk. "Maybe I should go over there and cheer her up. Show her a good time."

Mal follows his gaze to Jada and her friends, who are all still glaring at us. She waves and starts giggling. "You do that, Noah. Tell them you're in a band named Bird Poo."

Noah drops his head. "I hate you so much."

———

WE MEET WGBT's very own Julia Jenson outside the warehouse. It's hot and muggy, with people hanging out, skating, smoking, laughing and making faces at the camera. Music pulses from inside the building, the thump of the beat hitting my chest as a round of preshow jitters takes hold.

Kids rush up on Mal, gushing about the video, the podcast, her style. Mal nods through it graciously while Noah works the phone, updating the socials. Poor Julia doesn't seem too fond of her surroundings, muttering under her breath about hoodlums before asking if we can go somewhere more private.

We lead Julia and her camera guy to the backstage loading dock where it's quieter, but the clicks and clacks of the skaters echo around us as the music thumps over the speakers. The camera guy looks around, fussing over the lighting, the noise, and everything else until Julia tells him to shoot it.

Julia gets things rolling when Mal nudges me. We both turn to Noah, who has changed into a leather vest, and it's like we've silently agreed to let him have this interview. It's our gift to him.

"Okay, I'm here downtown in the warehouse district music scene with Clear Spring's very own teen band, The Wide Awakes."

Mal tenses at the words "teen band" as it's clear this thing is going to be every bit as corny as we thought. Naturally, Julia zeroes in on Mal because it's easy to do. She's a stunner on camera.

"We have Malorie Kamel," she says, butchering the name. "Of Clear Springs High. Well Malorie, it must be quite exciting, all this sudden attention. Between the viral video and now the big forthcoming appearance at the Charlotte Warped Tour, it must seem like a dream come true."

Mal tilts her head. "Oh, totally. But let me say, none of this would be possible without the backbone of our band, the *heartbeat* if you will, Noah Connors."

Julia blinks as Mal thrusts Noah front and center. Noah shoots her a look, then stammers out a hello. Julia nods, politely. "Noah, um..." She refers to her card but it's too late. Welcome to the Noah show.

He slicks back his wavy red hair. "Hey JJ. So, check it. Is this live?"

Julia flinches. "No. cut." She turns to Mal. "I was hoping we could," a quick survey of her surroundings before she turns to the camera guy. "You know what, just keep rolling."

She goes through the introductions again. And once again, Noah takes center stage. "Shout outs to Daris and Dorin. What's up, bros?"

Mal and I take a half step back, smiles spilling as Noah shouts out the entire town.

"...Kelly, what's up girl? Stu at the carwash. And can't forget..."

Julia glances at me before she tries to steer things to Mal. "Malorie, the Warped Tour, that must be a dream come true, am I right?" Her tight smile finds the camera, but her eyes are sharp with annoyance.

Mal nods, and right on cue, Noah slings an arm around her and takes it from there. "You know it. We're going to do some damage. The tour, this show? There's no telling what's next. Big things, Jules, big things."

"Great. Well, that's all for now. We'll return with some footage of these guys onstage."

Mal plops down beside me on a stack of pallets, quaking with laughter as the camera lights flick off and Julia eyes me closer, not exactly hiding her irritation as we break into giggles.

Julia looks around. Then at Mal. "You all aren't high, are you? I mean, this isn't—"

"Are you referring to drugs, ma'am?" Noah asks, still beaming from his performance.

Julia Jenson storms off, her cameraman hustling to keep up. When it's only the three of us, Noah smiles at Mal and me. "How'd I do?"

Mal pats him on the chest. "You did great, Noah. Really, really great."

I get to my feet, wiping my head. I turn to Mal, and it hits me all over again. She's too big for this, too good. None of this will last.

"Myles." Mal looks me up and down. "What?"

I shake my head. "Nothing. Let's go."

She doesn't move. The music cuts in the warehouse, only the skaters. Garrett is about to bring us out. Mal stares at me, gauging me. Then her smile returns.

She finds Noah and taps his cheek. "Well boys, are we ready to do this?"

"You know it." Noah grabs his sticks. I smile and do my best to show everyone I'm fine. Mal nods to the door.

"I'll go find Garrett."

When she's gone, Noah laughs. "Well, that interview was fun."

"Yeah."

He looks me over. "Thanks."

"For what?"

He rolls his eyes. "I know Julia Jenson wasn't there to interview me. She's here for you and Mal. It was cool of you guys to let me shine."

She's here for Mal, I think to myself but laugh it off. "And shine you did."

He glances at the door. "Listen, man. Thanks for the other day."

"Any time."

He nods. "So is this the part where we hug or what?"

Mal busts back in with Garrett trailing behind her. He claps his hands. "You kids ready to do this? You did mention The Spot? Skate Night every Friday night?"

We stare at each other. Garrett laughs. "What good are you? Okay, no worries, I'll get up with Julia. Let's get ready to rock!"

He turns to a panel on the wall and flips some switches. A hush falls over the warehouse right before the place erupts.

Garett smiles. "Showtime."

29

GARRETT TAKES THE STAGE AND MOST OF THE SKATING halts. He makes a few announcements about another upcoming competition and plugs the Facebook stream. We wait in the wings, where Noah bangs his sticks together as Garrett, in his best announcer voice, asks if everyone is ready for The Wide Awakes. The crowd comes alive. Garrett waves us on, and Mal hops for the stage then stops. She shakes her head and motions for Noah and me to catch up. Together, we storm the stage.

Mal takes up her bass and Noah finds his stool. The applause dies down, and the room grows quiet save for a few hushed conversations as Mal stands over the packed house. She takes them in like a general looking over a battlefield before she throws her hands up and a new rush of cheers hits the stage. I duck under the strap of my guitar and open my eyes. My breath catches when I manage to face the crowd.

There's an energy in the warehouse tonight. The whole place acts as one pulsing body as they chant and boo and yell and cuss and dare us to entertain them. It's perfect, or it should be. But I can't get my mind and my body to work together.

Mal moves to the mic stand. I glance back to Noah, who's

focused and ready. Not me. The live stream consumes me all over again. How Mal's so good at this, the way she sets her chin out and takes the mic with a playful smile. She clears her throat. "This first one goes out to all the *booooooring* guys."

They eat it up. She checks over to me and winks. I know what's coming, but I'm a bit slow and flub the first chord. Noah and Mal recover and we open hard, tearing into *You Wanna*.

I'm ripping into the chords, and Noah is doing his thing. Mal hops and shakes and skips with enough energy to power a city.

You wanna do the same things
You wanna go and play games,
You wanna make me stay
You wanna get in my way

I keep my head down and take it out on my guitar, but I can feel the mob weaving and waving and shouting as our sound bounces off the walls. I try to push it out, to force myself into the moment, where there is no Hank. No Nan. No dead father and no drama. It's in the beat and the buzz, and I can feel it in my feet and running up to my chest. It works. I get through the song, and we roll into another. For a while, it's perfect.

Until it isn't.

The reason we're here: a lucky video with a shining star. It's what everyone can see right now. In person, on the stream. The girl is on her way to bigger things. Bigger than me.

People are typing comments as we play, as Mal whips the skaters into shape. She knows the camera is rolling, while kids are still pouring through the doors, running around, jumping into each other, looking for someone to knock into—to share the joyful anarchy they're feeling.

By the time we get to *Can't Keep Myself*, Mal is drenched from her workout on stage. I'm turned to the side, trying to stay ahead of it, but ever since that last time here, it's been different. She's so gone, and I'm so here.

Another flub as I turn to see how they watch her. Mal whips her head to me, but I can't meet her eyes. The crowd doesn't seem to notice, bobbing and rocking along. From there, I keep my back to the crowd. Noah is completely entranced with the beat. I'm left watching my two best friends transport themselves to another world. Leaving me here.

I miss it again, my hands like the bricks I spend so much time laying. Usually my hands are part of the guitar, or the guitar is a part of me. But now, my back to the crowd, I struggle to keep it going, to get there with them.

We bang into *Your Kiss, My Fist*, the way we have to do the song now. At one point, Noah takes over, banging away for a solo. I'm happy to let him take it from there. I look to the rafters, to the bricks and the concrete of the warehouse, where men toiled away for life. Where Hank wants me to work. Maybe that's where I'm headed.

After the show, neither Mal nor Noah says a word about how awful I played. Mal gets mobbed all over again. She even signs a few autographs. Noah does Noah, running around and networking.

I keep waiting for Noah to say something about it. For Mal to ask. But they don't, and somehow, their silence only makes it worse. Because I'm left alone with one terrifying thought: If I'm messing up like this at the warehouse, how the hell am I going to play the tour?

30

"Easy dude."

Noah shoves me out of the way to rearrange his set. I've backed Barbara down the driveway, a few feet from the side porch, and now I can't help but laugh watching him take a step back, tilt his head, and then dive in again. Mal sits on the porch smirking, although it would probably be funnier if it weren't for the fresh tire tracks in the grass left by the U-Haul Noah's dad used to pack up and officially move out of the house.

I stand back as Noah fixes the blanket so it's perfect. We've just finished our last practice in the basement, and like every practice this week, things went really well. It's been a crazy week, too crazy to think, but we've found our groove. Our set is thirty minutes long, and we've narrowed down our setlist. Noah, of course, wanted to go loud and fast. Mal wanted to mix it up. I was just glad no one mentioned me sucking last Friday at the warehouse.

Noah recorded our sessions without telling me and put them up on YouTube and Soundcloud. Basically, our demo is out there, five original songs and two covers, if you want to count *Kiss on My Fist*, a cover song.

Mrs. Connors walks out to the porch, her phone stuck to her head. "Yes, hmm, hmm."

She looks up, covering the phone with her free hand. "Noah, we have a meet and greet at the tent. We have to be there by one." Mrs. Connors sees me and frowns. "Myles, are you sure you can't make it?"

Mal watches me. We've hashed this out. She wasn't thrilled at first about me meeting them down there, but Mr. Irvin and I have to see the Town Heights project through. I convinced him not to hire another body, and now we're down to the finishing touches at the absolute last minute, and I should be through by ten at the latest. It kind of works out better anyway because Hank will be at work and out of the way.

I nod to Mrs. C. It's a five-hour drive to Charlotte. We go on at seven. Again, I do the math, talking more to Mal than Noah's mom. "It's fine, really. I should make it by three, at the latest. We can probably get done early, I hope."

Mrs. C. grimaces and gets back to the phone. She's thrown herself in as our chaperone, making calls and booking rooms. She and Noah even had The Wide Awakes shirts and gear printed off, and she's going to work the merchandise booth. Noah says she's keeping herself busy so she doesn't have to think about his dad moving out.

Once she's gone, Noah throws an arm around Mal and smiles at me. "Looks like *we're* the couple act now."

Mal ducks out of his grasp and rolls her eyes. But I've made up my mind, even as Mr. Irvin would gladly let me skip out, but I can't. I need to finish this job with him. We can cash in, and I'll be on my way and should get down there with plenty of time to set up for soundcheck.

It's a decent plan, and we're sticking to it. I figure I'll play it like it's another warehouse gig and then pay the price for taking the car and leaving town when I get back. Maybe he'll make me change the oil again or wax the car. Whatever it takes, this will happen.

Noah does one last check-through of his set. Everything is cushioned and meticulous. He nods at it, talking to it, before he turns to me and sets his hand on my shoulder. "Okay dude, it's time for a talk." He looks me up and down. "About your image."

Mal sets her chin on her knees, watching from a distance as Noah gestures to my pocket tee and faded jeans. "This won't cut it on the big stage, Myles."

I sigh. "What do you suggest?"

"Glad you asked." He holds up a finger. "One sec."

He rushes up the porch and barrels inside. When he's gone, Mal gets to her feet. She approaches slowly and frowns. "I still don't like this plan."

"I know, but I can't ditch Mr. Irvin. We're on a deadline."

She closes her eyes and smiles. Something about the gesture makes me ache for our rock at the overlook. She folds her arms across her chest. "That's sweet."

"Hey, I'm a sweet guy."

She nods, lifting her head and squinting her eyes at me in a way that makes my heart twist in my chest. "You are."

The door swings open and Noah busts outside. "Here." He hands me a pair of Ray Ban Aviator sunglasses. High end, silver frame. Mirrors.

I look them over with a chuckle. "Um…"

He shrugs. "My dad left them. His fault."

I try them on. Noah shrugs. "You're still a dork, but it's better."

I turn to Mal, who nods, a small smile on her lips. "Your shield."

Later, we're in the basement when Noah pulls up some videos of last year's Warped Tour. Mal is into it, but the first thing I see is the crowd. A wild, massive, sea of people. I wander upstairs and find the bathroom, run some water over my face. With all the excitement, all the buzz about the tour, I've managed to cover up my biggest fear. But like a well nurtured plant, it keeps finding ways to sprout up, grow, stretch itself out to remind me.

Back in the basement, Noah shakes his head, talking about how badass it's going to be, this tour that we've decided will fix everything. And maybe that's it, the pressure, what his tour means to us, but seeing that crowd numbs my feet and turns my breathing shallow.

It's like one big comment section.

31

Mr. Irvin picks me up at seven Saturday morning. I walk out, relieved to see Barbara loaded down and safe. I'd checked on it from my window at six when Hank fired up his truck this morning. When he backed out, I laid my head down and exhaled. A few hours and I'll be on the road.

My boss is all ready to go, smiling more than usual, and I can tell he's relieved we're actually going to pull this off on time.

"Myles, I really appreciate all your help with this."

I shut the door, and we back out of the driveway. "Hey man, just doing my job."

"You do a fine job, too. I'll say that."

It's bright and sunny. All the bricks are laid, the pavers set. We drive out to pick up the first load of mulch. My feet won't stay still, my leg jack hammering along as Mr. Irvin laughs and asks what's going on. I tell him the Warped Tour is today as the first load of mulch comes crashing into the truck.

"What? I knew it was soon, but it's today? Why didn't you say so?"

He almost looks upset with me. I glance around. "We need to finish up, right? I was the one who said I'd get it done. I can't leave you to do all the work. Besides, as long as I hit the road before ten or eleven…"

He watches me closely for a minute, his smile gone, his eyes moving left to right with his thoughts. "Okay, well let's get you on the road then." He shakes his head. "You should've said something sooner."

Mal texts around eight. A picture of Noah asleep in the passenger seat, reclined back, head tilted to the side. Mouth open.

> Mal: It drools, too.

Damn, I wish I were in the car with them. But I'll be there soon enough.

Mr. Irvin whistles, and it's nice to see the whole project come together. A few guys come out to start planting, and we follow behind with the mulch. I can't help smiling. That we did this together, the two of us, feels good. But the closer we get to finishing, the more my heart thumps. My stomach twists. Soon, I'll be on the road.

All week, I've ignored the voice in my head whispering how I'm not ready for this, how I couldn't even play the warehouse. How it's too big for me, and I don't belong anywhere near that stage. I swallow it down. The sun is out, Mr. Irvin is whistling, and I'm determined to make this day the best one of my life.

Mr. Irvin keeps checking to see if we're doing okay on time. He's more concerned about me than the biggest contract he's ever landed. I laugh because the dude is unbelievable. I should have never told him about the show. We bust it and finish up around nine thirty to get packed up. Mr. Irvin has his check notebook out.

"You need to go to the bank, cash this?"

I just want to get to the car. "Nope, I'm good."

"Okay then."

I find my things and start gathering them up as we near the house. My breaths are already short and shaky as I pick up my thermos from the floorboard, ready to run inside, take a quick shower and get on the road. As I ball up my trash, Mr. Irvin brakes to a stop and groans in a way I've never heard him do before.

"Oh boy."

Something about the way he says it makes me turn to him. At first, I'm afraid he's having a heart attack or something from all the work. But his eyes are straight ahead, brow furrowed. Then I follow his gaze to Barbara.

The back is empty. Shiny pieces of Noah's drum set are strewn out all over the yard. The floor tom is off to the right, and the snare and some cymbals are on the other side. The road show gray of the bass drum glitters in the sun. Mic cords, the guitars, everything is out in the grass.

Mr. Irvin looks down, says, "Oh, Myles," but I can only stare dumbly through the windshield. The amp. Everything. All of it is unloaded and out of place. Mal's bass guitar lies cushioned in the grass.

I open the door, fighting for air through the ice pick that's punctured my lungs. I shiver in the ninety-degree day. Mr. Irvin's door opens and shuts behind me as I turn one way then another, unsure what to do or where to start. Empty heaves find their way up my throat as I suck down breaths. I lunge for Mal's bass guitar and inspect it, turning it over, scrunching up my nose because tears are burning behind my eyes. "I thought he was at work."

Mr. Irvin stands behind me. I look to him for an answer or explanation, still willing myself not to cry, not to believe this really happened. "I thought he…"

I thought he might let me have this. Just this once I thought he'd let me have this…

I bolt over to the wagon. The doors are locked. My hands shake as I reach in my pocket for the keys. I unlock the door and hit the power lock to pop the back locks, but nothing happens. I put the key in the ignition. Nothing.

I smack the steering wheel. I told Hank days ago we had a show tonight. I never said where, but he knew we had a show. I covered every base. I made sure everything was right. "Goddammit!"

Mr. Irvin calls my name. I ignore him, hot tears scraping my cheeks. The Ray Ban glasses Noah gave me rest on the seat. I want to smash them on the ground. I pull the lever and pop the hood. I leap out and stomp around the car where I find the latch and throw the hood open. Only an empty rectangle where the battery should be.

I'm still gaping at it when Mr. Irvin comes around. I slam down the hood as hard as I can. My knees bow out and I stumble. Everything feels loose, like I'm out of control.

"Myles."

I kick at the tire, kick it again and again until Mr. Irvin says my name in a way that I have to stop and look at him.

He glances around the yard, then to the tire I was kicking. "Look. Tell you what. Let's load it up in the truck, figure something out."

I'm dizzy from the shallow breaths, from the panic, from the rage taking hold in my chest. I turn to the house, wipe my eyes. My hands are trembling. Mr. Irvin shakes his head, some firmness in his voice. "Nothing else you can do here. Got it?"

He's right. I could go in there and start screaming at Nan, but it would do no good. I swallow down the rage. "Okay." I nod. "Okay."

We pick up each piece. We move the rakes and shovels and set a tarp over the mulch. We load down the amps, use a blanket to pad the drums and my guitar. A few times, the pieces of Noah's kit slide over each other, and it feels like I'm cutting my own skin. I wince, but Mr. Irvin says, "It's all right," in that way of his. It might be the only thing keeping me from giving up altogether.

The whole time my phone dings. More pictures from Mal. They have no idea. Nothing seems real anymore.

I gloss over the yard to make sure we got it all. It hurts to even look at the bed of the truck, our things back there with the rakes and tarps.

I'm filthy, covered in mulch. For all my planning, I never thought this would happen.

Mr. Irvin backs out. He doesn't say anything as we start up the road. I'm looking off and trying to figure something out, but my thoughts are jumbled by the quaking panic rumbling through my body. I can't stop crying. The radio hums low.

When we arrive at his house, Mr. Irvin shifts the truck in gear but doesn't kill the engine. He arches his back and reaches for his wallet.

"Why don't you take the truck?"

A spark of hope. He's pulling out money, but I can't accept it. I shake my head. Another burn of pressure to my eyes. "Mr. Irvin, I—"

"No, no. Now, listen to me." He gestures with his head toward the bed of the truck. "We'll knot everything tight, double check it. It's not quite eleven yet so you should be fine."

His voice is steady and sure, and he's got this look in his eye I've never seen before. Usually he's light and easy going, but now he's not asking me, he's telling me what I'm going to do. "I'm sure you won't have any trouble, but you have my number. Anything happens, I've got the car here. I can come down."

Since spring, I've been working with this old man who whistles and jokes while hauling loads of bricks or sand. He's taught me how to set a corner pole and build a lead at the edge when laying the bricks. He talks so openly about fears and passions. Now he's trying to teach something else, and it's all I can do to manage a breath and try to move the weight off my chest.

"Go do this, Myles." His stormy eyes hold a spark of intensity. Not angry or violent but urgent and hopeful. It's like he's trying to fill me with the courage and strength I don't feel right now.

"Here," he says, shaking a handful of twenties at me. "For gas, and don't you dare say no because we don't have time to argue."

I do what he says. We get the rakes and shovels out of the way and secure everything in the back. I thank him again and he shoos me off. I start down the road, fixing mirrors and getting a feel for the truck and trying not to focus on anything but driving.

It's going on 1:00 as I get to the Virginia/North Carolina border, when my thoughts shift from dizzying rage to reality. I'm still wearing my work clothes, stained and sweaty, but I keep following the GPS to Greensboro then the Interstate and then my exit. My phone is less than halfway charged and keeps dinging with happy messages from Mal.

At first, it's simple driving. Math. How long until I should get there. How the papers on the dashboard flutter in the wind. Then, as I hit Greensboro and the busy rush of the Interstate, it's more about seething over Hank and what he did. After that, as the miles pile up and Mr. Irvin's clarity and strength begin to waver, I catch myself in the mirror. I'm struck by the fear staring back at me.

Now it's all about me.

My foot eases off the gas. I swallow dryly as I trail behind a tractor trailer and check the rearview. The tarp is still secure, tied tight and sure-knotted by Mr. Irvin.

I turn the radio off, then back on. I search for a station and spend the next couple of hours slogging through delays, detours, lane closures and construction. When traffic halts, and I'm at a complete stop with nothing but the tight grip of doubt that's been slowly squeezing in my chest since Mal told us about the tour, I realize it's no longer about *getting* there. I'm worried about *being* there.

A gust of my breath hits the windshield as a much heavier doubt consumes me. I'm not good enough to do this. The moment is too big for me. I relive the warehouse. How badly I played. How all eyes were on Mal.

I mentally reread over every comment about myself until it's like I'm sitting at the table with Hank. I see him shaking his head, stroking his goatee. He knew I couldn't do it all along.

My phone lights up.

> Mal: Are you close?

Every hope and dream our band ever had rests in the back of the truck as I hit a snag and crawl down I-85.

> Mal: Okay, so Noah can't do interviews
> anymore...

I DRIVE around the gleaming buildings of downtown Charlotte. Signs and exits and arrows send drivers all over the place. I've made it, or at least the truck has made it. But I'm still scattered in the yard back at Nan's house.

After only a few more exits, everything starts squeezing in. Cars fight for space. "All right," I say to the phone, searching for my exit, refusing to admit how this is going to play out when I already know. It's already happened. I feel it in my limbs as I try to merge into the right lane where traffic is backed up.

EVENT PARKING signs direct the clogged lanes. Drivers fight for position, trying to merge with the vans and campers, smaller cars packed with clothes, coolers, and bikes on racks. I'm still trying to get over, but everything is bunched up. When things grind to a halt again, I check my phone.

Mal: I need you here!

My chest tightens. It's four o'clock, and I'm pushing it. Still stuck in traffic, waves of vehicles converge on the tour to watch the bands. This is not the warehouse. This is the real thing. Real bands. Real exposure. And I have our equipment in the back of a pickup truck because Hank threw it all over the yard.

I tap on the wheel, nodding, talking through my ragged breaths and begging the doubt to go away, to stop climbing up my chest to my throat. I get back to the radio dial. Someone honks, people hang out of the windows as we inch forward.

EVENT PARKING

Almost there. A single raindrop hits the windshield. And that drop is too much weight.

I can't do this. I knew it all along. Before I left, before Hank ruined everything. I've always known.

I throw my head around and look over my left shoulder. Semi-trucks go screaming past the congestion. Mostly everyone else is turning off, heading to the event. My hands shake, and my breaths grow raspy. I go to pull out of my lane and nearly get sideswiped as a truck lays on the horn. I brake, waving frantically, eyes pooling, wishing I could overcome this.

Then I spot an opening between trucks.

Again, the right lane scoots forward, and we start to move. Then, in my mirror, on my left, I spot an opening in the left lane. An escape.

Before it's too late, I take the clearing and gun the truck for the left lane. The rebuilt engine catches, before I roar ahead into the stream of moving traffic, away from the stage, my band, and every hope and dream and lie I let myself believe for so long.

<h1 style="text-align:center">32</h1>

I'M SIX YEARS OLD, PLAYING MUSIC WITH MY DAD IN THE kitchen. It's late when he busts into my room, wild-eyed and excited as he rouses me from bed. He wants to jam and needs me to hold the tambourine.

I do my best, but I can't keep up with him. I shake the tambourine, but it's offbeat—*too fast, no Myles, too slow.* I try again, still in my pajamas, wiping my eyes. My hair is spiky from sleep. I switch hands, jingling, concentrating to get it just right for him. But I can't do it.

He stops playing. I stop, too. He makes a phone call and says we're going to a friend's house. I smile, happy to be included.

It's dark in the car, only the greenish glow of the dashboard as my dad fiddles with the radio, lights a cigarette, and drives fast. He tussles my hair, singing along to the music. It's loud. He's loud. Everything is so loud.

He parks the car and gets out. The door shuts, and off he goes, singing to himself. Suddenly it's quiet, and I don't know if I'm supposed to follow him into the house or wait but then he's inside and I'm in the car. The dashboard is dark, only the smoke from his cigarette remains. I can't tell if he's forgotten about me, but I'm too scared to move.

It gets cold fast. I shiver. I can't sleep. Moments pass, hours or minutes, and I keep waiting for the door to open, for the dashboard to light up and glow, for the heat to turn on and my dad to tussle my hair and light a smoke. But he never comes back.

And I never see him again.

MY PHONE CONTINUES to light up with messages the entire drive back home. I ignore them and tuck the phone away along with the guilt, the urges, the sharp pangs of urgency—the voice screaming in my head that I've thrown everything away. I simply drive. I let the tarp snap in the wind, breathing the swirl of dirt and dust from our jobs.

An hour later, when it's too late to change my mind again, I pull off for gas. I follow the signs to the station, the evening sun level with my eyes as I drive down a curb-less, single-lane road and through an intersection. I pass the station and have to turn around in a gravel lot, in front of an abandoned house. I stop there as it fully hits me what I've done.

It's exactly seven o'clock. We're supposed to be huddled up, laughing at our luck, filled with magic and ready to take our shot, ready to drink in the biggest moment of our lives.

Hank was right all along.

EVENTUALLY, I get back on the road. The blanket of night helps my drive. Tucked away, with nothing but a void of blackness surrounding me, I'm able to simply hold the steering wheel and press the gas pedal without much thought. It's a little after eleven when I get to Mr. Irvin's house. The porch light is on, but the windows are black. I take a minute to sit in the truck, not really wanting to wake him but not sure what else to do.

Thing is, I have a few thousand dollars' worth of equipment I need to put somewhere, so I force myself out of the truck and walk to the door.

Three quick knocks, and I wait. A light flips on, then another. Mr. Irvin appears in the room. He walks to the door and looks out. I just want to run, but I can't outrun the shame. It lives inside me. Its weight like a heavy awning over my eyes, forcing me to stare at the ground as he unlocks the deadbolt.

He opens the door and I expect something like, "Myles?" and for him to ask what in the world I'm doing here. But he doesn't. He sets a hand on my shoulder and looks past me to the truck.

"Hang on," he says softly. "I'll help you get everything unloaded."

I stand in the quiet house as he gets changed, the hardwood floors whining under my fidgety steps. He returns dressed in khakis and a frayed button down. I start to put an explanation together, something about traffic or rain or anything, when it all sort of falls out of me.

He reaches out and catches me as I fold over and break. With a gasp, I try again, but I can't choke out the words. Mr. Irvin sets an arm around me. "Myles, son. Hey…"

I fall into him, and he wraps me up. I sink my head into his chest as a shuddering, hiccupping sob overtakes me. I try to tell him but only roll my head and wail as I manage to fall apart over and over again. He rubs my back. My shoulders convulse as it rolls through me. The day's anguish, its failures and regrets, the doubt that's been eating away at me from the inside out until it finally consumed me.

At some point, I get myself together enough to pull away, set my palms to my eyes. The realization that I'm crying, where I am and what I've done fully takes hold. I start to apologize for being such a burden when I notice Mr. Irvin's eyes are welling.

His gaze holds no judgement or shame. Even tearing up, he's as comfortable as I've ever seen him. He patiently waits me out. It's not something I'm used to, this show of feelings, fears, crying—I've always been told it's a sign of weakness. But this man, with shelves full of poetry, who plays piano, who has seen war and death, even lost his wife and child, seems to be okay with the bouts of silence between tears.

He laces up his boots and we unload the truck. In the light of the garage, my heart drops seeing the dings and scratches on Noah's drums. Mr. Irvin carefully handles Mal's bass, complete with the new stickers she'd bought just for this tour. He sets it by the chair next to my guitar. When we're through, we stand in the garage and survey the wreckage. I'm expecting him to offer me a ride home, but he asks if I want to stay and talk.

I leave my phone in the truck. I can't face what it holds right now. Disappointing myself was one thing. Ruining this chance for my two best friends is an unforgivable sin.

Back inside, it continues to settle into my bones what I've done to them. It expands with every breath. "I'm so sorry, Mr. Irvin. It's just that, I'm… there's no coming back from this, is there?"

He removes his boots and grunts. "You'd be surprised."

I clasp my hands behind my head. "This was our shot, everything. For the band this was all we ever dreamed about. Now it's gone." My voice fades as the tears threaten to return. The hurt is catching up to me now. Sharp, painful breaths. I fight it off. "I want to blame Hank for everything, but I got to the show, thanks to you. I got there, and I couldn't do it. I physically could not do it."

He regards me for few seconds, as though fully digesting what I've said. I close my arms around my head until my elbows touch. There's nothing, now. Nothing left at all. Maybe this is it, what my father felt. What drove him down.

"Myles, have a seat."

I find the edge of the couch and set my forehead into my hands.

"Myles, I know," he says, something in his voice catching me. I raise my head, thinking he's going to tell me a war story. Or about losing his family. He's experienced a lot of awful things in his lifetime. More than I can imagine. He takes a deep breath. "What I mean is, I know all too well about regret."

I turn to him. His gaze finds the mantel. He studies the piano, the silent instruments sitting by the wall. "A few months after I came home, I wasn't sure what was supposed to happen next. On a whim, I reached out to the Frampton Academy. I was surprised to learn my offer was still valid." His voice falters. "They'd held a spot for me."

I wipe my eyes and take this in. "Wait, you mean the classical school. Like, the scholarship?"

He shifts in his seat, nods. "Yes," he says, his voice scraping over the word. I study him as a clock clicks on the mantel. "I'd seen so much by then, Myles. So many awful things. I'd done awful things, too. And after that, even after I'd called to find out, I couldn't get myself to go. I didn't believe I had anything good left in me."

I sit back on the couch and blink my eyes. Mr. Irvin waits for me. He doesn't try to hammer home a moral or message, just lets it sit between us in the dark, with only the clock ticking and the shiny instruments waiting. The books of poetry.

"What do I do now?"

Mr. Irvin rubs his hands on his legs. "That's the thing. I moved on, or, I lived with it and never looked back until it was too late. Well, that's not true. I always regretted it, always wished I'd done it, even the other day when we played together. Especially then. But this dream of yours, it's not gone, Myles. You can still go after it."

I rub my face. "I don't think so."

"It's just a different path now."

I want to believe him. I do. But there's no path that gets me back there. This was everything, and I threw it all away. I took the path Hank always knew I would take.

33

THE NEXT MORNING, I WAKE UP IN A STRANGE BED, ONLY it's not strange at all. The sun leaks through the curtains, shining on a polished dresser and a framed painting of a jazz musician. I stretch, still safely cocooned in the new day's grogginess until last night jolts me awake.

The shame avalanche comes crashing down all over again. My mind swarms with possibilities, but the only real outcome to this is facing my bandmates. Facing Hank. Facing myself every day.

Mr. Irvin has made coffee. I slide into the little bar that separates the living room from the kitchen. It doesn't seem like the same place in the morning sunlight as it did last night, when he talked about the war, and I confessed that I'm nothing but a scared kid in the small glow of the lamplight

I keep my head down when he asks how I'm holding up. I shrug and try my best to be polite. He offers a ride home, but I'm good to walk. I need to walk.

I retrieve my phone from the truck and walk back in to thank him one more time. He has the paycheck notebook out.

"Almost forgot to give you this."

"Oh, yeah. Well, you gave me gas money, and a truck to drive to Charlotte and back for no reason, so…"

He shakes his head. "You've earned this."

I accept the check, my gaze still on the floor. He offers breakfast, but I'm too fidgety to sit or eat. All I can think about is Hank, the band. Mal. How I'm ever going to fix things.

I thank Mr. Irvin again. As I get to the door, he calls out. "Myles, one more thing. If it gets too bad, or if… things don't go well, just knock on the door, you hear? Anytime."

This time I bring my head up and meet his gaze. Still, it was easier to face him last night in the dark when everything felt different. But I force myself to nod and thank him again. I don't know what would have happened without hm.

Now, all I can think about is Mal and Noah, and what I've done to them.

34

IT MIGHT BE THE FIRST TIME IN MY ENTIRE LIFE THAT the sight of Hank's truck in the driveway doesn't set a hitch in my step. Not today, and maybe not ever again. What can he do to me after yesterday? There's nothing left to take.

I enter the living room to the familiar smells of a thick, meaty breakfast, Pine-Sol, and hopelessness. Pans sit soaking in the sink, awaiting Nan to degrease them. I start for my room when Hank calls from the den. "Myles, that you?"

"Yeah."

The deep grovel of his voice doesn't overpower me the way it usually does. I turn and stop at the doorway. He's on his recliner, wearing his usual basketball shorts. Diet Dr. Pepper on the table. It's three minutes after ten.

He's waiting for me to ask about the car. I should, but I can't bring myself to give him the satisfaction. He pries his gaze from the TV to me. I'm filthy, still in yesterday's clothes. He looks me up and down.

"You at work today?"

I shrug. "You could say that."

His eyes flick up at the sound of my tone. He cuts to the chase.

227

"The car." He's already shaking his head. "I don't know where you thought you were taking it, but—"

"Charlotte, North Carolina."

He stops, "What?"

I say it louder, pronouncing it as clearly as I can. "Charlotte, North Carolina. That's where I was taking the car. Our band was invited to play the Warped Tour. The local news did a story about it. It was a pretty big deal."

I blink once, forcefully, determined not to cry. He looks away and shakes his head. "Yeah, guy at work said something about it. It's why I came home and unloaded the car. You never asked to take it. And it's filthy, smells too. Need you to clean it out today. Carpet shampoo, the works."

I need to give the car a once over anyway to see if any cords or adapters were left behind. "Okay."

Hank nods, as though the point is settled. I turn for my room again when he calls me back. "You thought anymore about that position? They're looking to fill it early next week."

I stop. For some reason a smile emerges on my face. I'm almost looking forward to having it out with him for once. "No, not at all."

"Oh, really," he says, eager for confrontation. "Let me put it to you like this. You need to get your priorities in order. I'm only trying to help you here."

I start down the hallway but my strength falters at the sound of the recliner's lever. My throat dries as the panic sets in. This house has a way of chopping me down. The chair tips up, and he gets to his feet.

I'm almost to my room, but his footsteps ring through the kitchen, down the hallway. "How about tomorrow?"

At my doorway, I stop and turn to him. "What about tomorrow?"

He cuffs the back of my head. The thread holding me together snaps. I spin around, enraged. His eyes light up as he takes a small step back. But he recovers quickly. "You don't listen, Myles. I'll bring you in, talk about the position. Tomorrow."

Hank is the reason I didn't take that exit last night. He might as well have been sitting beside me, screaming at me. Telling me I couldn't do it. And up until now, part of me has always believed him. But I don't believe him now. I'm not missing any more chances. I'm through giving in to fear.

I close the distance between us, my shoulders square as I realize I'm at least an inch taller than he is. Somehow my voice is strong and steady. "I don't want the job. And I don't want you to touch me again."

"That right?"

"Yes, it is." I turn and walk into my room, realizing I'd rather be homeless than stay one more night here.

"Don't walk away from me."

I glare at him, almost daring him to walk in. When he doesn't, I grab a change of clothes and some money stashed in a drawer. I'm all set to turn around and leave when I see my notebook, turned to the song I was working on the other day. "Dashboard." A line on the page hits me hard. I'm still staring at it when Hank settles in the doorway.

"I told you not to walk away from me," he huffs.

I pick up the notebook and try to picture Hank in my room, reading it. Something about the thought fills me with rage. My knuckles go white as I grip my bag. Hank still leers at me, blocking my path as he has so many times. He throws his chest out before his gaze falls to my clenched fist. A burn of tears hits between my eyes as I realize I'm shaking with anger. I force it down and look into his eyes.

"I'm leaving."

"The hell you are," he shakes his head. He looks at the notebook. I set my jaw, determined not to let him take this from me. He shifts his weight again and inches closer the way he does to make me feel small. But not today. I left small back in the dark with Mr. Irvin last night.

I glare at him until he looks away. A single word leaves my mouth. "Why?"

Hearing the question, his confidence returns. "You got work to do, for one." He rubs his goatee, but I hold my ground. He nods to the bag. "Where do you think you're going, anyway?"

"Why?" I repeat it louder, my voice breaking some. His brow furrows.

"Why, what? I just said you've got chores to do."

I'm not letting it go. He's done this for too long. I'd rather be punched and kicked and beaten than wonder any longer. I only want answers. My eyes blur with tears. "Why?" I shout it at him, my voice ugly and breaking, a rusted hinge on the verge of collapse. "Do you think it helped me? When you beat me with a belt? Or your hand? When you stripped me down and told me I wasn't good enough?"

There's a squeak in the hallway. Hank turns his head, maybe to Nan cowering behind the walls. He takes a breath, shrinking before me. "I've told you why. To make you a better man. Look, Myles, it's like my father told me—"

"That's bullshit! I want to know why."

He takes a step back, eyes wider than I thought possible. "Now look, Myles. Listen to me. You think—"

"No. Not 'look Myles.' I'm done with 'look Myles.' I'm done." Another footstep creaks in the hallway, and I know Nan is there listening. "Look at me." I point to my brow. "Look at this scar on my face."

Hank shuts his mouth. I take a breath to regain my composure. "So you know, I took Mr. Irvin's truck. I got down there, to Charlotte yesterday, to the biggest show of my life, and I was too afraid." I stop and breathe. "I ruined everything because I was scared shitless." My voice breaks again. Hank blinks as I slap my chest and spread my arms out. "You win, Hank. You beat me. What else can you take from me? There's nothing left."

He glances right again. "What do you mean you got down there?"

His confusion is genuine and gives me an opening. I shoulder past him, his arm like warm butter as he grunts and falls back a step. I push through and charge down the hallway, past Nan gaping with her dishrag, ignoring her like she ignored me so many times when I needed her. When I get to the door, Hank has recovered. He sounds like himself again. "If you leave this house, don't you bother coming back."

I stop and turn around. I want to make this clear. "I'm not coming back, Hank. You're going to have to find the courage to climb that ladder on your own from now on." I look at Nan, still waiting for her to say something, anything. She doesn't. I shrug. "Goodbye."

The door slams behind me, as though sealing in all the fear and doubt and every hopeless night I spent on my bed staring up at the ceiling. I stumble out to the driveway but stop at the car. I reach in and grab the sunglasses. I set them on my face and hit the street.

35

My breaths come in wheezing spurts, a sharp pain crashing in and out as my lungs feel like a cactus in my chest. The clash with Hank has left my legs rubbery and my throat tight. The sweat on my back makes me shiver.

I power up my phone and send a text to Mal, then Noah. I try to call, but no one answers. My phone dies. There's nothing left.

Home, band, friends, it's all been swallowed up in one night. All I can think about is those few lines I found in my notebook. It's a strange time for a song to appear so loudly in my head, as though it wrote itself. I end up at the park, hiking down the trail to the overlook because it's the only sure thing in my life right now. A song in my notebook. It won't leave me alone.

I drop my bag and climb the rock, catching a whiff of myself. My shirt from yesterday is littered with dirt, sweat, and probably a few tears. My jeans are no better off.

Dashboard. My dad's face in its glow. The warning lights, the gauges, dings and beeps, the cold settling in as I await his return, his smile, for him to tussle my hair and tell me it's okay. *Dashboard.* Playing his guitar, Mal smiling at me. Noah behind us keeping the beat. The electrifying minutes as we play, where the world fades and everything feels right. The music is ours until we share it. *Dashboard.* Likes. Dislikes. Comments. Notifications.

For two years, I've only thought about the band. Music was going to be my way out of Nan's house. My only escape. Even as Mal was the voice and Noah was the manager, I'd always thought it mattered most to me—that I needed it more than they did. Now, sitting on the rock, alone without the soft evening glow, I gaze out to the trestle and realize it wasn't so much the band I needed, but them.

I set my forehead to my knees. I'm wondering for the thousandth time why I couldn't make myself go to the show when the faint chugging of a train passes through the trees. Some birds scatter off as its whistle pierces the cloudless day.

The train pulls across the horizon. I think of Mal, her little kid smile, how she scrambles to her feet whenever we're lucky enough to catch one. The way she points to the trestle, as though I have no idea where to look, until the cars rumble and click, one after another in rhythm like a song. I'm still smiling about it when the train passes, leaving me alone with my thoughts again. I turn to the notebook.

I write furiously, scribble it out and start over again. I think about the glow of the phone as I await the comments, the approval of someone, anyone, the crumbling hope when the people closest to you to leave you alone and cold again. I sing out parts of it, surprising myself at the strength of my voice, the conviction in my words, until the song appears. Then another idea hits, one I hope I have the courage to see through.

———

I'M NOT sure Mr. Irvin is expecting me back so soon when I show up at his door, again, with a bag of clothes in one hand and a notebook in the other, flushed and crazy about the song. My plan.

"Oh," he manages as I blow in and pace his floor, talking fast about how I stood up to Hank. How I saw the notebook and heard

Mr. Irvin's song on the piano, and it hit me all at once. I stop and start again, arranging words and thoughts that seem to be spilling out beyond my control.

"I want to do the song with you."

"With me? You want me to play?" he asks, as though he doesn't quite understand.

"You don't have to, but I was thinking. Can you wait a second? Let me just...." I rush to the garage and find my father's guitar. I rush back in and pull up a stool. "Here. Can I?"

"Certainly."

We plug in, and I strum out a few chords and explain what I have in mind. He rubs his chin, a small smile on his face. "That might work."

I get to my feet, excited but scared. My feet are like ice, but my brain is on fire. I run a hand through my hair. Mr. Irvin suggests I take a shower while he works through it on the piano. I laugh. "Yeah, that's probably a good idea."

The shower gives me time to second guess it all, but I push away from the doubt. I'm not backing out. I have to do this. I owe it to Mal and Noah and even more to myself. I charge my phone and find that I have no new messages. I figured as much. What I did isn't the kind of thing you just brush off and move on from.

Mr. Irvin sits at the piano, ready and waiting. We go through a few practice sessions, working it out. My foot bounces with excitement because it works so well, our songs—our regrets—fit together perfectly. There's only one problem.

"I hate my voice."

"I know the feeling," he says. "But trust me, it's not as bad as you think."

"Gee, thanks."

He laughs. "Let's do a full run, and don't be embarrassed on my account."

I laugh, nod, and take a breath before plowing through our new version of *Dashboard.*

We cut and add words and verses. I have three pages of scrawl to work with, so I tinker with it until I realize I'm stalling. After an hour or more, I declare I'm ready as I will ever be. Then I drop the bombshell on him.

"I want to record it, post it to our channel. Sort of an apology to Mal and Noah."

Surprisingly, Mr. Irvin doesn't flinch. "I'm old and out of friends, so it won't bother me at all."

We fill the house with nervous laughter. Then all goes still. I swallow it down and set my phone in place. Then, I press the button and try to forget about it.

"My name is Myles Bennett and I'm the guitarist for The Wide Awakes. Because of me, we didn't make our set at the Warped Tour, and I'd like to publicly apologize to my bandmates and best friends, Noah and Mal. I'm sorry. I know that isn't good enough, but..." I shift, my fingers finding the chords. I nod to Mr. Irvin. "Hopefully this song will better explain it."

I turn to Mr. Irvin. "On piano here is Mr. George Irvin, and together we're going to do a song we've been working on all our lives. It's called *Dashboard*."

We count it down. Mr. Irvin's fingers find the keys, and I strum out the opening chords, which match up to his notes. I close my eyes and take a deep breath. And in that moment, it feels like a snowy morning under the pines. It's where I need to be to sing my song. My confessional, apology, my promise to myself that I will see this through.

I manage to forget about the phone, and we simply play. We arrive at that magical place and capture four and a half minutes of freedom. I close my eyes, leaving my dingy room and find myself back in the car, the closest I've ever felt to my dad, my fears, and myself as we climb higher and higher before crashing down to an end. I press stop and look at Mr. Irvin. He nods.

"That was something."

The world returns, and I exhale. Mr. Irvin has a gleam in his eyes, and I feel it, too, as the song exits the room. I may never make things right with Mal and Noah again, but I want them to know I'm trying.

I don't even watch the video. Noah gave us the login for the band's YouTube channel a long time ago, but I almost hope he's changed the password as I get logged in and find the place to load new videos. I glance at Mr. Irvin, and then I upload *Dashboard*.

Mr. Irvin smiles at me. "I've always wondered what I'd do with that piece. Turns out I was just waiting for you to come along and show me."

We sit for a minute in silence as the song is posted. I don't care about likes or comments or anything else. I only want two people to see it.

36

I WAIT. MAL DOESN'T RETURN MY TEXTS, AND I SPEND THE day hanging in some sort of in between. The song was all I had, and now with it done, I don't have anything else to focus on. I've stood up to Hank, but it's left me here, with nowhere to go and unsure of what's next.

Mr. Irvin must sense my discomfort because he suggests we head out to look at a few upcoming jobs. I'm thankful for tagging along. On the way out, curiosity gets the better of me, and I check the video. I'm surprised to find it's doing well. Again, I don't know how this stuff works, but it's closing in on a thousand views and most of the feedback is positive. I'm surprised at a few that mention my singing. Words like *soulful, real, raw,* and *heartbreaking*.

Mr. Irvin sees me smiling. "How's our video doing?"

"Pretty good. Seems the piano player is a big hit."

Mr. Irvin throws his head back.

We putter around town and check on a few leads, enough to keep us busy while we wait on the next big job. Mr. Irvin has something on his mind, though, judging by the way he's gazing through the windshield when we pull off the road and come to a stop. I'm thinking it's the video when he kills the engine and pulls the keys from the ignition.

"Myles, look. Earlier when I said you could stay whenever."

Damn, I've already overstayed my welcome. "Yeah, I'll figure something out. I didn't mean to be a pain."

He shakes his head, removes the keys from the ignition. He starts fiddling with the keyring. "No, not at all. What I'm trying to say is, well... here." He takes off a key and offers it to me. I stare at it in his rough, big hand. I open my mouth but can't find anything to say. He nods. "Like I said, you can stay as long as you need."

I look to my lap, then back to his hand. He nods again, and I reach out and take the key. "Mr. Irvin, I... It would be just for a bit."

He closes his eyes. "As long as you need. It's my pleasure."

"I don't know what to say. Thank you."

"You're welcome. And this way you won't be late."

I laugh and slide my hand across my eyes. "And you wouldn't have to pick me up."

"Right."

We price out a few jobs. It's around four in the afternoon when my phone buzzes, and my heart flies with hope. I glance down, and when I see Noah's name, I almost hyperventilate.

Noah: Where you at?

I give him Mr. Irvin's address, take a deep breath and exhale with a nervous laugh. I check my phone again just to be sure and realize my hands are shaking.

Crazy to think facing my friends might be harder than facing Hank.

37

When we get back home, Mal's sitting at the curb. Mr. Irvin says something, but I don't hear anything as I watch Mal get to her feet and shield her eyes from the sun. My legs tighten, then push me back into the seat. Mr. Irvin pulls in and parks the truck. I draw a sharp breath.

When I emerge from the truck, I'm no closer to figuring out the right words to say to her. We meet in the driveway, and she gives me nothing to go on, her face devoid of expression and her arms crossed over a lavender Warped Tour t-shirt. She stands a few feet from me with one foot out, toeing at the curb. I open my mouth to speak, but a searing panic floods my chest, my thoughts tripping over each other while evacuating my head.

Mr. Irvin goes straight for the garage. Mal watches him with interest, still clutching her arms over her chest as the door to the house opens and shuts, leaving me alone to face whatever happens next.

She takes a breath and glosses over me. Her eyes are puffy, glistening and shining in the sun. She doesn't look angry, or even upset, maybe a little concerned, but mostly blank. It leaves me trying to fill in the void. For reasons I can't explain, I say, "Where's Noah?"

She takes a quick glance to the road. "He's coming. I asked him to let me talk to you first."

Her voice is soft, weak, and I don't know if that's good or bad. She seems perfectly content to hold me with her eyes. It's more than I can take. I drop my arms to my sides. "Mal, I'm so sorry."

Her mouth tightens. She's still clutching her elbows. I can't read her, so I dive into an explanation, talking fast, trying to stay ahead of what I'm feeling. "Hank came home early and sort of ruined things, but Mr. Irvin let me drive his truck. I got all the way to Charlotte, then I sort of crumbled. I can't believe I did this to you guys, and I'll spend my life trying to make it up to both of you."

I'm still talking when Mal unfolds her arms. She closes her eyes and steps forward suddenly, taking my face in her hands the way she did in the basement before we kissed. It works. My mouth stops, and I'm silenced by the blinding urgency in her eyes. She pulls me to her, and our lips meet, slow and deliberate, then building as my confusion melts into hunger. She surprises me as her mouth opens wider and I kiss her back with everything I've held in since the tenth grade, since her arm brushed against mine in art class.

She pulls away, her hands sliding from my head to my shoulders. Her eyes search mine as she tilts her head, almost with a smile, her voice low. "I had every intention of never speaking to you again."

I'm too afraid to smile or even move out of fear it will make this less real. But she comes in and kisses me again, deep and intentional, and then I'm pulling her into me. She laughs a little, and I kiss her forehead, her nose, and her lips. It's as natural as all the times we've written songs together and spilled our secrets to each other. I guess we're sort of doing both.

When we break apart, she's fiddling with her hands, but she's not acting worried like last time, not surprised or afraid. Instead, she looks almost relieved. Certain.

She grins. "Oh man, let me tell you something. Noah and I were discussing ways to torture you. We were going to make you suffer something terrible. And then Noah found the video and," she shakes her head. "Now I'm here, doing this."

"What changed?"

Her eyes fly open. "You did."

<h1 style="text-align:center">38</h1>

"So, do you want to hear about it?" Mal asks.

We've managed to make our way into Mr. Irvin's garage, with the normal smells of oil and grit mingled with the pleasant aroma of Mal's lotion.

I suck in a breath and let it out. "Yeah."

She looks over her bass for damage and sets it down. Her shoulders go up as she takes a deep breath. "Around four, I started to panic. I was thinking maybe you were stuck in traffic or having car trouble." Her eyes catch mine. "*Hank* trouble. So, we kept texting. I called, even left messages. We watched StatBoy go through soundcheck, and they were really kickass, but nothing felt right. There was this little voice in my head telling me you weren't coming."

I wipe my palms on my jeans. "Yeah, I..."

She shakes her head, cuts her eyes to me. "Hang on, Myles. Let me get this out."

Mal takes a seat but then quickly changes her mind. She stands. She leans against the refrigerator and arches her back. My breath catches. Even after the kissing, and well, the kissing, the guilt of what I did to them keeps ringing inside me like a bell struck by a hammer. Especially now, seeing how hard it is for her to talk about.

A few seconds go by as she gathers her thoughts. She places both hands behind her back and gazes off. "So, it's time for us to set up. and Mrs. Connors, who, wow, really came out of her shell by the way, was getting worried. She was talking to the staff and asking for Nan's number. Noah was grumbling, being all Noah because it was looking like we were going to miss our soundcheck. We sold like four shirts by the way," she laughs. "Still have a few boxes of them to go."

"Well at least something good came out of this."

Mal gives me a hint of a smile. "Hang on, now. Lots to tell. Things were getting hectic, but we were still more worried about you than anything else. Even Noah was more worried than pissed, and we were sort of wandering around lost when some dude with an Irish accent called for us, like, "Hey you two. Wanna help us out over here?' and we looked up and it was Nash Finnegan."

I grab the sides of my head. My eyes go wide. "Liar."

She shakes her head. "Myles, you should have *seen* Noah. I had to do the talking, at least initially, because Noah's jaw dropped like a cartoon. He was com*pletely* fanboying."

"I don't believe this. You guys... *Noah*, met Nash Finnegan?"

"It was something. We met all the Finnegan brothers, and they were asking about us and talking about *our* videos and how they loved our cover of *Your Kiss, My Fist*. It's a thing now, by the way."

"This is... I don't even know."

"Myles. Please. It gets better."

"How?"

She closes her eyes. Her little smile grows a bit more. "Once Noah was able to form words, he and Nash Finnegan make some sort of redhead connection. I'm serious, it was like, spiritual or something."

I keep my hands on my head as Mal continues. "As this is happening, six turns into to seven and still no you, and yeah Noah is bummed, but he's connected himself to Nash Finnegan's hip.

Meanwhile, I'm blowing up your phone, but it was still nice to see Noah so giddy. Mrs. Connors eventually came over and said that it looked like we were going to have to cancel. unless we think we can still be able to go on, which, I mean, how? So they bumped up the next band to our slot, and that was that."

I stare at the tattered and stained Persian rug on the floor. "I thought you said the story got *better*?"

Mal holds up a single finger. Her eyes flash in the dark garage. "Quick note, Nash Finnegan likes your raw ability. He said you remind him of himself when he was starting out. So there, that said I never, *ever* want to hear a word about the comments. Ever. I'm serious."

I roll my eyes. "He did not."

"I promise on my bass guitar." She walks over and taps the guitar twice. "After our set was canceled, I roamed about the restricted area, sort of star gazing and sort of sulking, when I nearly run into some chick and she's like *sorry* and I'm like *sorry* but then she looks at me and smiles. Myles. It was Mia Ramos!"

I drop my hands. "What? No. Mal, holy shit. *What?*"

Mal lets out a smile almost too big for her face. It reaches her eyes, and I can't help but smile back. She throws her hands up. "Right? But hang on, she's like, 'I was just coming to watch your set.'"

"She said that? Mia Ramos was coming to watch *us?*" Mal turns to me, and I realize what I said and what it means. "Shit."

Mal gets back to the story. "I told her I wasn't going on, and she was like, 'The hell you're not.' She took my hand." Mal holds up her left hand. "This unwashed hand. And led me to a tent where there was a little jam session going on. She pointed to a stool, and I took a seat. Myles, I can't even describe it."

"Hold on, hold on. So you jammed with Mia Ramos?"

She bites her lip and nods. "And Party Trash."

I look out the open bay door. "Wow." Suddenly I'm filled with too much at once. I'm heartbroken for not showing up. I'm jealous, regretful, and confused, but also so happy for them.

"Yeah Myles. It was a life changing moment. It was surreal and amazing, and I still can't believe it happened. I looked around and thought I was dreaming. I was surrounded by phenomenal musicians from all over the world. And it was when I realized something."

She steps closer, looking at me in a way that nearly brings me to my knees. She takes my hand and laces her fingers through mine. "None of them were you."

I turn to her. "Mal," I start in a whisper, her warm hand in mine, not sure if this means what I think it means. I wonder if my body will ever stop having a chemical reaction to her. Probably not. I hope not.

She grips my other hand in hers. "I've always hoped you would see what I see." She presses her body against me, knocking back a lock of hair from her eyes. "And when I saw that video, your song, I realized you'd found it." She smiles. "You see it now. Right?"

I smile at her, wobbly, dizzy, unable to look away from her eyes. "I think so. I mean, as terrible as I feel about flaking out, which is pretty damn terrible, I stood up to Hank. I was in my room, and I saw that song, something I'd written down, and it fell into place. Maybe like, saying goodbye to the house meant I could say goodbye to my dad. Everything sort of rained down on me. Does that make sense?"

She nods slowly. Then her face changes. "Wait, what do you mean, *goodbye?*"

I can't help my smile. "Oh, I'm staying here for a while."

Her mouth falls open. "What?" She drops my hand then snatches it up again, her blue nails digging into my palm.

"It's true."

I shrug. I knew she wanted me out of that house, but it isn't until she wipes her eyes with the back of her hand that I realize just how much it means to her. How much I mean to her. "I'm so happy for you." She glances to the garage door. "I need to meet this Mr. Irvin guy."

"You will, and I can't believe it either. But, I still ruined everything. I don't know how to make it up to you."

Mal stops, then shoots me a sidelong glance.

"What?"

"Well, you did basically ruin the Warped Tour."

I pinch the bridge of my nose. My gaze falls to the floor. Mal steps closer, pressing against me. "But that make it up to me thing? You might get another crack at that."

I draw back and take her in again. I feel like I'm on a seesaw with Mal. Kissing her. Letting down the band. Kissing her. Ruined the Warped Tour. "What are you saying?"

A blast of music erupts from the street as Noah's car pulls up to the curb. I tense up, unsure whether he's going to hug me or punch me. Mal nods towards the car and pats my arm. "Good timing. I'll let him tell you."

I'm still staring at Mal, wondering what's going on when Noah slides out of the car and comes waltzing down the driveway. He throws his hands out. "Well, well, well. Look who's posting videos now."

My head drops. I look down, half ashamed and half ecstatic at how the three of us are together again. But Noah is smiling as he holds up his phone. "Almost three thousand hits, my man. Not too shabby. And old dude isn't bad on the piano, either."

I throw my hands up. "Noah. I'm so, so sorry, man. I know that's not good enough, but I promise I'll never do it again."

He stops. His face balls up. I'm waiting for his response when he brushes by me and kneels to the floor. "Who the fuck stacked my set like this?"

Mal clears her throat. "Noah. Focus."

He leans in, inspecting his bass drum. "Well, I mean, the humidity levels—"

"Noah!" Mal lunges for him but I take a step forward.

"I can explain. I mean, I can try at least."

Noah pries his gaze from his set as he gets to his feet. He looks me over, and I prepare for an outburst, for him to lay me out worse than ever when he makes a bee line for the fridge. He slings the door open like he's at home, finds a can of Pepsi and cracks it open. He takes down half of it and burps. "Dude, you missed out so hard."

"Yeah, man, I don't even know where to start. I'm sorry."

"Well, you should be. But at least my main mucker, Nash, made up for it."

"Huh? Your what?"

Mal shoots me a smirk. "Don't. It's useless."

Noah launches into the story of meeting the Finnegan brothers, only his version differs from Mal's version in that Noah and Nash Finnegan tore up the night and howled at the moon. Mal interrupts him with corrections from time to time, like when Noah claims he and Nash spent most of the time backstage talking music, the industry, and women. *Noah, it was ten minutes, and you were circling him like a puppy.* But nothing derails his monologue.

"I have Nash Finnegan's number. We're boys now. And it looks like," he looks at Mal. "Did you tell him."

She shakes her head quickly, bites her lip. "I was waiting for you."

"Okay, check it out." He smiles and glances at Mal again. She nods like crazy. "Nash Finnegan loved our videos so much we're opening for The Finnegens in D.C. All of us, The Wide Awakes. And you're coming. I don't give a shit if Mal and I have to duct tape you to the car. It's happening."

I look at Mal then Noah. "What? Is this for real?" I turn to Mal as the goosebumps dot my skin. "Why are you just now telling me this?"

Mal glances at Noah, gives me a coy smile. "Because other things were happening?"

"Damn, already?" Noah crushes the can. "That was fast."

Mal slaps his arm, and he jerks back. I wait for the worst, for Noah to explode. Instead, he laughs at her. "You tell him how many times you watched the video?"

"Shut. Up."

I watch them go back and forth until Mal breaks her glare away from Noah and takes my hand again. Things are weird, granted, but a good kind of weird.

Noah laughs. "You're so far behind, dude. Mal and I bonded and did some team building at the Warped Tour."

Mal rolls her eyes. Noah is unperturbed. "Between hanging out with cool people, worrying about your sorry ass, and talking things out, we realized what we have with the band. Cue corny music." He nods to Mal. "Then Mal saw that song you did, and, bro, she's probably responsible for a thousand of those views."

Mal wide eyes him, grits her teeth. "Noah."

"I'm just saying. Anyway, Mal finally realized..." he sweeps a hand in our direction. "All this. While I realized, hmm... what did I realize?"

Mal reaches across me and slaps him. "Ouch. We need to have a talk about your anger issues. That's next, little lady."

Mal leans in toward Noah. "Noah realized we were his two favorite people in the world, and he wants what's best for us."

He rubs his arm. "What she said." So yeah, dipshit, we're opening for The Finnegens!"

I look from him to her and smile. As they start up with more stories about the bands, the people, and all the other craziness of their grand fifteen hours on tour, I realize how much I lost, gained, and discovered in between it all.

Mal launches into me with a hug. Noah takes it better than I thought, slapping my back before he stands. Then he closes his eyes and mutters what might be a prayer as he looks over his set again.

39

NOAH LOADS UP HIS SET AND SAYS HE NEEDS TO CRASH, so we make plans to practice tomorrow. Once he's gone, Mal turns to me, still flushed, her eyes heavy but fighting through the lack of sleep as she scoops up my hand and smiles.

It's hard to believe such a bleak night could lead up to this. When I invite Mal inside and Mr. Irvin looks at her with that big, twinkly smile of his, it hits me how much these two people matter to me.

I don't know what else to do but make introductions, even as they've sort of met already. "Mr. Irvin, this is Mal. Mal, Mr. Irvin."

"Please. Call me George." Mr. Irvin takes her hand in some chivalrous way. Mal raises her eyebrows, delighted as he bows. "Well, Miss Malorie, it's nice to finally meet you."

Mal makes a beeline for the piano. She runs a hand over the cherry wood top. Mr. Irvin's eyes light up with his smile. "Ah, do you play?"

Mal grins. "I took lessons for five years."

"Really?" I say.

She shoots me a devilish grin. "I still have *some* secrets."

Mr. Irvin chuckles. I don't know what exactly we're doing here but bringing them together feels right.

Mr. Irvin suggest veggie packets, and I offer to step out to the garden. When I return, Mal is playing parts of *Dashboard*. Mr. Irvin winks at me as though to say, *You've got yourself a fine girl, here.*

I don't know what I have or don't have, but Mal keeps my hand in hers. She looks at me a bit differently, touches me more. She keeps asking me about *Dashboard* and the lyrics, nudging me about how perfect it was.

By the time we sit down to eat, it's like Mr. Irvin and Mal have known each other for years. At the table, Mal looks over the spread, and her eyes go wide. "Yum."

Mal sits next to me, our legs touching. I'm thinking it's going to be all small talk and rainbows when she asks exactly how I stood up to Hank. Mr. Irvin excuses himself, and Mal watches him retreat before she turns to me. I tell her more about the notebook. The song. How it all came together at my darkest moment.

I even tell her about the memories of my father. How her voice came to me and saved me when I needed it. Mal's chin quivers as I go into the details about how I left Nan in the hallway.

"Myles." She closes her eyes. "I'm so sorry."

"Yeah, well. I'm sorry I flaked."

"No, it's..." She scoops up my hand and blows out a deep breath. "I'm so glad this is happening for you."

Mr. Irvin returns, and Mal and I perk up. I can tell he's being careful about what to say, but he shouldn't. The guy has saved my life.

Mal's smile turns contemplative, as the evening sun streams through the back windows, kissing off her shoulders. She's yawning, and her eyes are glazed. It's clear the last couple of days are catching up with her, but just when I think she's going to stretch and announce that she's beat, she finds the tongs and goes in for seconds on the veggies. "So, George, we've got another gig. We're opening for the Finnegens in D.C."

"Oh?" Mr. Irvin glances at me. I know what he's thinking as I stop pushing around vegetables. My heart is a battering ram in my chest. Mr. Irvin excuses himself yet again to refill his water. Mal stares at me.

"You're doing this, Myles."

"I know. I want to. I'm not letting you guys down again."

"But?" It's like she's reading my mind. "Whatever is going through your head, stop it now, got it?"

I take her hand. "Okay," I say, and for the first time, I mean it. I don't want to miss out on anything else. Music is what I want to do, so if I'm good enough for Mal, I'm good enough for anything else.

Mal nods as though it's all settled. She passes me the bowl and raises her voice to Mr. Irvin in the kitchen. "Well, would you gentlemen mind playing that song for me again?"

40

Mr. Irvin's garden is still going strong, a thick jungle of leaves and sprouts, where beanstalks grow like vines, stretching upward for sunlight. The smells mingle, from herbs to chives and to the sharp scent of tomatoes the size of baseballs. I find him out back, shovel in hand, fiddling with the hose. Once again, I'm caught between asking if he needs a hand and not wanting to bug him.

"Ah, Myles. Perfect. Could you grab that coupler for me?"

I dive in, and soon I'm drenched as we rework the sprinkler system. The evening is still warm and muggy, and neither of us have anywhere to be and so he shows me how it's laid out and irrigated like an outdoor grocery store. Strawberries, squash, pumpkins and corn, everything. The dude is a genius.

It's easier when we're busy. We clean the sprinkler heads, unclogging the dirt and making adjustments. Mr. Irvin nods and grunts as we chase down the kinks, find the places where roots have wrapped themselves into the lines. Soon I'm talking to him, telling him things again. Mostly because I can. Hank isn't around to tell me I'm wrong. What I can't do. What I won't do. I tell Mr. Irvin how much I enjoy our work. How maybe I want to run my own business down the road.

Our work finished, we sit at the patio table, admiring the garden. Mr. Irvin thinks it's a fine idea. He says he'll show me all he knows. Covered in mud, sweating through my shirt, I realize this is real. Living here. Him. My life. I just gaze out at the garden with a smile.

Mr. Irvin has a shine in his eyes, as well. "Yes, this is one of the better years."

I can't say I agree with him, but things are looking up. He sips vinegar water, his favorite elixir. Regular water for me, as we sit with our big ideas, the rattling of a woodpecker somewhere over our heads. "So, how are you feeling about the big show?"

I shrug. "I'm good, actually. I've sort of come to a realization."

Mr. Irvin sips his water. I smile at him as I sit back. "Mal's right. I play music for me. It's what I love. For so long I let other people determine how I felt. But how I feel about music? It's mine. I have control over that. I'm done letting people take it away from me."

"That sounds like wisdom to me."

We sit for a while, letting the evening roll over us, but just as I think we're done, he sets his cup down and smacks his lips. "I spoke to your Nan today."

I open my mouth, to speak, protest, gasp, I'm not sure. I sigh like a ball losing air. He closes his eyes and shakes his head. "She would like to see you."

"I'm not sure I have anything to say to her."

"I know you're upset, but..." I'm already shaking my head. "Very well. I just wanted her to know where you are. That you're okay."

"I'm sure she's concerned."

Mr. Irvin looks out to his garden. He fixes his hat and unknowingly scrapes dirt across his forehead. "You should see her."

I stop. All those good feelings sinking into the dirt like hose water. I wipe the dirt from my pants. "You've got to be kidding."

He shakes his head. "When you're ready."

"I'll never be ready to do that."

"I see."

THE SETLIST COMES ALONG. Noah's been busy posting, and the YouTube channel is getting major traffic. Meanwhile, *Dashboard* has nearly 10,000 views. Mal wanted to put it on the EP, and I agreed under one condition: she does it from here on out. Once I heard her sing it, while playing Mr. Irvin's piano, I knew that's how the song needed to be played.

As much as I fought it, I've been thinking about Nan. Mr. Irvin planted the seed and now, removed from the creaky floors of the house, I'm starting to see things his way. For all her faults, she's all the family I've got. After practice, I tell Mal and Noah I have to go do something alone.

Mal gets to her feet and wraps her arms around me. She whispers all the hope I need into my ear, then seals it with a kiss. Noah nods and wishes me luck.

Ten minutes later, I pull up to the old house in Mr. Irvin's truck. The tightly-coiled dread twists in my chest, but I breathe my way through it. I park behind Barbara the Beast, step out, and run a finger along her fine wood grain panels.

"Hey old girl."

The wagon is dusty, the windshield sappy with grit. I'm sure the battery is dead, and it breaks my heart. Thankfully, Hank's truck is missing. No surprise he refused to see me. It's for the best. Can't say I miss him either.

The grass in the lawn has grown thick and curls over itself. The leaves clog the gutter, falling to the porch. I'm hit with an urge to go find the ladder. But for now, I'm here for Nan.

I knock at the door. I'm only a few weeks gone but now firmly a guest. I picture Nan pausing *Law & Order*, getting to her feet, and grimacing as she walks to the door. She opens it a crack, even though she's expecting me.

"Hi, Nan." I force myself not to drop my shoulders or give up too easily. I'm determined to make this as painless as possible. Mr. Irvin and I have talked a lot about holding grudges and what it does to your soul. It's because of him I reached out and decided to give it a try.

"Myles." She motions for me to come in, where I'm hit by the smell of breakfast, bleach, all the smells of a former life. Nan's life is one of making meals and then cleaning the mess.

"So," I say, forcing myself through this. "I just wanted to say—"

She shakes her head. "I've got a few of your things here. You can check your room if you'd like, for anything else."

I nod, realizing it's going to be a business trip. I walk down the hall, as I've done so many times before. I feel the familiar creaks of the planks under my feet, hear the whine of my door hinges. I look at the tiny single bed, the dresser, the stains on the wall beneath my windows. everything clenches inside of me. My limbs are heavier, and there's a faint throb in my ears. This is where dreams go to die. I say yet another silent thanks to Mr. Irvin. He saved my life.

There isn't much to gather. The important stuff I'd already taken. What remains is in trash bags, ready to haul away. I check the drawers, and they're empty. The bed is made tight, and the floors have been scrubbed. I glance up. How many nights did I stare at that ceiling and hope for this day?

After another check through the closet and under the bed, I grab a few boxes of books, and that's all that's left. Only Nan. I know I have to say something to Nan.

I load up the truck and turn to Barbara again. I promise her I'll drive her someday soon. At least I hope so. When I get back to the porch, Nan stands there, expressionless, the rag in her hand.

She looks older outside. Weaker. It occurs to me that one day she'll be gone, and like Mr. Irvin said, I don't want to live with regrets.

I step toward her, watching her eyes widen as she takes a small step back. I ignore the hesitation and bring her in to me with a hug. She stiffens. I'm expecting her to push me away, to tell me that's enough. But she doesn't. Instead, she sniffles and sets her arms around me tightly. I'm surprised at her strength, the hurt in her voice. "Oh, Myles. I was always so afraid you'd turn out like him."

"I won't, Nan."

"Do you promise?"

"Yes."

I nod, keeping her in my arms. She buries her head into me, sobbing. "I'm so sorry, Myles."

"It's all right, Nan." I wipe my eyes. "I'm okay now."

She looks me over again, and I know she sees my father. But I'm so happy I did this. I let her cry the tears she should have shed years ago. She shakes her head, and then sobs some more.

Outside the house, on the slanted stoop, I'm not thinking about Hank or how much I hate this place. I'm just thankful to be leaving the right way because I have so much to do. I don't want anything holding me back. Not anymore.

We let go of each other, and she looks down and wipes her eyes. She tells me to take care. I tell her I will. It feels like I'm leaving to travel the world even though I'll be right across town.

As I walk to the truck, it hits me. I turn and smile because this doesn't have to be the end. "Hey Nan. Want to go to the market on Saturday?"

The storm door squeaks as she stops and smiles. My nan actually smiles. She bows her head. "That would be nice."

"It would."

"I'll see you at six. Don't sleep all morning."

I can't help but laugh as I get into the truck and wave to Nan. Then I drive to the park.

To celebrate things, Mal meets me at our rock. The glittering river below us flows like it always has, like it did yesterday, the day before, like it will after we're gone. But today I don't think about where it's going, I just appreciate the movement.

I hold Mal, enjoying the warmth as the sun finds her skin, as though it belongs there. She hums out a tune, but there's no notebook today. I didn't bring my guitar. She settles against me, and I trace my fingers down her arms. I convince myself it's a day worth celebrating. I'm with Mal. We're going to D.C. tomorrow to open for The Finnegens. I'm as good as I could be.

Mal opens her eyes and halfway turns to me. "We have another podcast."

I laugh. "Oh no."

She closes her eyes. "Not Ripcast. Another one." She glances up to me. "Bigger. And we're bringing Noah."

"Really?"

She nestles into me. "Hmm, mm."

"When were you going to tell me?"

She throws her hands out. "Right now. I'm telling you right now. And there's something else, too."

I squeeze her arms. "Yeah?"

She turns her head and her lips meet mine. She breaks away with a smile. "That."

I go to kiss her again when the heavy chug of an engine approaches from within the trees. Mal's eyes light up as the whistle pierces the calm evening sky. She shoves me away, leaps to her feet, and points to the trestle.

"Train!"

41

"THIS NEXT SONG IS A NEW ONE..."

Mal's laughing too hard too hard to finish the sentence. She stands over the weaving mass that is the crowd—a few thousand people caught in her web. We've just finished the most incredible set of our lives, and Mal is on fire. Noah is beasting. And I'm in the moment, riffing, coming off a guitar solo that's left the crowd cheering for this encore.

Sweat trickles down Mal's temples, smearing the eyeshadow until it looks like she's crying. She's as gorgeous as ever, and for a second I'm caught in her web myself. There's nowhere else I'd rather be.

Noah brings us back with three thumps of his kickdrum. Mal turns to me, her eyes swimming with a fervent energy, but there's something else too. It's an *I told you* so moment, one she's rightfully earned. I make a face at her, but she was right all along, I needed this. I needed to hold the buzzing guitar in my hands before the maniacs in the front row. I needed to see for myself how they lean closer, arms slung over the guard rails, soaking it in with goofy smiles and phones aimed at us. It's hard to believe I ever doubted I could do this.

We're cheesing hard, all three of us. We're almost too happy for punk, as Mal clutches the mic stand with both hands, again casting a sly glance my way. "This next song, it's... Ah, whatever..."

Feedback screeching, Mal swings her bass around, and we launch into *Oh That's Nice*. Mal gets the bassline rolling. I come down hard on the chords. The first few rows of the crowd shift their attention to me. And yeah, in the back of my head—in the front of my head—I know there are some agents and scouts out there who came to see her and her alone. As a band, we've talked a lot about this lately, and part of our plan is to be open and grasp the reality of things. Even as I've told Mal the decision is hers to make, she's made it clear she doesn't want to sign without us.

Then again, she might not have to.

Just offstage to my left, Nash Finnegan scrunches up his face in rocker ecstasy. He bangs his head to the beat, a long, gangly figure with sleeve tattoos and black Doc Martins. We're still flying high after he took us out to lunch earlier, answering all Noah's rapid-fire questions. He had a long talk with Mal about the agent thing before he led us on a walk down to a few clubs he played ages ago, when he and his brother were just starting out. He told us how so many times he almost quit when the crowd turned on him. Mal slid her hand in mine when he said it and gave it a squeeze. Message received.

Nash is almost forty now—not that you'd ever guess to see him rock a stage. On the way back to the hotel, he talked of how his kids are in middle school and the family tours with him in the summer. It sounded awesome to me, but Nash said he's seen a lot. He wants a break from the road.

He glanced back at us, leaving that last statement dangling before us. Then he announced he and his brother had started their own label, Finnegan Records.

Noah's mouth fell open. Mal's eyes doubled and she mouthed, "Oh my God." Nash laughed, as we sort of fell into each other on the sidewalk. His daughter, Brigid was a huge fan. She'd recently found our page, and it's all she listens to lately. He said she'd begged him to come along and wants more than anything in the world to meet Mal after the show.

I stood with Noah and Mal on a D.C. sidewalk as Nash Finnegan spread his arms wide and said he'd love for The Wide Awakes to be the first band he signed. I'm not sure how Mal or I responded, but Noah's ugly cry is aptly named.

We play the song fast, as Mal hops in place and the crowd goes nuts.

When I look left again, Brigid is bouncing along next to her dad. She watches Mal the way one looks at the sky on the Fourth of July, tugging like crazy on her father's arm. Mal turns to me with a dazzling smile.

There's no stage bigger than the one you're standing on. And Nash is about to join us on this grand stage of life and make an announcement that will change us forever. And I have no idea what will happen next.

But I can't wait to find out.

ACKNOWLEDGMENTS

Any thanks here must begin with Joel Brigham. Joel saw something in an early version of this story and picked it out of the tangled weeds of Pitch Wars. There were characters, there was music, but the soul of this book has a lot to do with him. Thanks Joel, for the countless hours of support, notes, feedback, texts, phone calls, and everything else. And it still doesn't seem like enough. So many times you talked me down and convinced me to rewrite a third of this book. Looking back, it's hard to believe the story was ever any other way!

Much love to Brenda Drake, Ayana Gray, and the entire Pitch Wars team. To think I made the cut on the last year of this amazing contest is special to me. And hey, it only took six tries!

Special thanks to Michael Dolan, for understanding what this book is really about. To the entire Winding Road team for being so close and supportive.

Thanks to Donna Stone, and Nic Molyneux, for reading early drafts and offering feedback. To Diane Fanning, forever my mentor. To my dad, Wayne Fanning, for nurturing a love of music. To Mom, Ivy, Taylor, Marley, Sean, Dean, Brandon, Ray, Phil, Adam, Dem, and anyone else who introduced me to some kind of music at some point in my life.

Most of all, thanks to my wife, Anne, who supports and encourages me to keep writing. To my son, Simon, who encourages me to stay young. And Bella, my little person, who encourages me to open the freezer and get out the ice cream.

ABOUT THE AUTHOR

Pete Fanning is the author of several middle grade and young adult books. He lives in Virginia with his wife, son, baby girl, and two very spoiled dogs. He can be found at www.petefanning.com, where he's posted over 200 flash fiction stories.

9 7 9 8 9 8 7 1 7 3 7 4 9